PULLED WITHIN

MARNI MANN

To those of you who have scars, whether they cover your surface like Rae's or are embedded under your skin, I want you to know you're not alone.

ONE

Drew...that bitch. After seeing her with her best friend Gianna tonight at the bar, I couldn't get her off my mind. Pacing Brady's bedroom wasn't helping me forget the too-confident grin that spread across her face whenever our eyes met. Every time I blinked, the memory would rewind: She'd taken Saint, my ex-boyfriend, away from me. She'd won. I'd lost everything shortly after she'd arrived in Bar Harbor. The wounds were still fresh. I didn't need her teal stare covering me in salt on top of it all.

I wanted to complain about her to someone who'd complain with me; I wanted to be reminded that what she'd taken from me wasn't such a big loss. I wanted to hear someone agree that she and Gianna should go back to Florida where they belonged. But there was no one to call. My best friend Brady was gone; he'd skipped town a month before, and I hadn't heard from him since. Aside from him, there was only one other person I wanted to talk to.

Darren, my brother.

And, well...I couldn't call him.

Thirty-two days, I thought. Even with no Brady to lean on, I'd feel a little relief in thirty-two days.

I left my phone on the dresser and crawled on to Brady's bed. Before getting comfortable, I wiggled a bag of weed out of my back pocket. Two perfect little buds sat in the center of my hand. They were darker than the last batch I'd bought; the tips were whiter danker—just how I liked it. It was only a dime; I couldn't afford anything larger. And I hated to waste it in anger just because Drew had gotten to me…especially since I didn't have a job and couldn't afford to buy any more.

Another reason I hated her.

Had she not messed with Saint, one of the few guys I'd actually cared about, and Brady, who had become my family, there was a chance I would have liked her. She was nice enough…and unlike most people, she didn't stare at the scar on my cheek. But there was no way I could show any softness toward someone who had stolen from me.

I'd been robbed once before. That thief was fucking dead to me.

Now, Drew was, too.

Thirty-two days.

I packed the small glass pipe with just enough for a few hits and popped the end in my mouth. My phone rang as the fire sprouted through the lighter. Who the hell would be calling me this late? Brady's boys only sent text messages, and the last time I'd heard from my mom, she was working day shifts, so she'd be asleep at this hour.

There wasn't anyone else.

I knew I probably had enough time to sneak in a quick hit before the call went to voicemail. But I was too curious to risk it. I rushed across the room and grabbed my phone from the dresser. I didn't recognize the number.

"Hello?"

I walked back to the bed, waiting for someone to respond. I slid all the way to the far end, crossed my legs, and leaned against the wall with the bowl balanced on my thigh. My fingers tapped my knees and traced the white stitching that ran down the inside of my jeans.

"Hello?" I repeated.

"Rae…"

My back jolted off the wall, and my eyes widened. His voice was hoarse and scratchy, but it was definitely him. "Brady? My god…where have you been?"

"Rae…"

"Say something. Say that you're all right."

"Shit…Rae."

Brady had two voices: sober and wasted. I knew both so well. This was definitely his wasted tone. And he was on more than just booze… something else had been mixed in. Something a lot stronger than just weed. Whatever it was, he'd probably crushed and snorted it.

"*Shit* what, Brady? Talk to me," I demanded.

"I'm…"

I could picture him running his fingers through his shaggy, dirty blond hair, his lids half-open, looking from side to side to figure out where he was. It was normal for him to black out. But I couldn't tell from his voice whether he was waking up out of his high or if he was actively in the middle of one.

"Brady, you've been gone a whole month and no one has heard from you. You need to tell me where you are."

"I'm in…Bangor…I think?"

"Bangor?" I slid to the end of the bed, my feet falling onto the filthy floor. I'd mopped it many times, but nothing helped get rid of the stickiness that had permanently sunk into the wood. Brady was no neat freak, and his mess only got worse when he started using again. This was the disaster he'd left me with. "What are you doing in Bangor, Brady?"

Bangor was about forty-five minutes from Bar Harbor. I wondered how he'd gotten there. He'd left his truck here, at his apartment building, and had shut off his cell phone. Before he'd taken off, he told me he didn't want to be found…but someone must have helped him. It wasn't one of his boys from around here.

"I'm in trouble." It sounded like his lips were having a hard time keeping up with the words.

"How much trouble?"

"A lot." He breathed loudly. "It's bad. Really...fucking...bad."

I moved to the dresser and hid the bowl in one of the drawers. Something told me I wouldn't be smoking tonight. "Tell me what to do."

"Come get me."

"Should I bring one of the guys?"

"No. They can't help me." There was rustling in the background. Banging. A shout that didn't come from Brady...or maybe it had. *"Wake the fuck up."* His voice was so raspy; it was little more than a whisper. I wondered who he was talking to, and if they were as wasted as he was. "What's the address here?" There was mumbling that I could barely make out. "Write this down," he said finally.

There wasn't anything on his dresser to write with, so I sprinted over to the nightstand. Inside the drawer I found a box of cards. I grabbed a few, along with my broken eyeliner that rested on top. "I'm ready." He gave me the address, and we hung up.

With liner smeared all over my nails and my fingers smelling like bud, I threw on a jacket, grabbed my purse and went straight downstairs to my car. Since it was three in the morning, the ride to Bangor wouldn't take long. There was nothing but blackness on the road. No other drivers, no sound. The occasional glimpse of a deer.

Boredom.

I blasted tunes to fill the stretching silence and counted the streetlights to keep my mind focused. When I got to one hundred, I started over again.

I hoped I could get him out of whatever trouble he was in. I couldn't lose him. I couldn't get through the next thirty-two days without him. In the past, drugs had taken him to some dark places

—not just with the law, or into a psychological hole with real lines of powder surrounding him. He'd had to deal with some disturbing people...the cocking of a gun was probably the most innocent of the noises I'd heard during those exchanges. Each time, I'd cleaned him up. I could do that again. It couldn't really be as bad as he'd said it was.

Or maybe it could.

I'd help him either way.

His directions took me to a duplex. I found him on the staircase outside, stretched across the second step. His neck was tilted and hung over the side; his body lay limp. He was missing a shoe and had no jacket on.

My fingers shook as I turned the car off. My breath pounded against the inside of my throat before it released its vapor cloud. It wasn't smoke that came from my mouth, but crisp November air.

When I reached the steps, I stood frozen. Too afraid to wake him; too afraid to even touch him. I could taste the salt as it dripped onto my lips. Tears for my best friend...or what was left of him, anyway.

The streetlamp showed dried blood caked across his mouth, and in the corners. Both eyes were black and swollen; his cheeks matched. His bare arms were marred with scratches, deep wounds that looked fully infected. His hands were crossed over his chest, gripping his T-shirt like he was using it to bear the ache—or take the edge off, at least. Nothing but more drugs could take away the incredible pain he had to be feeling.

"It's bad, isn't it?"

I jumped from the sound of his voice. It was even raspier in person than it had been on the phone, like his throat was coated in resin. "I thought you were sleeping."

"My eyes are swollen, not shut."

I squatted onto the bottom step and gently pulled his head onto my lap. My fingers slid through his greasy hair. It was the only part of him that wasn't covered in blood. I didn't know if the massage would make him feel better. I had to try something. I'd never seen him like this...not this messy or bruised. Not this broken. "Fuck, Brady. What the hell happened to you?"

He slowly reached for my free hand and used it to pull himself up. He sat on the second step above me and leaned forward, his hands covering his forehead. Even through the hair and dirt and swelling, I could tell how much weight he'd lost in his face.

He looked hollow.

And he smelled like something wicked. The stench of pee came from his jeans, a huge wet spot circling his zipper. He also reeked of chemicals, of unwashed skin and something metallic, which I figured was the blood.

He wobbled on the step, flinching each time his body rocked or his thumbs grazed his temple. It wasn't a whimpering cry, like a wounded animal might make as it lay in the middle of the road. This was deep, guttural. Primal. He was more than just battered physically.

He was crumbling mentally, too. Right in front of me.

My heel slipped on the wood, and I stood to regain my balance. Brady responded so quickly. Before I could move, he'd clamped his arms around the back of my legs and pressed his cheek against my thigh. "No," he cried. "You can't leave me."

My shoulders melted and slouched from the sound of him. I tried to stop my own sobs from matching his. "I'm not going anywhere. I would never leave you."

He tilted his neck to look up at me. His hands tightened. His lids were so dark and swollen, I couldn't see his pupils. But I knew he was staring at me; I could feel his gaze, and the tears that dripped off his chin soaked through my jeans. This was only the second time he'd ever cried in front of me.

The first was the morning after I'd gotten my scar.

"Help me," he begged. "Help me, Rae...I hurt so fucking much."

TWO

"Rae!" Brady screamed. "*Raaaaaaae!*"

For the two hours we'd been back in Bar Harbor, he'd been shouting my name non-stop. He'd even yelled when he was in the shower while I was sitting just a foot away on the closed toilet seat. He was in agony.

So was I.

His muscles ached so badly that he couldn't get comfortable in the bed. I'd covered him in a blanket when he shivered, but he'd just kicked it off. His skin throbbed too much. The fan didn't help; beads of sweat formed and pooled across his body regardless of the air it blew on him. The only thing that would make this go away was more drugs...but they were the reason he felt like this in the first place.

There was nothing I could do to help him.

That didn't mean I'd stop trying.

With a bowl of ice and a wet washcloth, I crawled behind him in the bed. "I'm here," I whispered as I placed the damp cloth over his forehead. We didn't have any paper towels, so I wrapped the ice in a piece of toilet paper and ran the cold nugget down his arms. He was in one of his hot phases. I could smell the drugs seeping out of him. And the booze.

And the vomit he'd gotten on himself since the shower.

"Kill me." He was tucked in a ball, his head resting on my lower thigh. His hands were just above his hair, wrapped around my leg, squeezing. There was dirt under his nails and cuts all over his knuckles, but they were still the same hands: kind and patient. Fingers that weren't always wise with their decisions but had faced demons for years and had clawed their way through to survive. "Give me a fucking needle, a knife—anything. I just need to end this."

The toilet paper wasn't holding up, so I used straight ice cubes on his skin. "You're going to get through this, Brady." I remembered when he'd said those same words to me.

"No, Rae." His body started shaking and still burned to the touch, even though he was freezing. "I can't do this."

I'd said those words once, too.

I leaned down to lend him some of my warmth, covering his neck with my arms. His hands released my thigh and reached up, grazing my chin on the way to my hair. A gasp shot through my lips. My body began to match his, tremors tormenting my whole shell. His fingers twisted into my strands and pulled them taught against his palms.

It was too much.

My eyes filled with tears, but I said nothing.

"Shit, Rae, I'm so sorry." He knew…he knew I couldn't take it —anything but touching my cheeks or my hair. "I didn't mean to. I forgot…"

I wiggled out from under his hands and moved to the far corner of the room. I didn't want to leave him, but I needed some kind of comfort, and the walls gave me that. They hugged me; held me. Supported me. So I rocked between them, my arms clinging to my knees, bunched together as close to my chest as I could get them. My ass rolled back and forth, back and forth over the sticky, filthy floor.

"Come back," he begged. "Please...I need you. Rae, I fucking need you."

Back and forth.

I covered my ears with my hands, my face tucked into the darkness. At some point, I'd wondered if I could handle Brady's hands being there, tangled in my hair. Just his. No one else's. Today had proved I couldn't.

Thirty-two days.

"Please, Rae...*pleeeeeeeassssse!*"

Back and forth.

"Call my dad," he yelled.

I was in the bathroom, rinsing the bucket from his last round of puking. I held my breath, but the smell was still seeping in some-how. I was doing everything I could not to gag.

"Do you want him to come over?" I asked as best I could.

The physical withdrawal he was going through could last up to a week; we didn't have that much time before we'd be kicked out of this apartment. The first eviction notice came just before Brady had taken off. The second had been delivered yesterday. We had seventy-two hours to pay two months of back rent, or we'd have to leave. I didn't have the money. I knew Brady didn't either.

"I want him to come get me."

He didn't want me to take care of him?

I left the bathroom and sat on the bed. He was on his back, his knees bent, staring at the ceiling. I touched his arm, and his hand closed over my fingers. "I just want to help you." My voice was so soft...so fragile. I almost didn't recognize it.

"I've hurt you," he said, "and I'm just going to keep doing it. I need help, Rae...real help this time." His teeth chattered. I covered him with the blanket, but he kicked it right off. Beads of sweat ran into his eyes. When I tried to dab the beads, he clenched down on my skin with his nails. "Call my dad...*please.*" His eyes rolled back

9

into his head. Spit flew from his tongue and landed on his lips, strings of white goo stretching between them. "Tell him I need rehab."

I was relieved that he wanted to get help. He never had before, which meant he'd inevitably gone back to using after every one of his breaks. Internal silence would be impossible for him, every addict I knew had told me that, but rehab would help him identify his demon and teach him how to quiet it. And then, once the facility thought he was ready—or once his money ran out, whichever came first—they'd spit him back onto the street. I'd be there when it happened. I'd make sure he didn't fall again. Or I'd try to, at least.

But I had no idea what I'd do in the meantime.

I'd sent Brady's dad a text when we'd gotten back to the apartment. He probably wasn't awake to hear it. I was happy the ringing had woken him. "Shane," I said, holding the phone up to my ear. "Brady's here."

"What? When did he get back?" The sleep in his voice began to vanish. "How is he?"

Either in person, on the phone, through text, or during our weekly lunches, Shane and I had talked about Brady almost every day since he'd disappeared. It was comforting to have someone else want Brady to return as badly as I did. But having Shane to talk to did more than just comfort me where his son was concerned. It was a reminder that not all dads were assholes.

Not like mine was.

Not long after Brady had taken off, Shane had called his connection at the rehab center. He wanted to be prepared for when Brady came home...if he came home at all. He'd been told there was a waiting list. But Shane had done most of the carpentry work at that facility, so they knew him well. If anyone could get Brady moved to the top of their list, it was him. "He wants to go to rehab," I said. "Can you help him get in?"

"You're at the apartment?" he asked.

"Yes."

"I'll call you right back."

Setting the phone down next to me, I ran my hands along the ends of his hair, careful to keep my fingers off his sweating face and the beard he had yet to shave. I didn't touch him enough to hurt him, just enough to let him know I was still there.

He could barely open his swollen lids. Through the slit between them, the light blue of his irises looked foggy. He was an overcast morning. "How did I get here?" he asked.

"I practically carried you from the shower."

A drop fell from the corner of his eye when he shook his head...just one. It slid slowly to his mouth. Most of the blood was gone from his lips, but there was still evidence in red. "No...how did I get *here*?"

He meant his addiction.

It was something he'd struggled with for a long time. Sometimes, he used several times a day; sometimes, only once. And sometimes, he went weeks or months without touching anything. But he'd told me the urge was always there.

My stare drifted to the corner of his room, where my clothes were folded in piles on the floor. My shampoo was in his shower. My rotten loaf of bread was in his kitchen. I didn't know how I'd gotten here, either.

Thirty-one days.

"I'm no better...no different," I whispered. "You know that."

"It took me further this time." He rubbed his knuckles over his chest. When he'd gotten out of the shower, I'd noticed all the bruising. Someone had beaten him, and it didn't look like they had used their fists to do it. "It got so fucking dark out there."

He hadn't told me what had happened on the streets. But I knew dark. Most of my life had been continuous cloud cover.

"Your dad's getting you help. You're going to be okay."

He mumbled something I couldn't understand. I didn't need to I saw the uncertainty on his face. A few of his boys had gone to the same rehab. After getting out, they hadn't stayed clean for more than a few days. I had no doubt this knowledge was among the many things eating at him.

"Don't think beyond right now," I continued. "We're going to get through this moment, just like we're going to get through the next."

I needed to take my own advice.

My phone began to ring. Shane's name appeared on the screen.

"They can get him a bed in two days."

"Two days?" I echoed, but with greater disappointment.

"No…I can't wait two fucking days," Brady groaned.

I agreed. There was a good chance he'd change his mind by then. We needed to get him in sooner.

"But he's in rough shape, Shane, and he's so sick."

"They're going to write him a prescription that will help with the withdrawal. I'm on my way to the pharmacy to pick it up, then I'll swing by the apartment." He hesitated. "Do you think it would be best if Brady stayed…with *me*…in the meantime?"

A tiny bit of Brady's swollen lids popped open. I wasn't on speakerphone, but Shane spoke loud enough for him to hear. "I've gotta go to his place." He wiped the back of his hand across his forehead. His skin was drenched. "The meds aren't going to do shit. I'm only going to get sicker."

I pressed the phone against my shoulder so Shane couldn't hear what we were saying. "I'll go with you. I'll—"

"No." He sat up and moved to the other end of the bed. When his back pressed against the wall, he winced. "I don't want you to see me like this."

"Brady, I want to take care of—"

"You've done enough. I'm not dragging you down anymore. Tell him to come get me. Now."

All I wanted to do was care for him. It hurt that he wouldn't let me, but I had to do what he'd asked. I pulled the phone off my shoulder and held it to my cheek. It pressed against my scar. "Come get him, I guess." I didn't try to hide the emotion in my voice, and I didn't say anything more. I ended the call and stared at my hands. It was too difficult to look at him…I had to think very carefully about what to say. He felt horrible, and I didn't want to make him feel worse.

"Dad can afford to take a few days off," Brady said. "You probably don't have any time off yet, and I'd never let you use it if you did."

He was assuming that I'd sorted out my life in the month he'd been gone. That I'd gotten a new job after losing mine at Saint's restaurant. That I was paying for the apartment and the utilities. That there were more than a few bills in my wallet.

None of that was true.

His arm shot out from his side, and he grasped handfuls of air. "Bucket…*bucket!*"

I'd left it in the bathroom. I sprinted out of the bedroom to grab it. As I rounded the corner of the kitchen, I heard him retching. I backed up, peeked around the doorway, and saw him on his knees, throwing up on the bed. Yellow bile. It formed a puddle on the white sheets. Sheets that I had to change—*again.* He didn't have an extra set, or a washer and dryer. But it didn't matter…I'd figure it out and get it taken care of. Because he needed me to.

Brady.

My family.

"He looks a lot worse than I'd imagined," Shane said, shutting the passenger door.

We moved a few feet away to keep Brady from hearing us. He didn't seem to care that we were chatting, or that his dad didn't immediately get in the truck. He leaned his head against the seat and covered his forehead with the back of his arm.

"Wait until you see his chest," I told him. "It looks even worse than his face."

Shane's hand rested on my shoulder. His hands were compassionate and calm...loving. Just like Brady's. "What happened while he was out there?"

I shrugged. "He didn't tell me."

"I hope it's nothing like I'm thinking."

I glanced over at the window. Brady hadn't moved. "He has to *stay* in rehab. He can't check himself out. We can deal with whatever happened on the streets after he finishes the whole program."

"You're a good friend to him, Rae." A furrow formed between his blue eyes—eyes that were so kind and understanding. "I know how worried you've been. I hope this means you'll start taking better care of yourself."

If anyone else had said that to me, I would have probably flipped out. Not that they would have deserved that reaction; they would have been entirely right. It looked like Brady and I had been struggling with the same demon.

I'd lost weight recently...too much of it.

It was impossible to hide the amount since it had shed from my face and arms and thighs. My eyes were sunken. Mirrors only revealed how dark my scar had gotten without any fat to plump up the skin and make it thicker. And there was nothing I could do about it for thirty-one more days.

I didn't bother with the fake smile. Shane knew me too well for that. "It's almost December. So...you know."

"I know, kiddo, but you've got to start eating."

I nodded. He'd said the same thing to me every November since I was sixteen. He knew his words weren't going to change how little I'd be eating—or how little I would be keeping down. He also knew I would gain the weight back after December seventeenth. "Give him a hug for me when you drop him off." I took one step back, then another. I waved good-bye and moved to the entrance of the building. I rested my side against the doorway, watching as Shane climbed inside the truck and started the engine. The truck stopped as Brady's window aligned with me, and the glass slowly rolled down.

"Rae!" Brady yelled. "Come here."

I walked back over and leaned in through the open window, glancing between the two men inside. Air conditioning pumped through the vents. The droplets on his forehead told me he was having another hot flash. "Are you going to be okay?" he asked. His fingers lifted and curled around mine. He'd picked off a scab on his knuckle; blood that had dripped a few inches along his skin was already dry.

He was in the middle of his own personal storm, and he was wondering how I was doing. But this wasn't about me. It was all about him. "I'm fine." My voice would have convinced anyone but Shane and Brady. I couldn't be any stronger than that—not even for them. "Just go to rehab and get sober...for us. Everything will be better after that. I promise." He knew that was a lie, too. Brady couldn't make everything better. He'd tried...for years. And here he was again, in the same place he'd always come back to. I hoped this time it would end differently.

"You sure? Cause if—"

"I'm sure." My hand clamped down on his, and I squeezed. It was the closest thing to a hug I could give him without causing more pain. I couldn't hurt him any more than I already had today, and I couldn't risk him coming too close to my hair...not even unintentionally.

I pushed off the door, rushing toward the building. This time, I didn't stop in the doorway, and I didn't look back. I walked straight up the stairs and headed for the bathroom. The piece of bread I had eaten earlier—the one I'd picked the mold off of—wasn't sitting well in my stomach.

I wasn't surprised at all.

THREE

"I understand. Thanks for letting me know."

I dropped my phone onto the bed and stared at it as if it had just slapped me—and really, it felt as if the words on the other end actually had. I'd been waiting over a week to hear back from the managers of those two pubs. Each of them told me the positions I'd interviewed for had already been filled.

There was nothing left in town for me to apply for.

Bar Harbor was too seasonal. Most of the restaurants and many of the shops shut down during the winter months and reopened again in the spring. I'd applied to the pubs that stayed open all year...and a boutique, and some warehouses. Even several office jobs. I tried for every position I found in the paper and online: twenty-seven in total. With no experience at anything other than serving, I didn't expect to get those jobs. I just hoped something would come through regardless. I figured after being at Saint's lobster pound, the Trap House, for four years, one of the pubs would appreciate my experience and hire me.

I'd figured wrong.

Fucking Drew. She made me lose my job, in addition to making me lose my boyfriend.

She put me in this situation.

I couldn't think about her. I had to find a new job, no matter what had gotten me here. My Uncle Irving ran a small convenience store in town. There was a chance he would help me out if he had extra shifts available. I hated to ask him, but not because the only time I went in there was when I needed something.

It was more because of his hands.

They looked so much like *his*.

That was why I only saw my uncle when it was necessary. Using that as a reason to keep my distance wasn't exactly fair to him. Even though Uncle Irving had nothing to do with it, what had happened to me wasn't fair, either. After all this time, I still wasn't able to separate the two. But I had no choice.

With one day until my eviction and no other way to make money, I walked to his store. It was only a few blocks from Brady's apartment. He was waiting on a customer when I got inside, so I hung around the chip display. He'd owned this place since I was a kid; my brother and I used to come here for candy. Uncle Irving would give us small paper bags and let us fill them to the top with whatever we wanted. We always chose the gummy stuff: worms, bears, fish. Those were our favorites. Then we'd help him stock the shelves to pay off everything we'd eaten. We didn't mind. Darren and I got to do it together, and that was all that mattered to us.

Uncle Irving smiled when he saw me. "Rae, my girl! What brings you in?"

I dragged my eyes away from the candy aisle and the hunks of penny gum that I remembered Darren chewing so he could blow bubbles in my face. I slowly glanced at my uncle, my eyes moving to his hands even though I didn't want them to. They were harsh, weathered from hard work. His face was entirely different. There was a softness to it. A weakness, too.

He knew there was a reason for me coming here. My past had obviously set a precedent, and I was thankful for that.

"I wanted to see if you had any extra shifts I could take."

He moved out from behind the counter with two plastic bags in his hands and began walking down the aisles, dropping things in them as he went. "Extra shifts?"

"Yeah...I could use some hours, if you have them."

He stopped when he reached me and handed the bags over. They were full—and heavy. "These are for you...take 'em. Don't know what you've been eating, but it ain't enough. You're all skin and bones. Has your mama seen how thin you are?"

I shook my head, holding the bags back out to him. "No...I can't take these." It would all grow mold, just like the bread had.

"Please, take 'em or I'll be offended," he said. He wiped the corners of his mouth and crossed his arms over his chest. All IAllAll I could focus on were the backs of his palms while he gripped his biceps. His hands were really starting to wrinkle. To age...

My stomach began to twist.

"Saint not giving you enough shifts? Thought things were real busy for that boy."

He didn't know. It had been months since I'd last been here, and I was selective with what I told my mom.

"I don't work for Saint anymore."

He stood a little taller, his eyes narrowing as his hand reached up and scraped along the edge of his jaw, clenching and unclenching. His fingers knotted into fists. I read his body language as a sign of protection. "If that boy crossed any lines, I'll—"

"No, no, it was nothing like that." I almost laughed at his response. Hands that looked so much like my uncle's hadn't shown the same concern when it came to the safety of others. "It just isn't easy working for your ex, you know? Especially when he's dating someone new."

That wasn't totally a lie. It wasn't the whole truth, either. But he didn't need the truth because whatever I told him, he'd then go tell my mom. The less she knew, the better.

He nodded. "I know how that can be. I'm sorry, my girl, but I've got nothing to give you but a few bags of food. Only servicing the townies until summer, so I've cut down on my help.

Your mama asked for some shifts, too. Had nothing to give her, either."

I should have known she would have asked him for hours. It was November after all, and December seventeenth was quickly approaching. My body dealt with the upcoming date by rejecting anything I put in my stomach. Mom just worked herself to death.

My fingers tightened around the plastic handles of the bags. "It's okay. I've got some things going on up in Bangor. I just wanted to check with you first to see if I could save myself the commute."

"Whereabouts in Bangor?"

I avoided answering, leaning forward instead and blocking his hands with the bags so he couldn't use them to hug me. "I'll stop by again real soon so we can catch up." Then I planted the quickest kiss possible on his cheek. His scruff was so sharp, it practically bit me.

"Good to see you, Rae," he said as I walked out the door. "You be careful." I raised one of the bags to wave without bothering to turn around.

Once inside Brady's apartment, I dropped everything on the kitchen table. My stomach was growling, but I knew it wasn't from hunger. Still, I needed to put something in me. It had been hours— no, it had been a *full day* since I'd last eaten.

Rather than fiddling with the wire tie, I ripped a hole in the plastic bag that held the loaf of bread and shoved a corner into my mouth. I washed it down by sticking my face under the faucet. I rolled the rest of the slice into balls and slowly popped them in one at a time. They were just a little smaller than the penny gum from Uncle Irving's store. They didn't taste nearly as good, and they definitely didn't make me smile.

And they hadn't come from Darren's sweet, innocent hand.

Still, I was grateful for my uncle's gesture.

I plowed through several more pieces, and was full by the time I'd devoured the last bite—full *and* exhausted. There wasn't time for a nap...I might have lied to my uncle about having an opportunity in Bangor, but that didn't mean there wasn't one waiting for me. I had enough gas to get me there and back, and maybe even enough to stop at several places along the way if the first one didn't hire me. Someone would give me a chance. They had to.

Time was working against me, as it usually did.

Thirty days…

FOUR

"Can you start right now?"

The casino was my first stop once I'd arrived in Bangor. Rumor was that I'd make more here in a night as a cocktail waitress than I'd make if I did two double shifts at the Trap House. This was really the only place I wanted to work, but I never expected there to be an opening.

I kept my unscarred cheek pointed toward him and leaned forward to make sure I'd heard Kevin, the beverage manager, correctly. "You mean you want to hire me now? Like, this second?"

"It's short notice, I know." He pulled out a pile of papers from one of his desk drawers. "One of my waitresses just up and quit, so I'm understaffed for a poker tournament starting in an hour. Consider it a tryout. If you do well, I'll hire you full-time."

I watched his hands as he placed the sheets in front of me. His nails needed to be cut. There were thick, curly black hairs on both sides of his knuckles. *Masculine, but harmless.*

"So what do you say, Ms. Ryan?"

I continued to stare at him, keeping my neck turned to hide my scar. That was how I always spoke to people—never straight on. They didn't need to see my marred skin, and I didn't need to witness them gawking at it. That only led to questions…questions I'd never answer. But Kevin needed to know exactly who he was hiring and what his customers would be viewing whenever I approached their table. So I held my breath and slowly turned my face. He didn't flinch; his eyes didn't move from mine. I waited several more seconds before I said, "Yes, of course I can start right now."

He placed a pen on top of the stack of papers. "Excellent." He leaned back into his seat, his fingers gripping the armrests. "I don't have time to check out your references. I'm assuming they'll be good?"

I nodded and wiped my palms on the side of the chair. They were slick and clammy. *Who could I use as a reference?* Saint wasn't an option, or the other servers I'd worked with. They'd kept their distance because I'd been dating their boss. Shane and Uncle Irving would have to do.

"Then if you don't have any questions, take those sheets into the HR office and fill them out there." He tipped his head toward the stack. "Once you're done, head over to the employee locker room. I'll have Christy meet you there. She'll get you a uniform and show you around, and at the end of the night she'll tell me how you did. If you don't hear from me in the morning, plan on coming in tomorrow night, too. By then, I'll have a schedule worked out…I'll slip a copy into your locker."

I was sure I had some questions; I just didn't know what they were. This was all happening so fast, but that was the speed I needed. Last month was the first time I'd missed making my monthly deposit, money I'd been saving since I was sixteen. Money that couldn't be used to cover the rent. Because Saint had fired me, I already had a month to make up for, and I didn't want to miss another one.

"No questions," I said, reaching for the pen and the papers.

"Good." He slid his mouse over the pad, turning his computer screen from black to white. "Take a left just outside the door. HR is at the end of the hallway."

I stood from the chair, my purse swinging from my shoulder and the papers and pen in my sweaty hands. My neck turned again, moving my scar away from him. He'd seen enough of it. "Thanks for the opportunity." I pulled my skirt down as I walked. It was the longest one I owned, but it was still too short. I didn't have the cash to pick up something more appropriate, not even for an interview. Thankfully, it hadn't worked against me. It might have even worked in my favor.

"Rae?"

I stopped in the doorway and turned around to face Kevin again. "Yes?"

"Today is an important day for the casino. I'm counting on you."

"I won't disappoint you."

"Good." His eyes went back to the computer screen.

I followed his directions to HR. It didn't take me long to fill out the paperwork. Most of the sheets asked the same questions. For the address, I used Brady's apartment. I didn't know how much longer I'd be living there. Now that I had a job, I could hopefully work something out with the landlord. I reminded myself to call him in the morning.

I handed all the papers to the secretary, and she opened a small map and highlighted the route to the employee locker room.

"A map?" I asked.

"Trust me, you'll need it. This place is harder to navigate than downtown Boston during rush hour."

I hadn't ever been to Boston, or to another casino. And I hadn't seen much of this place so far, but the few areas I'd been through were huge. I was grateful to have some sort of direction.

"Thank you," I said over my shoulder as I followed the bright yellow line on the map. I hadn't gotten more than twenty yards before I hit a dead end. Either the map was outdated, or I didn't know how to read one. Either way, I was standing in front of a bathroom. I turned around and circled the section of slot machines looking for someone to ask.

"Employee locker room?" I said to an attendant who was exchanging a customer's slot ticket for cash.

"That way." She pointed behind me. "Second left after the blackjack tables."

I followed her instructions, ditching the map when I passed a wastebasket. The door was unmarked. It had to be the one.

I was barely inside before I heard my name. "Rae?" When my eyes met the girl who had spoken it, my lids widened. It felt like the highlighter had leaked from the paper, bled onto my face and circled my scar—flashing vividly, grabbing her attention and immediately revealing my flaw...and there wasn't a single blemish I could find on her. It was exactly how I'd felt the first time I was in Drew's presence after finding out she was dating Saint.

Beautiful people made me want to hide under an umbrella.

"Christy?" I asked, confirming what I already suspected, knowing I would be spending the next several hours with this beauty.

"That's me." Her piercing aqua eyes never blinked, and they never strayed from mine. "I'm so glad you made it, girl. When I called HR, they said you left ten minutes ago...I was getting ready to come look for you."

I shrugged a silent apology. "I got so lost."

"No worries." She waved me over. "This place is crazy-big, and that damn map they give you is useless."

It was larger than any building in Bar Harbor, even the hotels. But the size of this place wasn't what I was thinking about at the moment. It was *her*. She wasn't simply beautiful; she was intriguing, too. She was one of those girls you gazed at because you wanted to know her story—the reason she made the expressions she did, the reasons she chose to highlight her dark hair with caramel streaks, what gave her movements such fluidity. Was she a dancer? A swimmer? Were other parts of her body covered with the lightest patch of freckles like the one that spread under her eyes and nose? Even that was perfect.

Damn her.

I stopped a few feet away. "Yeah, it's huge. I threw the map away. It didn't help at all."

Even though I had my smooth cheek pointed at her, she was looking at my scar. Her pupils traced each swirl and jagged edge on my skin. I'd known this was going to be one of her first moves. I'd encountered enough girls like her—the kind who didn't care how obvious she was as she examined me, scrutinized me. She didn't blush when our eyes finally met. She didn't even look sorry, though she didn't look grossed out, either. She acted as if it was something that needed to happen, and now that it had, we could move on. It wasn't comfortable for me, but I was relieved that we'd gotten it out of the way.

"Ready to get dressed?" she asked. "You've got a great body… the uniform is going to hug you just right."

I did a quick scan of the black skirt she wore, which was much shorter than the one I had on, and her skin-tight tank top. Her breasts were twice as big as my B-cups, and her lips had to have been plumped. Her eyes followed mine as I returned her scrutiny. But unlike her, I actually did blush when I realized she'd caught me. "Is that what I'll be wearing?" I asked.

She turned around to show me the rest. I wasn't surprised by what I saw: more perfection, in the form of an ass that pushed out against the pleats of her skirt, and legs that were thin but held just the right amount of muscle. She opened a door along the back wall, grabbed several items off the shelves inside and handed them all to me.

I unfolded the short black skirt and held it out. It looked small enough to fit a doll…and the tank was narrow and barely stretched. "I might need a bigger—"

"They're both your size." She glanced at my feet. "Seven, right?"

I nodded.

She walked back over to the closet and removed a pair of knee-high leather boots, placing those in my arms as well. "There's one last thing…" She moved over to the closest row of lockers, punched in a code to open one and reached inside. "You'll want to wear this, too." When she pulled her hand out again, there was a black bra strung around her fingers.

"Is that yours?"

She nodded. "The casino should really give these out as part of the uniform, but they don't, so..."

"So you want me to wear *your* bra?"

She looked at my breasts, then back at my face. "Unless you have a push-up in your purse, then yes. You'll thank me later...I can promise you that." I owned three bras. They all had a bit of padding, but I wouldn't consider any of them a real push-up. "This little gem will earn you at least three hundred tonight," she added.

I nearly choked. "That's how much you make?"

She puckered her glossy lips and cupped her hands under her own bra, lifting and pushing to readjust her perfect breasts. "At least. But wearing that baby, *you'll* probably make closer to four."

I held out my hand and wiggled my fingers. "Give it to me."

She smirked. "Thought so."

There was something about her that I liked. She owed me nothing—shit, she didn't even have to be nice to me—but for some reason, she was helping me out.

"Bathrooms are in the back." She reached into her locker again and removed a small black bag. "Since you don't have a locker yet, feel free to use mine. I'm just going to touch up my makeup, and then we can hit the floor."

I carried the clothes and boots to the back of the locker room and changed in one of the stalls. The skirt barely covered the tiny pair of boy shorts she had given me. I kept my panties on under them. It felt weird to think of going without them; I didn't need my stuff rubbing all over the company-supplied uniform, regardless of how sexy the outfit was. The tank had a hard time stretching over my pumped up breasts, and they spilled out the top once it was fully on.

I'd never had this much cleavage before.

When I returned to the main room, Christy had added a pair of false lashes to her eyes, and red tint to her lips. It looked like she'd sprayed her long curls to keep them from straightening. "Ready?" she asked.

"I think so."

She gave me a short black apron that I tied around my waist, and I followed her out the door.

As we walked through the different sections of the casino, she described the types of customers who gambled in each area, what they drank, and the amount they usually tipped. There was a definite divide.

"Do you earn as much in the poker room?" I asked. It sounded like the table game players tipped the most...but that wasn't where we were headed.

She winked at one of the dealers. "Hell yeah. It's the only place I like to work." She brought me into a large square room that was completely filled with tables. There were men everywhere— leaning against the back wall, waiting in line by the entrance, chatting in groups by the teller, sitting in chairs around the tables, moving through the aisles. Most of them were in their twenties, thirties tops. There were very few women, aside from the handful who were playing. The rest were either serving or dealing.

"I can see why," I said, searching the faces closest to me, taking in all their scents. I had never been around so many men at once. And because most of them were so focused, it gave me a chance to stare without being noticed. I couldn't stop.

She laughed for the first time in our short interaction. It was such a simple sound, yet she made it sensual. "It's like a locker room, isn't it?"

We stopped walking and stood near the far wall. I glanced in her direction as her eyes met mine. "But they're dressed...unfortunately."

I heard the sound again. This time it was even lighter. "I hope they stay that way." She reached for my hand. "Come on." There was a door just to the side of us marked *Employees Only*. She pulled me through. "Most of the guys in here will only order beer, but let me show you how to enter mixed drinks and special orders just in case." She typed her employee code into the computer and pulled up the drink options. After a brief demonstration, she had me type a few fake orders. That was all it took before I could operate the system on my own. It was almost identical to the one I'd used at the Trap House. "You're going to start with two hundred, and that's how much you'll return at the end of your shift. Anything over that amount you keep. Questions?" She handed me the wad of cash.

I stuck it into my apron. "Nope, I've got it."

"We'll each have five tables. I can help out with yours until you get the feel of it, if you want."

The casino wasn't really all that different from Saint's restaurant. The orders were mostly drinks, which made it much easier. Food tended to make things a bit harder, with all the ingredients and cooking processes to memorize.

"I think I'm good," I said. "I'll come get you if I need help."

She smiled, her red lips parting to show perfectly white teeth. It was no wonder she made that amount each night. I didn't like girls *that* way, but even I'd tip the hell out of her. There was a huge difference between Christy and me, something that went well beyond our appearances.

She was perfect, and I was...not.

I had no idea how these guys would react to the mess on my face. Unless they were from Bar Harbor, their assumptions would be far from accurate.

I packed the other pocket of my apron with a pad of paper and several pens. Then I straightened my back and followed her to the door.

Before she opened it, we both adjusted our bras. "Your nipples are going to ache by the end of the night," she warned me, "but the money will be well worth it. Promise."

I laughed, my smile spreading as wide as it could. "They already do! I'll tough it out." The bra felt like a set of clamps, not just holding me up, but binding me, too. There was pain starting in my shoulders and in the center of my back where the straps dug into my skin. But pain was part of my life.

All that mattered at that moment was how much money I was going to make.

Her fingers tapped my wrist. "I figured I was going to like you. I was right." She released me and moved through the open door before I got a chance to get a good look at anything besides her black nail polish. "Those are yours." She pointed toward the row across from us. "Mine is the row to the right. Let me know if you need me."

With the pad in my hand, I walked to the first ten-top and began taking their orders. Christy was right: they mostly wanted beer. But their tips were consistent, and they drank fast. After a few rounds, I started ordering ahead so their drinks would be ready before they asked for them. That allowed me to turn the bottles even faster. The players seemed to appreciate not having to wait, and their tips started to increase.

Every hour, we took a fifteen-minute break. Those moments went by so fast, I barely had time to sit and take a sip of water before we had to report back to our tables. My feet throbbed inside the boots; my nipples had been hard and aching for hours from the constant rubbing and squeezing of the bra. The spilled beer felt like glue on my fingers, and every part of my body reeked of cigarette smoke. Still, none of that mattered. Cash was building in my apron. The wad had become so big, I had to break it up into two separate folds, and the other pocket was almost overflowing with chips.

"Rae?" a man said from behind me.

I was setting my last bottle on one of the tables, and I froze from the sound of him speaking my name. The depth of his husky voice was a sound I knew without having to see who it belonged to—not just because I'd heard it so often, but because it used to vibrate across my skin and sear into my memory.

I didn't turn around. I just kept facing the table.

I wasn't ready for those eyes, that mouth; those hands, so achingly familiar. The memory of them hurt. They'd left me too suddenly to represent anything but pain now.

"Rae," he repeated. "It's me."

There was nowhere to go. If I wanted to move around him, I was going to have to turn and face him. So I did...but slowly. I kept my breath in my lungs so he wouldn't see how he'd knocked the air out of me. My stare moved from the ground to his boots. I didn't recognize them...and of course, I wouldn't have. Why would he still have the same boots he'd had so long ago? But they were definitely something he'd wear—full of style and terribly expensive.

My eyes moved up the height of him. His dark jeans outlined the muscles in his thighs, and his shirt hinted at what was beneath the thin material. I knew what was under it: the feel of his skin, its taste, its smell. I knew the warmth of his arms, and how much it had stung when they'd released me...forever.

When my eyes reached his neck, my entire body stiffened. My mouth turned dry and my hands started to shake. The tray was empty, so I flipped it around and clutched it against my chest like a shield. "Hart Booker," I whispered. It was so loud in that room from all the chatter and the clanking of chips. But he nodded, and I knew he'd heard me. Then I dared to look at his face...finally. A few days' worth of medium-brown scruff covered his cheeks. His eyes—the lightest blue, almost silver—glimmered back at me. They weren't always that color, but when they were, they could be the most honest eyes I'd ever looked into.

It felt like I'd been swept up in a storm of moments from my past, a whirlwind of every memory from every year we had been apart. The heat from those memories turned my face red. Sweat covered my body. Lightning flashed around my cheek.

I couldn't stop it.

I didn't want him to see me like this...in this outfit, in this casino. So scarred.

Where the fuck was my umbrella?

"You've been walking by my table all night," he said. "You look so different...I wasn't sure it was you at first. But I'm glad it is. I was hoping I'd see you while I'm in town."

You look so different...

Hart had graduated high school and left Bar Harbor when I was a sophomore. The scar came my junior year. It was a part of me he hadn't seen, a part that hadn't existed the last time we were in each other's presence. The way my body was angled, he could see the whole thing, and I couldn't change that now. I was frozen. I hated that he still did that to me.

He'd broken me.

So how was it possible he could still affect me like that? Or that I would allow him to, after all these years?

"You've worked here for a while?" he asked.

Did it really matter? I wasn't sure why he was talking to me now...he hadn't even told me he was leaving Bar Harbor. I found out from his friends...and from him not returning any of my messages. No good-bye, no explanation. No call after all this time. And now he wanted to ask me questions about my *job*?

What about *me*? What about what *I* felt?

"Rae?"

"Yes," I said. What had I just answered? "I mean, no, I haven't."

He was several inches taller than me, but he was somehow able to look up at me through his lashes. His gaze was more than intense. It shook me. It wrapped its power around my limbs, my body. It felt as if the ground beneath me was convulsing and quaking.

"Are you living up here in Bangor?" he asked.

I held the tray even closer against my body as my stare traveled from his eyes to his lips. They were pale red, full, and hinted at the grin that used to melt me—that was melting me now, in spite of everything. "No," I finally said. "I'm still in Bar Harbor."

"Do you have a place in town or—"

"Boss man just walked in," Christy said in my ear, standing

directly behind me. She pressed close to my side as I forced my attention toward the entrance. She was right; Kevin had just walked in and was scanning the room. "He's going to check your tables and make sure all the players have drinks. Just wanted to warn you."

"Thanks," I whispered over my shoulder. A gasp came through my lips when I reconnected with Hart's stare. He was stirring up emotions that I couldn't control. I had for so long, and I wanted to now…or maybe I didn't. I was too swept up to know. But I couldn't lose this job before it had even really started. "I've got to go."

"Okay. I'll catch up with you later." His lips remained apart, like there was something more he wanted to say. But he didn't. He didn't turn around, either.

So I did.

And I instantly regretted it.

As much as he'd hurt me—and as much as I needed to check on my tables so I didn't get fired on my first night working—something was pulling me toward him. But when I turned around to tell him I'd find him after my shift, he wasn't there anymore. I did a quick search of the other aisles, the chairs, the backs and fronts of everyone nearby. I found nothing. He was gone.

I knew I was running out of time so, using the notes I had taken earlier, I hurried into the back room and ordered the list of beers that were the most popular at my tables. Packing the bottles onto my tray, I returned to the main room just as Kevin was checking my row. He nodded as I passed and continued to watch while I traded the players' empty bottles for full ones.

I kept up the same pace the rest of the night until last call. Time hadn't dragged at all, but my feet certainly had and my nipples felt like they were on fire. My apron was full of cash and chips, so that was what I'd focused on—and on Christy, who had pulled me into the back room to go over the closing duties after we'd dropped off the last round of drinks.

When she went to the bathroom, I took the opportunity to peek into the poker lounge. Most of the tables were empty except for the stragglers who were sitting around bullshitting and a few other players waiting in line at the cashier window. None of them were Hart.

"We have to stock the glasses, refill the napkins, and make sure the station is clean. Then we can go home," Christy said from behind me. I hadn't realized she'd returned, or that I was still staring at the exact place where I had spoken to him.

I felt like I was standing outside after a storm had passed, surveying the devastation. Broken branches and leaves and tiny pebbles had collected around my feet. The sky was black; I could taste the earth in the air. As I took my first step, my shoes squeaked with moisture.

I was completely drenched.

FIVE

"Do you know what the rain is?" he asked.

I was curled in a ball in the corner of the couch. A candle flickered on the table. It was the only light in the house; we'd lost power from the storm. He'd even let me take the candle into the potty with me, but he told me not to flush. I kinda liked that. The noise the toilet made could be so loud and scary at night.

I pulled the blanket even tighter around me. "No...what is it?"

"It's the tears from all the people who cried today. The sky pulls them out of all the tissues and sleeves and holds them up there until it's full. Then, it comes raining down on us."

A chill ran over me, covering my skin in tiny bumps as I remembered how mean the rain had sounded. It felt like our house had been shaking. "Why did the storm sound so angry?"

"The sky doesn't just take tears; it also takes the sounds that people make. That yelling you did while you cried this afternoon came right back at us, didn't it?"

I couldn't control my temper sometimes. I wanted to. I tried really hard to. I just didn't want Mommy to go to work because Darren got so sad whenever she left. And what made him sad, made me sad.

"So if I cry softly, it won't thunder as much?"

"Come on over here, Rae."

I glanced toward the rocking chair where he was sitting. The candle lit up his face and his open arms. With the blanket still around me, I tiptoed over to him. He pulled me onto his lap, tucking my legs into the side of the chair and wrapping his arms around me. We swayed back and forth.

"You're a good girl. You have no reason to be shedding those tears, and especially no reason to be yelling like that."

Back and forth.

Mommy said I was a strong girl, a smart girl. He always said I had the prettiest smile of all the girls he'd ever seen. Strong, pretty girls didn't need to cry. Darren didn't need to cry, either. I wanted to tell him that, but he was in his room. He was always in there. He said he didn't like hanging out anywhere else in the house. He was so silly.

I stretched my hands out of the blanket and placed them on top of his. His knuckles were so rough and hard. Chapped like my lips after I cried. They held me tight, but it didn't hurt.

"Rest your head on my chest and let's see if we can get you to sleep. It's past your bedtime, my good girl."

I pressed my cheek against his shirt. It was soft. Much softer than his knuckles, and the hairs around his neck tickled my nose.

Back and forth.

"I want you to think of good things. Pretty things. No more rain tonight, only rainbows."

His fingers moved out from under mine and he ran them through the loose strands of my hair. My eyes closed. My breathing slowed. His thumb dipped onto my neck, but the rest of his hand stayed in my hair.

Back and forth.

"You're such a good girl, Rae."

Back and forth.

"*Stooooppp!*" I screamed as my eyelids flew open. There was a noise other than my own voice, coming from somewhere around me. I ignored it. My hand immediately reached for my face, blotting the skin from the corner of my eye to my mouth. There was moisture, but it wasn't thick or metallic-smelling like blood. It was from the tears.

And my scar was still there.

Every time I touched my cheek after one of my nightmares, I hoped my fingers would pass over clear, unmarked flesh. That would never happen. But it didn't stop me from wishing.

I tried to slow my breathing, clawing the scarf off my throat and unbuttoning the top of my jacket. There weren't any hands around my neck, but it felt as if there were...as if they were squeezing all the air out of me. I couldn't breathe deeply enough.

I needed to concentrate on something other than hands.

His hands.

The noise...it hadn't gone away. It was an annoying mix of ringing and vibrating, and it was coming from the seat next to me.

My phone.

"Hello," I said as I answered.

"Ms. Ryan, it's Vince." Brady's landlord. *Shit.*

I used my sleeve to wipe the tears out of my eyes and off my face. Then I dragged it across the driver's window and the inside of the windshield to clear the condensation. The glass finally revealed that I was in the parking lot of the casino. My brain had been too foggy to remember this when I'd woken up from my nightmare. I'd only planned on taking a short nap after my shift. I'd been so damn tired. Something told me I slept a lot longer than I intended.

I turned on the car, waiting for the time on the clock to show. It was...eight.

In the morning?

Fuck.

"Hey, listen, I was about to call you. I—"

"Ms. Ryan, you said the same thing last week and the week before. I'm done listening to you. You were served an eviction notice seventy-two hours ago. In the meantime, you had every chance to pay up. I still haven't received a dime."

"I have money." I grabbed my purse off the passenger seat, frantically trying to unzip the top. I dug around inside until I found the wad. "I just got a job at the casino in Bangor, so I'll be able to pay you everything I owe you."

"You're going to bring me the money right now?"

My fingers tightened around the cash. "Not all of it. Just some of it, but I'll give you everything I have."

"How much is that?"

I calculated how much I would need for gas and my cell phone bill and an extra twenty in case something came up. "Around three hundred."

"Three hundred isn't even close to the amount you owe me, Ms. Ryan."

"I know, but—"

"I want you out. You have one hour...or your things will become my property."

My forehead dropped to the steering wheel, the freezing leather practically piercing my skin.

My body swayed *back and forth.*

Was this really happening?

"One hour?" I repeated. "That's all you're going to give me?"

"You heard me," he said. Then the phone went dead.

SIX

B rady's landlord didn't care that I'd have no place to go once he kicked me out, or that it had taken me an entire month to find a job—or that three hundred and eighty-five dollars was more than I'd ever made in one day, and I was willing to give most of it to him. He just wanted his money—*all* of it—and I didn't have enough to make him happy.

I didn't bother putting down the phone. I just called Shane's number. "It's me," I said when he answered. "We have a problem."

"It's not Brady, is it?"

Shane had texted me the prior morning, telling me he'd dropped Brady off at rehab, that he was still detoxing pretty hard and the meds weren't really helping. But at least he was someplace safe, someplace that would help him get through this. From the sound of Shane's reaction, he had lingering fears that something bad had happened already...or that Brady had left.

"No, I haven't heard from him," I said, hoping it reassured him. "It's about his apartment."

Shane sighed in relief. "I'm in the middle of a meeting and can't really talk right now. Can you swing by my job site in about twenty and we can discuss whatever is going on?"

I checked the time; I had fifty-eight minutes. It would take at least forty-five to get to Bar Harbor. There was a chance Vince would give me a little more time if Shane were the one asking for it. I'd ask Shane to call him when I got there.

"That's fine," I said, "but it's going to be a little more than twenty. Where are you?"

"That old B&B at the end of Cottage Way. It's right off Main Street."

I put the car in drive and began to pull out of the parking lot. "I'll see you soon."

It felt like the drive took forever this time. Cottage Way was just outside the downtown area, only a few minutes from the Trap House and Brady's apartment, so I knew the area well. I hadn't been going out much—mostly because I didn't have the money—so I hadn't realized the old B&B had been sold. The place had been for sale for close to a year, and I didn't think they'd ever find a buyer. But something was definitely happening now. Workers in hardhats were rushing in and out of the building; tools and machinery were parked all over the front lawn.

Shane was standing on the front steps with Josh, one of his helpers, holding a set of blueprints. He stopped chatting when I reached them and gave me a hug...carefully, though, like he always did, knowing where not to touch.

"What's going on here?" I asked, secretly hoping some rich, out-of-town investor was making the B&B into a restaurant and needed to hire a full staff. I probably wouldn't make as much money here as I would at the casino, but it would save me hours of commuting and gas—and the uniform would likely be more comfortable.

"It's a huge renovation," Shane said. "We're gutting the whole building and making it into a place called The Harbor Spa."

"A spa?"

A twinge of disappointment fluttered through my chest. From the time I'd gotten my scar, I'd wanted so much to go to cosmetology school. I may not have been able to stand the sun shining on my face, but that didn't mean I couldn't help others glow in their own light. I'd been supporting myself since I was sixteen, which made it impossible to save enough for school. There was something more important I'd been stashing away money for. That took almost all the extra cash I had.

"It'll be a real high-end place," Shane said, his eyes wandering over the building, "nicer than anything we have now and ready just in time for season." The expression on his face was just like the one he wore when Brady did something to make him proud. Shane truly loved his job; I was envious of that. He turned his full attention to me. "Anyway, you said you wanted to talk about the apartment?"

My gaze moved to the ground. "With Brady gone and losing my job, I haven't been able to afford the rent. The landlord wants me out. Today."

"Today?"

I looked up, expecting to see disappointment. But there was only stress and worry on his face, which I understood completely. I was feeling the same things myself. "Like, in fifteen minutes," I said.

He ran his fingers through his hair. "I can't leave right now. I've got a meeting in ten minutes, and we're starting the plumbing this afternoon."

"I'm so sorry, Shane." And I really was. I didn't want Brady to lose his apartment or any of his things that were inside, because that would mean I'd be losing them, too. I just didn't know how I could save any of it.

He shook his head, pulled his hand out of his pocket and rested it on my shoulder. He was the only parent who embraced me...the only one I allowed to. He'd taken me in when I needed it. I considered him more of a father than my own. Mine had taken off before my brother had even been born and I hadn't heard from him since. If I knew anything of the word "father," it was because Shane had been in my life. "This isn't your fault, Rae. It wasn't your job to pay Brady's rent. How much does he owe?"

"About twenty-five hundred."

"Dammit." He shook his head. The dark circles under his eyes suddenly seemed even darker. "I don't have that kind of money right now. Brady let his health insurance lapse, so I'm paying for his rehab."

I hadn't even considered asking Shane for the money or anyone else. This was our mess to handle—mine and Brady's—not his. He'd given me enough over the years. And I knew even if we ended up being evicted, Brady would be fine. Once he was done with rehab, he'd just crash with Shane for a month or so until he'd saved up enough for another place.

My situation was a little different.

There was no way I would ever go back to Mom's house; those walls weren't home anymore, and hadn't been for a very long time. That space was dead to me. And I didn't want to squat at Shane's, either. Going back there would only remind me of how little I'd grown since I had left. I felt enough of that helplessness on my own. Sleeping on Shane's couch or in Brady's old bed would just rub that wound until it bled.

"Don't worry about the apartment," I said. "I just want to make sure I get Brady's stuff out before the landlord takes it all. Maybe if you talked to him, he'd give us an extension?"

He reached into his front pocket and pulled out his phone. "Do you have his number?"

I scrolled through my call log and read it off to him. He waited for the landlord to answer as I wandered off toward the water.

I needed to think beyond the apartment.

I hadn't heard from the manager at the casino, so I was pretty sure I had a full-time job. But even with making that kind of money, it would still take me a few weeks to be able to afford a place on my own. Where would I live in the meantime? Whenever this had happened before, when I was between crashing with the few guys I'd dated in the past, Brady was the one who took me in. That wasn't going to happen this time.

"Hi, Rae."

My breath got stuck in the back of my throat. I had to stop myself from choking. It was that voice again, the one that made my entire body melt...and that made my heart ache at the same time. I'd lost track of him at the casino. He'd so easily left me behind. *Again.*

What the hell was he doing *here* now?

"Seeing you at the poker room was a coincidence," he said as I turned around. His soft lips were pulled into a grin. "This time, it feels a little more meaningful."

I didn't bother telling him that, after I'd gotten out of work, I had checked the whole parking lot for him. I hadn't expected that he'd stick around, considering his tendency for leaving. Maybe I'd just been hoping it would be different this time.

"The poker room was definitely unintentional. But you're in *my* space now."

And he was. He was standing only a foot away, with his hands in his pockets. A fleece hugged his tall, tight frame.

His eyelids narrowed. His bottom lip was wet where he'd just licked it. "*Your* space?"

I didn't just hear his words when he spoke; I felt them push through my jacket and tickle the skin around my navel. Had I closed my eyes, I'd have seen his lips in that exact spot. His tongue, too. My back arching from the syllables he breathed over my flesh.

But I couldn't close my eyes...and I couldn't let any of that happen. I wasn't going back to that place with him. It had taken me far too long to recover last time. All he would get from me now were simple answers. "Yeah, this is..."

I stopped speaking when Shane joined us suddenly, his eyes bouncing from Hart to me. "Did I interrupt you guys?"

"No," I answered quickly, thinking of a question to fire off at Shane. "Is everything okay with the landlord?" I hoped it would make Hart uncomfortable enough to walk away. But he didn't. He just stood there facing me, his eyes never leaving mine.

"He's giving me a few extra days to move Brady's things,"

Shane said. He wasn't done speaking. I could tell that whatever was coming next, it hurt him to say it. "That's the only allowance he'll make. He doesn't want you—or anyone—living there, so that means you—"

"I'll head over there right now," I blurted out. I got it. He didn't need to say any more, especially in front of Hart. Not that it mattered, but Hart didn't need to know anything about my living situation. And it was a reason to make my exit.

"He wants you to leave your key on the kitchen counter," Shane said.

That spot inside my stomach began to thaw from Hart's silvery stare. It was the same spot that liked to shoot little bolts to the place between my legs, reminding me of the control he used to have over my body...and apparently still did. I only wished it could heat my face, too; it was the only skin that wasn't covered by at least a layer of clothes. And the colder it got, the deeper and redder my scar appeared. I hated that I couldn't hide it from him.

"No problem," I said.

Shane's hand was back on my shoulder, more fatherly concern filling his face. "You know you can always stay at my house. No one is using Brady's room, so it's yours if you need it. You still have the key I gave you?"

Hart had noticed Shane embracing me, and his concerned expression. He was processing the pieces he'd just heard, putting the whole picture together. His stance told me he wasn't going anywhere...which meant I needed to. "Yeah, I have it, but I'm all set. I have a place already." I hated lying to Shane after everything he had done for me. It was something I didn't usually do. I just didn't want him to worry, and I really didn't want Hart to be here while we had this conversation, either. "Thank you, Shane. I'll call you after I leave the apartment." I glanced at Hart. I had no idea what to say to him, so I said nothing. I raised my fingers and waved as I turned around and rushed to my car.

I slid into the driver's seat and watched the guys from the corner of my eye. I saw their lips move. I couldn't help but wonder what they were talking about, why Hart was at the construction site...what he was even doing back in Bar Harbor. Shane would tell me everything, but it would have to wait until later.

I put my foot on the brake and turned the key, and a sputtering filled my ears. The entire car shook. It sounded like it was trying to start; it just didn't actually fire up. I checked the key to make sure it was the right one. I tried tapping the gas.

Nothing happened, other than the noise attracting their attention.

This can't be fucking happening.

As my forehead pressed against the steering wheel, my skin chafed from the leather rubbing against it. I didn't care. All I wanted was to go to Brady's and grab my things and figure out where I was going to live. Hopefully, it wasn't going to be inside this car.

There was a knock at the window. I took a deep breath, slowly turning toward the glass and rolled it down.

"I think you're out of gas," Shane said.

Hart had followed him, and was already lifting my hood. It blocked my view of him, but I could hear him checking whatever was underneath. He closed it and walked over to my window. "Shane's right," he said. "Everything else looks fine."

I felt so stupid. I knew I needed gas, but I had left Bangor in such a hurry that I'd forgotten to get some. My eyes automatically closed; my head leaned into the seat. I needed to think—again— and knowing Hart's eyes were all over me wasn't helping.

"Shane," Hart said, "I know your guys need you right now. I've got some time before my next meeting. I can take her to the gas station."

My lids burst open and my head lifted. The spot in my stomach was boiling. I wrapped my arms around it and squeezed.

"Are you okay with Hart taking you?" Shane asked. He knew about my past with Hart. But we were adults now, and all of that had happened years ago. There was no reason for Shane to think I couldn't be in a car with him. But he didn't know what was going on inside me.

And there was plenty of reason for *me* to think I couldn't do it.

I had no choice. I had to get to the apartment. "I'm…" I glanced at Hart. The flirtatious grin on his lips, the way his long, harmless-yet-demanding fingers ran through the scruffy stubble on his face. It was too much. I couldn't do it. "I'm good, thanks. I'll just call a taxi so I can get my stuff."

My car door opened. "No need," Hart said. "I'll take you there. Come on."

There was no way he was taking me to Brady's. This whole situation was embarrassing enough.

"No, Hart, it's okay…really."

He just kept holding the door open, and I just kept sitting there, waiting for him to close it again. Finally, he reached for my hand. "Let me help you." It was an order, though a soft one that came from a sincere, helpful place.

"The man's offering to move you out," Shane said. "I'd do it if I could, but I'm stuck
here."

They obviously weren't going to ease up on Hart's offer, which didn't surprise me. I grabbed my purse and got out of the car. Hart's hand dropped when he realized I wasn't going to take it.

"Give him a real good workout, Rae," Shane laughed. "Maybe he won't ride my ass so hard this afternoon."

What the hell did that mean?

I didn't have time to think about it. I smiled at Shane, but it wasn't real. I was just trying to hide everything that stirred inside me. "Don't worry…I won't be easy on him."

"Good," Shane said. "We'll talk later."

I nodded as he walked away.

"Does that mean you're going to ride *me* really hard at Brady's?" Hart's lids narrowed again, and he gazed at me through his long lashes. "You know how much I liked it when you did that. And you know how much I liked to return the favor." His words could have been taken as an attempt at humor, but his tone told me he wasn't entirely kidding.

Goose bumps covered my skin.

"Where's your car?" I asked, breaking my stare away from him.

He laughed and held out his arm. "This way. After you."

I moved in front of him and headed down the long driveway. After a few steps, he caught up with me and led me to the black Range Rover that was parked in the street. I should have known he'd be driving something like that. Money wasn't something Hart or his family had ever lacked.

"Where are we going?" he asked once he got in.

"Turn around and go straight until you hit Main Street." I ran my fingers over the stitching of the leather seat, rubbed my knuckles—anything to keep my hands busy and my mind off him. I knew both were impossible. I had too many questions. I just didn't know why I couldn't bring myself to ask them.

He'd left Maine while were still dating—abruptly, with no warning, and no good-bye. It was the summer of his junior year. He just disappeared one day, and I hadn't heard much about him since. But that was my doing; whenever someone started talking about him, I walked away. It hurt too much to hear it. Eventually, I'd heard that Bar Harbor wasn't enough for him. His dream was to play professional baseball, but college scouts weren't exactly rushing to our town to find athletes. So he moved away and went to the best prep school in New England. Knowing he'd chosen sports over me and hadn't bothered to tell me hadn't exactly left the best impression.

I stared at his profile as he looked over his shoulder to back out of his spot on the street. I knew his face so well, but the years we'd been apart had only made him more attractive. More mature. His features were so sharp, so angled. He'd always been sexual, more so than anyone I had ever dated, but now it felt like there was a grown-up confidence that enhanced his physicality.

Sex poured from him.

He wasn't all tatted up like Saint—not that I could see, anyway.

He didn't have Saint's rugged appearance, or a bad boy exterior hiding an interior so battered and damaged that he was nearly impossible to heal. Hart was bold and smooth instead.

He was refreshing.

The only badness about him was the way he'd pleasured my body with his hands...and tongue.

I made myself not think about it.

He put the SUV back in drive and slowly turned around again, stopping when he found my eyes. I hated riding in the passenger seat. It positioned my scarred cheek closest to whoever was driving. He may not have been staring at it, but I could feel his questions regardless. I'd been so whole the last time he'd seen me. Now my skin was cracked, so thick and jagged that it barely looked like skin at all. But the memories inside me had made scars even worse than this, even worse than how I'd felt when Hart left without saying good-bye.

The countdown was still ticking away.

Twenty-nine days.

I made myself not think about that either, though it wasn't easy. I looked at Hart again. His eyes hadn't left me. He was looking beyond my scar, beneath the surface, trying to read my thoughts. I had no doubt he could do it, too. He'd always had the ability to hear the things I didn't say. Sometimes he'd tell me what he'd seen, but I had usually gotten the feeling that he kept most of it to himself.

His vision returned to the road. "I take a left onto Main Street?"

"Yeah, then a right onto Hancock. It's the third house on the left."

Slowly, the questions came. "So...you're living with Brady?" His hand casually slid around the wheel, pausing when it reached the top.

"I was just staying with him." The conversation he'd heard between me and Shane couldn't have made a lot of sense. "The landlord kicked us out—well...really, he kicked *me* out. I just need to get my stuff."

"You guys have been best friends for a long time." He was already digging around. "Still...just friends?"

I remembered all the conversations I'd had with Hart about this subject. He'd thought Brady liked me as more than just a friend. Saint had thought the same. Neither of them understood the level of friendship I had with Brady, what the two of us had been through together. Having been away as long as he had, Hart couldn't have known the half of it. I thought at least Saint would have gotten it, since he'd experienced some of my pain. But he never understood.

"Yep. Just friends," I said.

"I hear he's gone into rehab." I nodded. It felt like an interview. "Where will you be living now?"

I wondered how much more Shane had told him. I glanced out the window, tracing my fingers over the tinted glass. I wasn't giving him any eye contact while I answered. "I've lined up a place around here."

It was time to get the attention off me. It never should have been on me in the first place.

"You're living in Mass now?"

His grin was back. It was unsettling. "You've been looking into me?"

I didn't have a computer, and my phone only had features I could afford. I wasn't into social media...those sites were full of pictures of people who loved looking at themselves. I hated photos of myself—the old ones reminded me of someone I'd never be again, and the new ones told the truth about it. It hurt too much to look at them. "No. I saw your license plate."

"That's not what I was hoping you'd say."

Our eyes met briefly, once again triggering the jolt in my stomach.

"Being in Maine is one thing," I told him, "but what are you doing back in Bar Harbor?"

He shrugged. "I travel a lot for work."

I had no idea what his work was. "Baseball couldn't have brought you here."

His brows narrowed, a small line forming between them. "Baseball?" He paused. "You really haven't looked into me at all, have you?"

I shook my head. "No."

"Baseball didn't end up happening. I was injured pretty early on…my career ended before it really even started."

I could relate to that, more than he probably realized. But my scar hadn't changed only my career choices. It had changed my entire life.

"And why are you working for Shane?"

His hand moved down the wheel to hit the blinker. "Shane's working for me, actually. He's building the spa."

"He's working for you? Wait…" Hart's mom had once owned a spa in town; his dad was an accountant. After Hart left for prep school, his mom sold the spa and the family moved to Vermont. The spa had been sold several times since then and it was now closed. But now… "So The Harbor Spa is yours?"

"I partnered with my parents after I graduated college. So yeah, it's half mine."

I couldn't picture Hart working at a place like that. He'd grown into a sort of refined masculinity and was well-kept appearance-wise, but he didn't have the personality to be surrounded by so much vanity. I had no doubt his mom loved having him work with her. She had always been a bit controlling and a tad mouthy; having Hart in that position meant she could watch him closely. Hart had never confirmed it, but she hadn't been the biggest fan of me. "What do you do there?"

"I build the locations. Then I oversee the openings, making sure they're up and running to my standards." Locations…openings. There was more than one, apparently.

I turned my head toward the window again, scrunching my lids together while I waited for him to answer my next question. "So that means you're going to be here for a little while?"

"Six months in Bar Harbor, six in Bangor. Then another six in Portland. After that I'll hopefully be headed to a new location."

A year and a half in Maine.

I wasn't sure how I felt about that. In two short days, it had already become hard not to run into him. Eighteen months would only make it that much worse.

"I bet you're good at what you do...especially the taking off part." That slipped out. I didn't want to have a more in-depth conversation about it. I just couldn't help pointing out his flaw, since he was in full view of mine.

His sigh filled the silence. "Rae, about that—"

"It's that house right there," I said, pointing just ahead of us. Whatever the excuse was going to be, I didn't want to hear it. It wouldn't have stopped my stomach from jolting, wouldn't have made those memories hurt any less. I'd felt the heat return between us as soon as we were alone in the car, and even though it was tempting to climb over the seat, straddle his lap, and taste those lips I'd been missing, I couldn't do that. I didn't want to be hurt again. Saint was a brutal reminder of how bad it could feel to be cut loose. The pain returned every time I saw Drew. I didn't want another doomed relationship.

And casual sex would never work with Hart.

He turned into the driveway, and I saw Vince immediately. He was leaning against the side of his car, his arms crossed, the entire lower half of his face dropped in a frown. He looked like a pug.

He snapped like one, too.

Hart parked as Vince walked over to the SUV, stopping just a few feet from my door. "You're late," he yelled.

"But I'm here now," I replied once I opened the door.

He looked at his watch. "You have ten minutes before the locksmith gets here."

"Just give me a second and I'll get all my things out. Damn." I shut the door and hurried toward the building without even glancing behind me to see if Hart had gotten out of the car.

"Ten minutes," Vince yelled. "That's all you've got."

"Got it," I shouted back. "Again."

"Relax," Hart said. I stopped in the middle of the staircase and turned around. He was at the bottom, standing in front of the land-lord. "We heard you the first time."

"She was supposed to be here over thirty minutes ago."

Hart's back straightened, his feet spread apart, his hands stiff-ened at his sides. "That's not her fault; it's mine. So if you're going to yell at someone, yell at me. Or keep quiet; that would be even better."

"But she—"

"There's no way in hell you're going to keep talking to her the way you have been."

I couldn't see Vince's expression, but I saw the change in his posture: the way his shoulders slouched and his weight shifted between his feet. He slowly turned his head and looked up at me. "I'll wait for you out here. Let me know when you're done." His tone was entirely different this time.

Hart hadn't been an instigator in high school, and I'd never seen him in a fight—mostly because nobody had ever tried to fuck with him. Everyone had known that he stood up for what he believed in and didn't take any shit. It made disliking him even more difficult.

I couldn't think about any of that now.

Using my key, I trundled inside Brady's apartment, pausing in the middle of the living room to scan it all. He'd lived here for at least a few years. It was a good apartment. Great memories...some bad ones, too. Like the most recent ones of him detoxing on his bed.

Hart was suddenly in the doorway. "I think we're going to need a bigger SUV," he said. I glanced at my side, watching his eyes travel over the couch and the kitchen table, the pots and pans that covered the counter. "Do you want me to go—"

"None of this is mine." I moved into the bedroom, opened my suitcase and threw in all my clothes that were on the floor. I loaded it until it was so full I could barely get it closed. I packed the rest into garbage bags. Then I went into the bathroom and removed everything that was mine, making sure the lids were on tight before I stuck them in the same bag as my clothes.

"Do you have any boxes? I can start packing the rest."

"There's nothing else to pack." He stood in the entryway of the bathroom, and I moved past him, dragging the suitcase and the two plastic bags over to the front door. I checked all the surfaces one final time; there was nothing else that was mine. And since I didn't have enough room in Hart's SUV to load Brady's stuff, this would have to do.

I was going to miss this place.

"This is everything I own." The humiliation of it suddenly registered. I slowly met his eyes. In my head, I created so many different reactions that would come out of him, imagining his expressions, his words. His pity. I was waiting for one of those...or all.

He approached me and took everything out of my hands. "I'll carry this all downstairs. Do what you need to in here, and I'll meet you outside." His voice was gentle—a whisper. Compassionate. It wasn't one of the reactions I'd expected. "Don't worry about the landlord...I'll take care of him if I have to."

I watched him move into the hallway, focusing on the provocative curves of his hand as it gripped the knob and pulled the door shut.

I sat on the sticky floor, tucked my knees into my chest, and wrapped my arms around them. The air left my lungs. I tried to suck it back in.

Back and forth.

I hadn't shown any emotion while Hart had been in here. But now it was everywhere. In my liquid eyes, in my quivering lips, in my shuddering heart. Other than Brady and Shane, no one had seen me cry since the day I'd gotten my scar. And now Brady wasn't even here to see this. To hold me. To save me.

Back and forth.

I didn't need this apartment to remind me how alone I was.

Brady's boys were always around and available, but they were superficial. I needed someone much deeper. I needed Brady, and I couldn't have him. And no one else was here, because people like me didn't show their wounds easily. No one wanted to see this kind of damage. It was violent and disgusting, dirty and evil. It was destructive.

It had ruined me.

My face, my skin, and my soul.

I tried to control my breathing, to stop the tears from seeping out of my lids by rubbing my eyes over the knees of my jeans. A black smudge from the liner had smeared across the fabric. Brady didn't have detergent...he didn't even have hand soap. But I didn't have time to scrub it out, anyway. I didn't want the landlord to start mouthing off to Hart because I was taking too long. I'd dragged him into this situation, and it wasn't fair to keep him in it any longer than necessary. I wondered what he was thinking as he packed my shit into his pristine, gleaming Range Rover. I know what I thought.

That I was trash, littering his perfection with my fear and my failure.

Fuck.

I uncurled my body and went into the bathroom. My eyes lingered in the mirror above the sink. I couldn't stop staring. My mascara had dripped into my scar. The black mixed against the damaged skin, creating a deep, bruised purple. Like a storm gathering on the surface of my skin. It would have been perfect if this were Halloween. But this wasn't a costume; I couldn't take it off at the end of the night and return to the smooth, wanted face beneath it. My scar was permanent, a storm that would never pass. It glared back at me every day. It called out its existence whenever I touched my face.

It haunted my dreams.

SEVEN

"Let me bring this stuff to your new place," Hart said, moving to the back of his SUV. "I don't want you carrying it all by yourself."

He opened his trunk and placed the gas can back inside that he'd used to fill my tank. It gave me a second to think. If I agreed, he'd follow me to my new apartment and help me carry the two bags and suitcase inside. The problem was...there was no new apartment. And this was the second time he'd asked; the first happened just after he bought me the gas. I'd refused then, too.

This time was no different.

"I'll be fine." I glanced at the B&B again. It was going to make a perfect spa. It was horseshoe-shaped, which meant the whole backside would face the water. I remembered how relaxing it was to stare at the ocean from Saint's boat. A vision passed through my mind—a dream, really, of me somehow working in the spa, doing something I loved, with the sea being part of my daily view. It would be a long time before this place was ready for anyone to work here. And even beyond that, I wasn't willing to spend any more time with Hart than I already had.

Stupid dream, Rae.

"Thanks for your help," I told him sincerely. "You made this morning suck a little less."

He sat on the edge of the trunk, his knees spread far apart. One of them brushed against the side of mine. It tingled. "The morning doesn't have to be over," he said.

Sex drizzled from his mouth. He didn't even have to try. The way his gaze took all of me in didn't help matters. I knew if I spent any more time alone with him, I would be naked before noon. The tears I'd sobbed on the floor of Brady's apartment and the fact that I was homeless would be forgotten...until I got back into my car and had nowhere to drive to.

Spreading my legs for this man would just add to the day's problems.

That didn't mean my desire for him had disappeared. There was a lot of it, actually. And I didn't think I was the only one feeling that way. For someone who had left me so easily before, he seemed to be having difficulty doing it this time.

I didn't understand it. But I guess I didn't have to.

I reached around him and grabbed the two trash bags, leaving the suitcase for him to roll. "I have to go, Hart."

"Have to...or want to?"

Instead of answering him, I turned around and began walking. I placed the bags inside my trunk and held it open so he could do the same. I avoided his gaze as I moved to the side and unlocked the driver's door. I could feel him behind me—the heat of his silvery eyes as they examined my legs, my ass, the outline of my torso that could be seen through my jacket.

When I tried to duck inside the car, he blocked me.

"Look at me, Rae."

My lids closed and I took a deep breath. As calmly as I could, I turned. When I opened my eyes again, my vision was drawn to the spot where his jawline protruded as it met his cheekbones and angled up to his forehead. I remembered how my hands had once fit so perfectly there. I remembered too that after he was gone, my fingers still craved the feel of his skin.

It hurt to see him.

"What do you want from me, Hart?" I blurted out.

"I don't want you to leave. Just give me a few more minutes."

I wasn't holding back the pain or the anger anymore. "And what will you do with those minutes that will make any difference at this point?"

He moved closer, so I backed up. The frame of the door pressed into me...and his fingers, at the spot where we both held the window. "I won't be able to take it back," he admitted. "None of it. I know that. And you won't understand why I did it, but at least hear me out."

I didn't know if I wanted to hear any of it—especially today. Still, whether or not I wanted to, it felt like something he needed to say. In return for helping me, I'd give that to him. But nothing else.

"Okay. Tell me."

He scanned my eyes, his irises sliding *back and forth*. I had to force my body not to sway in the same rhythm. "I didn't want to go. My parents and coaches were telling me to leave because it was the best thing for my future." He sighed, a breath that sounded painful for him. "I believed them; that's what kids do. But I didn't want to leave everything I knew, everyone who mattered to me: you." His arms blocked me in. Every time he shifted, another gust of his scent filled me. He was cedar and musk, blending with the tangy smell of his skin. It only added to the other triggers that caused lightning flashes in my stomach. "When I tried to have a voice, they overpowered me. According to them, I didn't know what was best for me." There was a change in his tone, an underlying anger. I felt it, and felt for him because of it. "So they packed up my stuff and they sent me to a place where I could be a star. And it worked...until the injury happened in college."

He held my gaze as I tried to find the answer somewhere in there. The answer I'd been waiting to hear all these years. I couldn't see anything but myself staring back. "I haven't heard it yet."

"Heard what?"

I took a gulp of the cold air and held it in my lungs. "The reason you didn't say good-bye."

His fingers tightened on the window. They weren't squeezing me, but I could sense their strength just the same. "If my parents had given me the opportunity, I wouldn't have left at all. They knew that. I don't blame them for waking me up in the middle of the night, packing my clothes into the car and driving me away. That was smart. Had they given me even a little space, I wouldn't have gone."

I hadn't wanted to hear anything he had to say, and now suddenly I was addicted to his answers. But that one wasn't good enough.

"Do they not have phones in prep school?"

His body hadn't moved, but somehow it felt as if he was even closer now. "You're right. I should have called. But it was hard enough to know I wouldn't be with you anymore..."

"Maybe that didn't have to happen. Maybe I could have been there with you." They were so irrational, the thoughts of my younger self.

"You were in school, Rae."

"I would have chosen you over school, if you'd asked."

I couldn't believe I'd just told him that.

"You would have dropped out your sophomore year to be with me? Left your friends and family? I would never have let you do that. And even if I'd been that selfish, I didn't have the means to support you back then."

"So instead, you decided to never speak to me again?"

His gaze moved to my lips, then lifted once more. "I wouldn't have been able to live with myself if I'd heard how much I hurt you. I didn't want to be your pain, and I didn't want you to hear mine." His face clouded over. "I realized long ago how shitty that was."

I tried to move away from him. He wouldn't let me, but he kept his hands off me just the same. "Shitty? It's way more than that.

It's *unfair*, Hart. You didn't even give me a chance. I deserved that from you, at the very least."

"I would have told you to wait for me—I was ready to tell you, even as they were driving me out of town. *That* wouldn't have been fair, because I knew you would have."

He was right; I would have waited. He'd meant that much to me—more than Saint or any of the guys I had dated in between. All my relationships after Hart were about healing, finding others with the same wounds I'd suffered and trying to close them—with my hands, my heart, my body. With my words and my loyalty. But Hart was the only one I'd been with who hadn't needed to be fixed.

He was also the only one who'd been there before my scar. All the others came afterward.

I wasn't too blind to recognize that, in trying to heal them, I was also trying to heal myself.

"What are you doing back in Bar Harbor, then?" It came out as a whisper, and even that stung my already-burning throat.

His hand slid over mine and stopped just on the other side of my palm. "I'm building a spa."

"No, what are you *doing here*?" He could be as evasive as he wanted. I couldn't anymore.

Tiny flakes started falling from the sky. I felt them on my face. I glanced up, greeting the white specks of cold. They stuck to my eyelashes and melted on my lips.

"This was the first chance I've had to come home," he said. My neck slowly tilted downward until my vision fixed on him. "I've missed it."

I could tell he was waiting for something. Did he expect me to fade into his arms? To wrap my mouth around the sweetness of his? I wasn't the soft thing he'd left behind all those years ago. I was made of scars now, of storms and squalls that tossed me about and made my life unpredictable.

I was hardened.

"I get it," I said. And I did; I understood his answers, and the position he'd been in, even though there had been years in between for him to pick up a phone and offer an explanation. As fucked up as it was, a part of me was grateful for it. I didn't know what I would have done if he had come to my house to say good-bye, or if he had called me from prep school. Because he hadn't, my life had gone in a different direction, much darker than I'd expected.

And after all these years, he'd found me again, at what was possibly my lowest moment. What that meant or what was supposed to happen, I wasn't sure. I didn't know what either of us wanted. All I knew was *twenty-nine days*.

And he hadn't even apologized for leaving me behind.

I couldn't give in to him now.

"Don't ask for any more minutes," I said.

A playful look came over his face. I had to stop myself from smiling. "I won't...for today. But this won't be the last you see of me. You know that." He didn't make any attempt to back up or drop his hands from the window.

"Do I? This from the guy who leaves in the middle of the night without a good-bye and doesn't ever call." I knew this kind of bitterness would come out sooner or later.

I turned, ducked my head and dropped into the seat of my car. My hands fumbled with the key before getting it to start.

"You're not going to get very far with the amount of gas I just put in. Unless that's your plan..." The grin hadn't left his lips.

It made me angry more than anything. I didn't need to be rescued more than once.

Saved from myself, maybe. But that wasn't something Hart would be able to do.

"I'm headed to the gas station now."

He leaned against the open window, not far from my unmarked cheek. I'd washed off most of my makeup in Brady's bathroom; I knew how exposed my scar was. But I hadn't caught him staring at it. Not even once. Either he didn't want to see the way time had ravaged me, or he couldn't see it at all.

I didn't know which would be better.

I broke away from his gaze, trying to settle my stomach and get rid of his scent that seemed to have settled in my nose. "See you around." I put the car in reverse.

He pushed off the window and took several steps back. "Yes, you will."

EIGHT

As I filled my gas tank, I considered the places I could crash. I really only needed a few weeks before I'd be able to afford something on my own. Of course, I'd have nothing to fill it with, to sleep on, or sit on, but it would be mine. In the meantime, Caleb's house was probably the best spot for me. It was the biggest house and had the most room out of all the places Brady and his boys hung out. And since Caleb's parents had given him the house and it was all paid for, there wouldn't be a landlord to evict me. For now, that would work.

I got back in my car and texted Caleb and his roommate, Jeremy, to ask if I could stay for a bit. Their replies welcomed me to, for as long as I needed. I'd spent enough time there to know there was an empty bedroom in the back, and that I'd be sharing a bathroom with Jeremy. With my work schedule, I'd really only be there to sleep. It didn't matter how late or early I arrived; the guys would always be home.

Drug dealers didn't usually get out much.

Before he'd disappeared, the rumor around town was that Brady was dealing again. It wasn't exactly a lie. He did push the occasional ounce of weed or pounds for the guys who liked to buy in larger quantities. But he wasn't a street-level dealer, and he didn't do it every day. And he definitely hadn't made it a career. He just had a solid connection with a guy in northern Maine who grew it, and he liked to snort the profits. The real dealers were Caleb and Jeremy. They were able to get their hands on anything—heroin, meth, even bath salts. But since one of their tweakers had flipped out after Caleb ran out of meth, poured gas all over the front porch, and tried to blow up the house, the guys were more selective with whom they sold to and what they kept around.

A long dirt road led up to the house. The guys' cars were parked on the grass; they were the only ones there besides mine. I was thankful for that.

I waddled up to the front door with the two bags and my suitcase. After my double-knock, Jeremy answered and led me toward the back of the house. He scratched the top of his scalp as he walked, pulling his red strands in all different directions. I didn't know if it was gel or filth, but the hair stayed where he left it.

On the carpet of the bedroom was a bare mattress that he said I could use. A mound of crumpled clothes sat next to it, and even more were on the floor of the closet. There were splatter stains on each wall, and two empty condom wrappers in the corner. If I looked hard enough, I'd probably find the filled rubbers somewhere in there, too. The room reeked of sour milk. It could have been from the clothes, or the cans of beer that were littered throughout, or from any of the stains that had hardened on the carpet.

And Hart had wanted to help me move into my new place…

I made a mental list of everything I needed to pick up on my way to work, things that would make this room clean and livable. Then I joined the guys in the living room. There were pieces of bud all over the glass table. Some were small enough to be rolled; the rest were waiting to be bagged. Other empty cans had been tossed on the floor beside the couch. At least every wood-paneled wall had a hole in it, and they were covered in a blackish film that turned the grain much darker than it was supposed to be. The cleanest thing in there was the flat-screen that hung in front of us, and even that had handprints all over it.

"Thanks for letting me stay," I said, tucking my feet underneath me and leaning into the end of the sectional. "I just need a couple weeks and I'll be able to afford my own place."

"Don't rush out," Jeremy said. "There's way too much cock and takeout boxes and unused bottles of bleach up in here. We need a girl roommate." He put a glass bowl up to his lips and took a hit, holding the smoke in for a while before he finally coughed it into the air. Then he passed the bowl to Caleb. "The place is starting to fucking smell. Keep telling Caleb that, but he says he doesn't smell shit."

Maybe that was because Caleb couldn't smell *anything* past his hair. Since we'd graduated, I'd been telling him to cut it. He hadn't listened. The dreads made everyone think he was a hippie; his patchy beard and Birkenstocks only added to the image. He never dressed in anything other than a hoodie, jeans and wool socks—even in the summer. His teeth were starting to turn the color of resin. The truth was, he wasn't a hippie at all. He was just lazy, and grime—whether it was around him or actually on him—didn't bother him.

"How's my boy?" Caleb asked, smoke drifting from his lips as he spoke. He banged the bowl against his palm to empty it, collecting the ash and wiping it on his jeans. They were already so dirty, the streak was hardly noticeable. Scooping up a few buds, he packed the bowl again and handed it to me.

Smoke began to fill my mouth. I blew it out and said, "He's still in detox. At least that's what Shane told me in his last text. Brady hasn't called me since he left."

There was a knock at the door, and Jeremy got up to answer it. The living room was in the back of the house so I wasn't able to see who it was. Not that it mattered. Unless they were friends, the guys usually didn't let anyone in past the kitchen.

"When I heard Brady had been in Bangor," Caleb said, taking the bowl from my hand, "I called some of my boys up there. No one had seen him around. Whoever he was with is way deeper than the connections I have."

Jeremy returned to the living room, taking the same spot on the couch, reaching for the pipe as soon as he sat. "They wanted a dime," he said to Caleb.

I thought about Brady's face, and how beaten it had been when I'd picked him up. "Do you think he's in trouble?" I didn't know anyone in Bangor, so there was no one I could check with or call.

Caleb shrugged. "If he is, I've got his back. He knows that."

"Me too," Jeremy said. The whites of his eyes were now the same color as his hair.

Brady had helped out these guys so much over the years, especially when the cops had been tipped off and told that they were all dealing. When Caleb had a hard time moving the rest of his supply, Brady took care of it. The cops hadn't found anything in Caleb's house when they'd searched it.

"Hope Brady doesn't think he'll be getting any drugs from me when he gets out," Jeremy said. It was strange hearing those words come from someone who had a beer in his hand and probably more than a few pills up his nose.

Caleb laughed while he tied an elastic around his knots. "You said the same thing about Tiff when she went to rehab, and Evan, and they were just here buying shit from us last night."

"Brady's different," Jeremy said. He reached for one of the cigars on the table and sliced it open with a razor blade, emptying out all the tobacco. Then he wetted the leaves in his mouth and filled the center with weed. "We've known him since we were kids. Guy's got a chance to do something good, you know?"

"Whatever," Caleb said. He wiped his hands on his jeans again. "If Brady wants something, Brady's going to get something. I'm not denying my boy."

This was just another thing that would have to change once Brady got out of rehab. He couldn't come here anymore. I wasn't even sure if he could still be friends with these guys. I wondered if he'd considered any of that, since almost everyone he hung out with either used or sold. Most did both.

Pot and alcohol were the hardest things I'd touched. And I didn't consider weed to be all that bad, since it would soon be legal to buy it in Maine. Still, I'd give it up for Brady because Jeremy was right: he did have a chance to do something good with his life. More of a chance than the rest of us did. Shane was going to eventually give him the business. I wouldn't let him screw that up.

"Rae, you won't believe who I saw at the store the other day," Caleb said.

I knew exactly who he had seen. He'd directed the question at me, after all. "Who's that?" I asked, playing dumb.

"Hart Booker," he continued.

"No shit?" Jeremy said. He was holding the blunt against his lips, licking the inside flap before he finished the roll. "Haven't seen that kid since…damn, I can't even remember the last time."

Neither of them had hung out with Hart the summer before he left, which would have made it the end of our freshman year when they'd last seen him. He was an athlete; people in our crew were already stoners at that point. We partied in different crowds, which was why I was surprised Hart had even been interested in me. But we went to a small school where everyone knew everyone. And there was just something between us, regardless of who surrounded us.

Our paths had diverged, and though we'd ended up with very different lives, we were both in Bar Harbor once again. That was a strange thought.

"He bought that old B&B off Main Street," I said. "Shane's helping him convert it into a spa."

Caleb's brows rose, looking like he'd actually gotten a whiff of himself. "Sounds like I'm not the only one that ran into him."

I nodded. "I saw him today."

And yesterday, which was something they didn't need to know.

Not because I was trying to hide it, but because it just didn't matter.

And yet...he was still on my mind.

I didn't want this.

"Maybe he can get one of his girls to cut that fucking bush on top of your head," Jeremy said, looking right at Caleb. He stuck the end of the blunt into his mouth and lit the tip, taking long, deep drags to really get it puffing. "It looks like a nasty pussy, don't it, Rae?"

"I've got to get ready for work," I said, standing from the couch.

"Pass the blunt, Jeremy, and shut the hell up," Caleb said.

I reached the entrance of the hallway and turned around. "I won't be back until around four in the morning. Will you guys be up, or do you want to give me a key or something?"

"We'll be up," Jeremy said. "Just text us on your way home."

"Cool. Thanks." I went back in my room to grab what I needed.

With a change of clothes and my makeup bag in hand, I peeked into the bathroom. For someone who made fun of Caleb's bush, Jeremy wasn't any cleaner. The inside of the toilet was black. There was a layer of slime on the shower floor. The garbage can overflowed, and musty-smelling towels covered the linoleum.

I wasn't a neat freak, by any means. Living with guys since I'd been sixteen years old, I'd learned how to deal with messiness and even was a bit of that myself. But that house wasn't just a little messy. It was a health hazard.

I added a second bottle of bleach to my mental list and reminded myself to shower at work as much as I could.

Starting right then.

NINE

I looked at the chip Hart placed on my tray after I'd set his beer down. "A twenty-five-dollar tip is a little much, don't you think?" He was already on his third drink, and he'd given me just as much for the last two rounds.

"You're not just serving me beer." He folded his hand by throwing his cards out for the dealer to grab.

"I'm not?"

He shifted a little in his chair, turning toward me. His shirt was deep gray, almost charcoal. It darkened his eyes by several shades. "You're providing entertainment."

I glanced down at what I was wearing. The uniform hadn't changed, but it looked like it had gotten tighter somehow. It couldn't have been because I'd gained weight; I hadn't eaten anything since the day before. "You mean, my *outfit* is providing entertainment."

"No...I mean, your *smile* is." He crooked his finger to motion me closer. "Although that doesn't mean I'm ignoring your outfit. That would be impossible."

The encounters we'd had as teenagers were as sweet as they were sensual, and they'd bonded me to him. It was why I'd been so twisted up when he'd left. Still, I couldn't stop my mind from wondering how he looked underneath his clothes now. The thought made my skin break out in a sweat, even with the room as cold as it was. The freezing air made my nipples strain against Christy's bra. I hoped he couldn't see them through the padding.

I didn't trust what would come out of my mouth, so I kept it closed. But I widened my lips and smiled even more as I handed out the rest of the beers on my tray. Once it was empty, I returned to the back room to fill up again.

"That's the guy you were talking to last night, isn't it?" Christy asked, joining me at the bar. "The one at table eight."

I knew she'd told Kevin I'd done a good job; when I had arrived for my shift, a copy of the rest of November's schedule was in my newly-assigned mailbox, with a key for a locker. I'd be working five nights a week, all closing shifts in the poker room. They'd given me the best shift, and Christy's favorite section to work. I was grateful for that, and for her friendly interest, even if I didn't want to talk about him.

"Same guy," I said.

"What's his name?"

"Hart," I answered reluctantly. "His name is Hart. I've known him for a long time."

"So you guys are friends?"

I shook my head. "Maybe a long time ago. Not anymore."

"Well, friends or not, if he was looking at me the way he's looking at you, I'd wait until we were both walking out to the parking lot, push his fine ass against the side of his car and tell him how amazing I am when there isn't a pair of panties separating us. But I'm not you...and cock really isn't my thing."

My neck swooped to the side, meeting her wide hazel eyes. "You have no idea what you're talking about. He's definitely not looking at me that way." I was more interested in her piece of advice than her being a lesbian. It didn't bother me at all; I just hadn't pegged her for someone who liked girls.

"Oh yes, he is…and so are you. If you don't go for him quickly some other chick will."

"Good, I hope—"

"Hear me out, Rae. You're right: I don't know a thing about you two. Hell, I hardly know anything about *you*. But I've watched you two lock eyes all night, and there's obviously something going on." She was a little pushier than I liked. "I'm not saying you should fuck him right away; just show him why his eyes should stay on you, why your eyes are only on him and make him work for the rest. Chase it, you know?" She paused, glancing from side to side. There was no one around us except the bartender. She pulled me a few feet away so he couldn't hear us. "There's a blackjack dealer that works in pit two, the one right across from the buffet. She's been after me for weeks. Typical girly stuff, you know, sending me texts, flirting with her eyes and her tits. She hasn't let me touch her yet—we've kissed and shit like that, but nothing else, really."

I recalled the woman Christy had winked at when we'd passed by her table yesterday…the one with pink streaks in her hair. "What's your point?"

"That girl's got me crazy about her because she's playing hard to get," she said. "It'll work for you, too. It's obvious he wants you…and of course he does; you're fucking hot."

She didn't know about my difficult connection to Hart. She thought she was helping me out, but she was only making me angry. "You're reading this all wrong—there's nothing to chase. He's not trying to get with me, and I'm *definitely* not pursuing him. We have a history. That's it." I stepped back to the bar and grabbed the bottles that had been placed there for me, twisting off the caps before setting them on my tray.

Christy's eyes widened. "Wow. I pushed too hard…I'm sorry," she said softly. "And you're right: I must have read you both all wrong."

I lifted the tray and held it above my shoulder. The tone of my voice had been snappy. She hadn't deserved that, and I didn't want to make her feel bad for sharing her opinion. With Hart, things just weren't simple. "I'm sorry, too."

She gave me a warm, sultry smile and a wink. "Forgiven. Now get back to work."

Back in the main room, I passed out each of the bottles that were on my tray and took orders for several more. Just like it had last night, the front of my apron was filling with bills and chips. It seemed like the faster I moved, the more I earned. Knowing the amount I would probably make didn't stop my feet from hurting in the high heels, or my nipples from aching in that bra. It just made the pain more tolerable. It also helped energize me, which I needed since I really hadn't gotten more than a few hours of sleep.

Heading back to refill, I dropped the tray to my side and stepped away from the table. A hand stopped me from moving any farther. A hand that came from behind me and rested flat against my navel. Fingers that were full of strength and power... and lust. "I forgot to ask for your number this morning," Hart said.

The heat from his breath trickled to my neck and down the back of my tank top. I tried to calm the fluttering inside my throat. "I wouldn't have given it to you."

His hand tightened against me. "How can I get you to change your mind?"

"You can start by telling me why you think you need it."

His lips dipped to the base of my ear. "So I can call you whenever I'm thinking about you." The pad of his thumb grazed over the little ball that sat at the top of my belly button. It was connected to a curved rod and a small purple star that hung at the base of the hole. He knew the piercing was there...he was the one who'd paid for it. "Despite what you think, I'm actually a good guy." His other hand moved to my apron where I saw him drop something in. Then his fingers left my body, and I spun around.

A sudden coldness filled me, and I met his silvery eyes and half smile. "What did you just put in there?"

"I had a feeling you wouldn't give me yours," he said, his stare dipping toward my waist. "So I gave you mine instead."

Maybe he was a good guy and had just made some bad decisions when he was young. Or maybe he was an asshole. All I knew was I couldn't get hurt again, especially not by him.

"I'm not going to need it," I said.

"You never know...you might change your mind. In fact, I hope you use it tonight, to call me on your way home to let me know you're safe and that your car is acting all right."

My fingers drifted inside my apron, holding the small piece of paper with his number written on it. "Good-bye, Hart."

"Call anytime—doesn't matter how late," he said from behind me as I walked away.

I didn't believe my safety was the real reason he wanted me to call. If he really wanted to be friends again, he was coming on strong, especially because he knew how I felt about him. The only other reason was...sex. Of course.

That wasn't going to happen. None of it was.

I'd tried so hard to keep my past behind me. Hart was a major part of that past.

As far as I was concerned, that's where he'd be staying.

Christy and I walked out to the parking lot together. I was relieved to be wearing my own boots—ones that didn't pinch my toes—and going without a bra. As I'd thought earlier, the pain had been worth it. I'd made even more than last night, largely due to the hundred dollars Hart had tipped me before he left. Several hours had passed since he'd taken off.

I could still feel his fingers.

I hated that.

"Are you going to keep driving back and forth to Bar Harbor?" she asked, pulling a hat down over her dark locks. "I'm a Bangor girl...you know I have an apartment not too far from here."

I finished buttoning the top of my jacket, tucked my scarf inside, and shifted my messenger bag. It was heavy; I wasn't used to carrying a bag in addition to my purse, but now that I was having to shower at work, I had to bring so many extra things with me. "Yeah, I'm commuting," I answered. "I mean, I've never lived anywhere else. I'm comfortable being in a place I know so well."

"Makes sense," she said. "I usually don't stick around here for very long. Just enough time to save a little cash before I head out of town again." Maine had a look, and Christy wasn't it. She should have been singing in some hip studio in Manhattan or painting in some Los Angeles loft. She seemed to be more than just *this*. "I've lived all over," she continued, "but always end up coming back home."

Home.

Brady and Shane had given me the closest thing I had to one of those. Still, nothing had felt right since I'd gotten my scar. That wasn't Bar Harbor's fault; that was my fucked-up past, though as long as Brady and Shane were still living there, I couldn't imagine being anywhere else.

"You think you'll stay a while this time?" I asked her.

So far, my conversations with Christy were usually pointed at me—the topics and the questions, the slow release of information that I was hesitant to give. I didn't like it. My scar looked even worse when the spotlight was on me. It was time to change that. It also helped keep my mind off Hart.

She turned toward me with a grin spread over her heavily glossed lips. They twinkled under the moon. It didn't sound like a nervous laugh. Christy was all confidence. "Doubt it. Rosie—pink streaks—wants out of Maine. Love...it's such a fucker, isn't it?"

"Love? Yes, it definitely is." It had been a while since I'd felt something that resembled anything even close to love. I still remembered it, though: the way it made me ache and quiver and feel so much comfort in the same breath; the way it felt even stronger when the sun was shining on my skin. Mostly, I remembered the hole it had created in its wake when it was torn away from me without warning.

It hadn't been filled since.

If I were going to that place again, I'd have to be honest with whoever it was—not just about my feelings, but about my past, too. There were things I'd have to admit out loud that I wasn't ready to say. I'd spoken those words once, to Brady and Shane. I didn't know if I could do it again.

"Sounds like you know exactly what I mean," she said.

I glanced at my feet, the heavy, clunky buckles much more my style than the spikes I'd worn earlier. "I do."

"And it was with Hart, wasn't it? That's why you got so upset when I pushed you."

I glanced up, noticing the way she stared at me. She already knew the answer; nothing I said would change that. My silence would only tell her more. Rather than give her the word she already knew was coming, I just nodded.

Her hand found its way into the palm of my mitten. She gave it a squeeze. "It's okay. I get it." It was the first time she had touched me for more than a few seconds. Even though I couldn't feel her skin through the thick fabric, the contact still made me jump.

She was a girl, I reminded myself.

Her hands weren't the same as *his*.

"See you tomorrow," she said, veering off to the right since we had reached her car. I watched her open the driver's door and climb in.

I couldn't muster a smile, but the hand she had touched went into the air and waved. I saw her wave back through the windshield as I continued walking down the lot.

I finally got into my car, waiting for the engine to warm and for the air to heat up before I pulled out of the spot. My phone sat in my lap along with the piece of paper Hart had given me. His area code was 617...Boston. I pulled off my mittens, typed the nine digits into my phone and hit *save*. Then I set my cell on the passenger seat and shifted into drive.

I didn't know if I'd ever actually call him.

If I did, it wouldn't be tonight.

TEN

I sent the guys a text once I got into town like they'd asked me to do. Jeremy replied instantly, telling me to knock on the front door so he could let me in. When I pulled into the driveway, I found an unfamiliar car parked beside Caleb's. I knew what all their friends drove…this wasn't someone they hung out with.

I slipped my purse and messenger bag over my shoulder and headed for the door. Jeremy opened it before I'd even had a chance to tap my fingers against the wood.

"Saw your headlights," he said, moving inside, letting me close the door. "Wanna smoke?"

I really needed something. "Of course."

I followed him into the living room and sat on the opposite side of the couch, dropping my bags beside me. The house looked even worse in the early hours of the morning. The flickering lamp next to me turned everything straw yellow. There was a thick haze that coated the walls, the coffee table…even the TV. A rotten scent filled the air. Jeremy made a snorting sound, then coughed up whatever was in his throat, spitting it somewhere on the other side of him. My boots had stuck to the floor as I'd walked to the couch. Now I knew why.

"Getting good tips up in Bangor?" he asked. He pulled the bowl out of his lips and handed it to me.

I wiped the end of the glass before sticking it in my mouth. It was so tightly packed, I had to take several puffs before I got a decent hit. "More than I did at the Trap House."

"Saint, that fucker. Glad you're not dating him anymore."

None of Brady's boys liked Saint; they all thought he'd ratted them out to the cops. But Saint told me he hadn't, and he'd never lied to me before. Still, I wasn't sure who to believe...not that it mattered anymore.

"Saw his girl in town the other day. What's her name...Drew? Wasn't she over here one of those nights when Brady got into it with Gabe?"

I nodded and blew a stream of smoke through my lips. That party had been the first time I'd hung out with Drew. I'd liked her then. I'd even thought she was someone I could become really good friends with.

Damn. Things had really changed.

"She's pretty hot," he continued, "but not as hot as her friend Gianna. That red hair of hers...shit. I'd be all over that."

"So why aren't you?"

I handed him back the bowl, and he gave me a look that I understood. Both of those girls thought they were too good for our crowd—Saint, too, now that he'd become this straightedge. After seeing Jeremy launch his snot rocket on the floor, I knew they didn't fit here. But Gianna...she was the worst one. "Fancy" was how I usually referred to her. The rumor now was that Saint had hired her to do all his marketing, or some bullshit like that, probably just so she could stick around Bar Harbor and be Drew's shadow. He'd never offered me a job like that.

I was only good enough to serve his fucking food and work in his fucking warehouse shipping packages during the winter.

"She's really..." My voice trailed off as I heard something behind me. It was giggling. Squealing, even. With the TV turned down and the back of my head leaning against the wall, I could hear the sounds even clearer. Caleb's bedroom was on the other side…and apparently his bed was as well. That explained the other car parked in the driveway, and the mystery guest I hadn't seen yet.

"Anyone I know?" I asked. I knew he'd heard her. It was impossible not to.

He shook his head. "She's ain't from around here."

The girl's laughter switched to moaning. I tried not to make eye contact with Jeremy when he passed me the bowl. Things were awkward enough; I didn't need to see his expression, too. But I wasn't going to my room until the bowl was cashed, even if that meant listening to Caleb hook up.

I'd heard worse sounds in the past.

Sounds that made me scream in my nightmares.

"*Caleb…Caleb!*" she yelled. "*Fuck me. Harder. Haaaaarder!*"

I leaned forward and rested my elbows on my knees as I exhaled another hit. My eyes were on the TV; it was on, but I had no idea what was playing. It didn't matter. Rays of heat had entered my chest and slowly crawled toward my throat. That was what weed did for me. It was gentle and filled me with wispy clouds and a soft blue sky. It calmed the storm, if only temporarily.

Jeremy's phone beeped and a few seconds later there was a knock at the door. He got up to answer it while I nursed the bowl. The wall shook behind me…which then rattled the couch. I felt like I was in a rocking chair.

Back and forth.

I'd never imagined Caleb on top of me, and I didn't find him attractive at all, but some guys gave off a vibe that hinted at how rhythmic they'd be in bed. Being that he was a stoner and on a constant delay, I figured he'd be a slow fuck. But he wasn't. His pace was fast.

Surprisingly fast, actually.

"We're having a party tomorrow night," Jeremy said as he walked back into the living room.

The girl's yelling started to get louder. The wall shook even more. The couch was moving so much, it began to squeak.

It was time for me to get out of there.

I kept my eyes on the weed, blowing out my final hit. "I have to work, but I'll be back around the same time as tonight."

His hand appeared at my side, reaching for the bowl. His nails were chewed and filthy. Simple fingers that I didn't fear. "It won't be a huge party...just the usual crew. Might want to padlock your door, unless you don't mind if your bed gets used."

The thought of that grossed me out. "I'll pick one up in the morning."

"You might—"

A crunching sound cut off his words, and we both turned around. We could see over the low back of the couch where the wall was beginning to cave. Not all of it...just a round section, level with my neck. Seconds later, there was another scream.

Her scream this time.

A cry so loud I could almost feel the pain that had caused it.

"*Fuck!*" Caleb screeched.

Whatever had hit that wall hadn't come all the way through; it had broken the drywall, and I'd heard it split open, but it had only dented the living room side.

"You're fucking *bleeding!*" Caleb shouted.

I glanced at Jeremy; he stared at me, the bowl still between the tips of his fingers, his mouth around the end. "What the hell?" I asked.

He shrugged.

"Your goddamn blood is *everywhere!*" Caleb yelled. "Jeremy, get the hell in here *right now!*"

Jeremy walked toward me, his fingers clamping my wrist as he lifted me to my feet and dragged me behind him. "You're coming with me."

I didn't resist. I just followed, hoping whatever was on the other side wouldn't ruin my high. I was too tired for this shit. I didn't even know if I'd bother to bleach anything before crashing.

"What's up?" Jeremy said, cracking the door a little. It was too dark to see anything.

"Turn the fucking light on, you idiot!" Caleb shouted.

Jeremy opened the door a bit more and moved inside. He flipped the switch and filled the room with light. The glow from the bulb was so mustard-yellow, it made the blood look almost green...and it was everywhere: All over Caleb's neck, stuck to the hair on his chest, the tips of his dreadlocks and splattered on the mismatched pillowcases. It was coming from the girl's head, dripping down her brows and into her face. Her eyes were as wide open as her legs; the top of her head was still inside the drywall. She said nothing. She didn't even cry out from the pain, which must have been incredible.

"Dude, you fucked her through the wall," Jeremy said.

Caleb stood from the bed, completely naked except for a pair of wool socks. His dick was no longer hard enough to fill the condom. It hung from him like a dead balloon. He yanked it off, threw it in the corner, and reached for his jeans. "No shit," he snapped. He pulled a shirt on over his head and moved closer to me. "You've got to take her to the hospital, Rae."

My neck tilted back like he'd slapped me. "Me?"

"That blood ain't stopping," Jeremy said. He had taken Caleb's place right next to the bed, looking at the wall and inside the hole. "Yup, she definitely needs stitches."

I turned toward Caleb, who now stood a few feet from me, and leaned against his dresser. "So why the hell would *I* take her?"

"I can't," Caleb said. "They'll think I fucking beat her. And Jeremy's too high to drive."

"I ain't high," Jeremy yelled back.

"Then why are you inspecting her like she's a piece of bud?" Caleb asked.

Jeremy stumbled back and held onto the window, but he kept his eyes on the girl. "Cause she's got nice tits. Shit, at least I didn't crack her head open with my dick."

Caleb was right: Jeremy was too messed up to go anywhere.

With so much blood coming from her head, she definitely shouldn't drive herself to the hospital. I wasn't sure I was the best person to take her, either; even though this had shaken me out of my high, I was still tired from the weed.

But Caleb was letting me stay at his house—for free. It was probably the least I could do.

The girl wobbled and swayed as she sat up. Blood dripped down her nose and into her mouth. She wiped it like it was a tear. "Stop staring at my tits, you flamer." Her voice didn't match her words. She sounded like a cartoon. "And you—Scarface? I don't want you taking me anywhere." She tucked her knees against her chest. "Caleb, you fucking asshole, I'm not going to be seen with some meth head that slashed her face open while she was tweaking."

Something dark began to fill my chest, like the gathering of a storm. My back stiffened; my eyelids narrowed. There was rage swirling inside me, ready to burst from my mouth. "What the hell did you just call me?"

"Caleb," she whined, "that *thing* is looking at me like she wants to eat me. Tell her to stop."

My nails dug into my palm. My pulse quickened, my heart pounding as if it was trying to break through my skin.

I wasn't a fighter. I'd slapped Drew once because I resented her. I couldn't stand the way she looked at me, like she pitied me, like she was sad for me. And aside from a few situations in high school, I didn't normally react with my hands. This girl wasn't going to get my open palm. She was getting my fist.

I took a step forward and was ready to take another when Caleb moved in front of me. His chest pressed against mine, his outstretched arms preventing me from going any farther. "Rae, she's already in rough shape." His voice was smooth like he was trying to calm me down. "What you'll do to her will only make it worse. It's not worth it."

An obnoxious and extremely fake giggle came from her lips. "Rough shape…*pleeease*. At least my face doesn't look like hers."

"Shut up, Becky," Caleb yelled over his shoulder. "Sit on that bed and stop fucking talking."

Whatever he was doing to kill my anger was overpowered by her irritating smirk. I leaned back and placed my hands on his chest. "Get out of my way," I shouted, shoving him as hard as I could.

He came forward again. "Jeremy," Caleb said, his voice still calm, "come take Rae to her room before she kills Becky."

"She's not going to kill me, baby." Becky giggled. "Scare me, maybe."

I lurched forward again; Caleb stopped me. He turned around and pressed his back against me, holding my arms down with his. "Shut the hell up!" he screamed at her. "Do not say another fucking word, do you hear me? You're lucky I don't come over there and knock your ass out."

I sucked in a breath as I felt Jeremy's hands on me. I waited for his fingers to lift and graze my hair or the side of my head. If that happened, the three of them would really see me flip out, but for a completely different reason.

He gripped my waist and my arm and gently pulled me out of Caleb's room and into mine. Then he stationed himself in the doorway to keep me from running back out. I leaned against the far wall and tried to catch my breath.

"She's a whore," he said. "It don't matter what she says."

He was right; it didn't matter. But I could still feel her words and her expression. It felt like they'd slashed my skin, like the pain in my scar was fresh all over again.

"If she knew what happened to you, she'd feel like a fucking fool," he said. He wiggled out the joint that had been tucked between his head and ear and handed it to me, with a lighter.

It seemed as if he had an endless supply of drugs on him at all times. I suddenly appreciated that.

I stuck one end in my mouth and lit the other. The weed wasn't going to soften her words, or make me forget them. But it would help stop my brain from wandering and help me fall asleep. And I was going to need it. On my way back from work, I'd heard on the radio that a rainstorm was headed our way. The thought of that made me suck down even more of the joint.

"You want some of this?" I asked him, nodding toward the weed.

He shook his head. "Nah, you keep it." He was lighting his own joint. I didn't know where that one had come from. This time I didn't care. He had given me my own, and that was all that mattered.

I finished it and crashed, without even bothering to clean the room like I'd wanted to.

My body still wasn't used to this new schedule, and as a result, I only slept for about five hours. When I woke up, I downed half a bowl of cereal and drove to work.

I sat in the back lot behind the casino, my hands circling the top of the steering wheel, even though the car was in park. I could feel what the lack of sleep and food were starting to do to me. My collarbone stuck out more than usual; my belt was on the tightest notch. I didn't like being this skinny, but there was nothing I could do. My body was completely in control until December seventeenth. Weed should have made me hungry; it didn't. I could feel the hollow of my stomach gurgling, trying to reject whatever it held but finding nothing of substance.

I just had to wait this out and continue eating tiny amounts for the next *twenty-seven days*. After that, my appetite would return. My hair would thicken, and my body would fill out again.

When this first happened five years ago, I tried to stop it from repeating the following year. To keep my mind straight. To forget the significance of that date.

To forgive what had happened, and the one who'd caused it.

I couldn't.

So I stopped fighting and I let it take over. My stomach. My dreams. And though things didn't completely return to normal after mid-December, they did improve. They became a little more tolerable. I could at least keep down the food I ate.

Without looking at the time on my phone, I knew I had to get inside for my shift. I wasn't ready. The mid-day sky had turned black, with a storm that hadn't yet released its rain.

Tears.

He had once told me that's what the rain was.

I hoped I wouldn't hear the storm over the clanking chips or the clinking glasses or the chatter. If the noises of the storm seeped through, I didn't know how I'd finish my shift.

As my eyes drifted down the sky, something else grabbed my attention: the movement in the car across from mine. Two girls sat in the front seat, holding their phones out in front of them. It looked like they were snapping pictures of each other, probably posting them all over social media or some shit like that.

They couldn't stop laughing.

One put lipstick on the other. With a glossy red mouth, she began to fix the other's hair, teasing the sides to curl around her face. I was only feet away, but they were too caught up, too busy to notice I was staring.

It didn't look like they worked at the casino. They were most likely just having a girls' day and had decided to spend it here. I had no one to do that with—no girlfriends to curl my hair or put makeup on to cover my scar. No one who wanted to take my picture.

No one who wanted to look deeper than my scar tissue.

I only had guys in my life. They fed me joints and made sure I didn't swing my fists.

Maybe that was all I needed.

ELEVEN

I gripped the handrail as I climbed up the basement stairs—not with just the tips of my fingers, but with both hands, leaning against it as I walked. The stairs were moving, shifting…wiggling underneath me. It was like a ride at the fair.

Or maybe it was just my eyes.

And that I didn't have any balance.

And that I'd chugged way too many beers over the last few hours at Caleb's party.

I was prone to losing control whenever I consumed anything stronger than weed, which was why I didn't usually drink. But tonight, or this morning—or whatever time it was—I wanted to lose control.

He had called, using an unlisted number.

Him.

Gerald.

Or I thought it was him, at least. There wasn't anyone else it could have been.

I also drank because it was raining. Storming. It had started when I was at work. Customers came in with their heads dripping wet, laughing about the sudden downpour. But once I was finished with my shift and ready to drive back to the house, the rain had cleared. Only a few times had it released even a sprinkling of tears. Or raindrops.

Whatever the fuck they were.

But as soon as I joined the party in the basement, the weather changed again. The thunder was louder than the bass pumping through the speakers. I felt both in my chest. The lightning lit up the small windows at the top of the ceiling—the ones Caleb had opened to let out the smoke. It let in the smell of the circling storm, of the heavy air.

Of mud from the ground wet with rain.

Rain.

I had grabbed a red plastic cup filled with keg beer and drowned it all out—the noises, the smells, the flashes of white light, the tears. *Rain and him.* I'd eaten a roll during one of my breaks. Other than that, my stomach was empty. The alcohol hit me quickly.

And hard.

I rounded the corner to the living room, holding onto the wall and keeping my eyes trained on the sticky wood floor. I didn't want to bump into anything, to touch any of the filthy surfaces that surrounded me. But the hallway was so slanted and yellow from the flickering lamp. Endless. There were way too many steps between me and my bed, but finally I collapsed on top of it.

My thumb hit a button on my phone, and the screen lit up. It showed a picture of Brady and me. He still hadn't called. I fucking missed that boy. He listened. Always.

My finger hit another button. Then a second one. The screen felt so smooth on my skin. Smooth and unmarred. I held it against my scar and rubbed the softness over my jagged edges.

"I hope you're not driving home in this weather," Hart said.

I jumped at the sound of him. "Hart? Where are you?" I glanced at the doorway, looking for him, and across the carpet of my room.

"At my house."

He was on the phone. The phone was...*on?*

"Did I call you?" I asked.

"Well, I didn't call you."

At least his voice was familiar. Not as familiar as Brady's, but it would do. And it did things...to my stomach, to my chest. But I couldn't fully feel those places right now. The beer had numbed them. It had numbed all of me. But I still remembered how much he'd hurt me.

I hated him for that. Yet I liked him in spite of it.

Shit.

"You've been drinking," he said.

"How can you," I stopped to hiccup, "tell?"

He laughed. "I think we both know the answer to that."

I pushed myself up a little, resting the back of my head against the wall and digging my heels into the mattress.

Everything was...*spinning.*

"Got a call today while I was at work," I said, just rattling off information I wouldn't have normally shared with anyone but Brady or Shane. "Fucker didn't even leave a message." My forehead dropped onto my bent knees, and I wrapped my arm around my head to block out some of the light. "Can you believe that shit?"

"Who called you?"

"The number didn't show up on caller ID...but I know it was him."

"Who is he?"

I hiccupped again. My forehead banged against the hard knob of my knee. "Ouch. My head hurts. Bet it doesn't hurt as bad as Becky's. You know Caleb screwed her so hard, her head went through the wall? Then she called me 'Scarface.'"

My stomach started to churn, flipping almost as fast as the room. My mouth began to water. I untangled from the ball I was in and searched the floor. There was a trash bag on the carpet—the one that had held my clothes. I reached for it and barely had it open before beer shot from between my lips. I tried to hold my hair out of the way, but I couldn't get all of it. My coordination was off; my balance was uneven. Each time I heaved, I leaned to the side and coated more of my hair.

When I felt like there was nothing left in me, I dropped the bag and huddled back into my ball. I couldn't make it to the mattress. I just stayed on the carpet, with the trash bag next to me, my puke-dampened hair dragging over my arms and the knees of my jeans.

"Rae?" Hart's voice was small, but I could tell he was shouting at me. "Are you okay?"

I lifted my head and opened my eyes, searching for his voice. My phone was on the floor. "Hart?" I reached over and grabbed it. "Hart..."

"Where are you?"

"Caleb's."

"Caleb from high school?"

"Yeah...high school, Caleb."

"Where does he live?"

I tried to bury my head between my stomach and my knees, and got a solid whiff of the puke. The bag had opened. The beer stared at me from the bottom of the plastic. It hadn't gotten only in my hair; it was on my shirt and my jeans, too. I was covered in it.

"I need to wash it off me," I said. "It's everywhere. It's all I can smell."

"Wash what off you, Rae?"

Hart's voice grew small again as I stood and dropped the phone. I held onto the wall as I moved into the bathroom. I stared into the mirror. The yellow light on the ceiling showed all the wet spots on my face and the round, chunky circles on my shirt. The front of my hair was soaked. The smell made me heave again, but nothing came out. There was nothing inside but a massive ache in my stomach and a cry seeping from my lips.

I looked up again, my eyes catching the mark on my cheek.

Twenty-six days.

I tugged at the bottom of my shirt and yanked it over my head.

Then I pulled down my jeans, turning them inside out just to get out of them. The black shower curtain was closed. There were white stains on the bottom of the fabric. They looked like snowballs. Snowballs that had gone...*splat*.

I pushed it open and stepped inside, turning on the water, and closing the drain with the metal plug. There was crusted goo all over it. It stuck to my fingers. I had nothing to wipe them on except the wall of the shower. So I did.

I sat at the edge of the bathtub, feeling the grime against my skin. It was slick and slimy. There were small slivers of bar soap sitting in the holder. I didn't know what it took to turn white soap brown. Whatever it was, Jeremy had discovered it. The bottle of shampoo behind me was nearly empty. I sniffed its cap; it smelled like pine trees. There was a long strip of black where the tile met the tub. It was mold. Something musty was on every surface in this entire house. I was probably coated in it.

I should have cleaned the bathroom.

As the water started to fill, I leaned against the back of the tub and placed my feet under the stream. The heat burned the blisters on my toes, the ones those damn heels gave me. Steam floated up to my eyes and made them want to close. The tub wasn't long enough to fully stretch out my legs, so I tucked them in and lowered myself as much as I could.

I'd left my shampoo in my room. My body wash, too. I hadn't even brought in a towel. *Shit*. It didn't matter. The water was washing my hair. My stomach wasn't flipping as much as it was before. Even though the spinning wasn't as bad, I swear I saw three eyes staring back at me. Maybe it was four...or two?

"Those are some nice tits," a man said.

I couldn't place the voice, though I knew I'd heard it before. It belonged to one of the guys who'd been in the basement. I just wasn't sure which one. There were a lot of them down there, and the beer made them all sound the same.

And it made me so tired.

I placed my hands over my breasts and drew my legs in even closer. "Are you talking to me?"

"Don't cover them up. I was enjoying the view."

"Towel," I said, pointing toward the sink. "Get me one." I realized that by pointing, I'd just uncovered one of my breasts again. My hand immediately returned to my chest, the movement sloshing water over my face. I wiped it out of my eyes—this time showing him *both* breasts. As I rubbed, I wondered if there were even towels in the bathroom. Maybe they were in the hall closet.

Was there a closet in the hall?

The heat made me yawn.

"I've never been jealous of Saint before," the guy said, "but now that I see what he used to fuck every day, I think he was stupid to give you up."

The water had almost filled to the top of the tub. My toes reached for the knob, but missed. I tried again. Each try threw me off-balance, my back sliding up and down the end of the tub. Water washed over my face. I spit it out.

It tasted dirty. As dirty as this stranger.

His nasty eyes were on me...I could feel them. I couldn't see him because he wasn't standing under the light.

But neither was I.

"Pussy fully shaved...fuck," he said.

I tucked my leg back in. Everything was now under the water except my face. "Stop staring at me and get me a goddamn towel!" The warmth was really working on me. Steam floated above the tub and there was a haze spreading throughout the room. I could almost taste its thickness as it mixed with the beer on my tongue. "I know you're there," I said. "I can hear you breathing." And I could hear my words slurring, but I couldn't form them any better. I had completely lost control. My back fell a few more inches and my face tilted to the side, resting on top of the water. My lips dipped and teased the pool; a tiny wave formed from the breath leaving my mouth.

My calm exhales made my lids even heavier.

"Stop staring at me," I whispered. "Please...stop."

I could feel the bubbles around my mouth. I could feel the darkness surrounding me. I couldn't see anything through it. My eyes were closed.

Everything had finally stopped spinning.

TWELVE

Drop, *drop, drop.*

It felt like someone was dropping a needle against the backs of my eyes, again and again.

The reverberation pulsed straight up to my head, then down to my stomach. Something had rotted in my mouth. My body ached. Even my toes throbbed. But the bed was surprisingly comfortable...at least I thought it was a bed. It was squishy, and there was something covering me. It was softer than the sheets I'd purchased the other day. And the mattress felt bouncier than the twin that was on the floor in my room.

It was probably the hangover making everything on the outside feel better to compensate for how sick I felt on the inside.

I slowly spread out: first my arms, then my legs, carefully lengthening each limb and stretching the muscles. I still couldn't open my eyes. My brain couldn't take the brightness I felt searing against my lids.

How many beers had I chugged last night?

"There's some medicine right next to you on the nightstand along with a big glass of water. You should take it...and drink every drop of that water."

My body froze. So did my breath. I knew it wasn't Caleb's voice that was telling me to take the medicine, or Jeremy's. And it certainly wouldn't be Brady.

"Hart?"

"Don't open—"

My eyes burst open, immediately meeting his concerned gaze as he leaned against the doorframe on the other side of the room. The sight of him was cut short when the stabbing in my forehead mixed with the sunlight that seeped in through the blinds. The pain became almost unbearable. "Ouch." My palms went to my head, trying to balance out some of the hurt.

"...your eyes," he continued, but it was much too late.

I rubbed, and the blanket fell out of my arms and to my waist, revealing a T-shirt...one that wasn't mine. I yanked the comforter off my legs and saw the pair of boxers I was wearing. Those weren't mine, either. I clenched my eyes as hard as I could and pushed my fingers against my forehead, trying to remember what had happened last night.

I couldn't recall any of it—not changing into Hart's clothes (or what I assumed were his) or coming to his house (where I assumed I was) or lying in his bed (which I didn't even want to think about).

Had he put me in these clothes?

Or worse: had we done something before they had been put on?

I squeezed my thighs together, searching for that satisfying ache I got after sex.

"Nothing happened," he said, as if he had read my thoughts in my body language, "if that's what you're wondering."

My eyes opened again, watching him move from the doorway to the end of the bed. His dark jeans hung low on his waist, showing the outline of his thighs, and his white T-shirt accented the curves of his chest. His hair was wet. And as a breeze of his cologne and body wash rushed past me, I found out that he smelled more than just clean. He smelled enticing.

I pointed at my T-shirt. "Are these your clothes?"

He nodded.

I wished I didn't need to ask my next question. "Did you…put them on me?" I held my breath while I waited for his answer. It had been years since Hart had seen me naked. My body had changed so much since then. Although I was too thin, I still had more curves than I did back then. And my breasts were larger, too…and I was fully shaved now.

And then, there was my scar.

Being unconscious meant I hadn't been able to see the look on his face when he examined it, hadn't known if he'd taken the opportunity to really stare at it.

"I did," he finally said. "You were naked when I found you. I was a gentleman, but it wasn't easy. Your body, Rae…it's only gotten better."

My eyes widened, and my body started to shake worse than it already was. "I was naked…" I took a breath, "…when you found me?"

He nodded.

How the fuck had that happened?

I couldn't remember.

"I think I'm going to be sick." I should have headed for the bathroom. Instead, I quickly swallowed the pills, pulled the blanket up to my neck, and leaned into the headboard. He had already seen me without these clothes on, but modesty wasn't the point here. All I wanted was to hide completely, to crawl underneath the comforter and make it all go away.

I was back to wanting an umbrella.

"Tell me where we are and what happened last night."

"Can I sit?" he asked quietly.

I tucked my legs beneath me to give him room and watched him carefully take a seat on the end of the mattress. His movements sent me another whiff of his cologne. It was impossible to ignore the smell, and the effect it had on me no matter how hard I tried.

"We're at my parents' old house. I bought it from them so it's now mine." I hadn't glanced around the room all that much, but what I had seen looked familiar. "Do you remember calling me from Caleb's?" he asked.

I attempted to rewind my thoughts. The last thing I remembered was the railing, the one that bordered the stairs in the basement. I remembered how I'd held onto it with both hands. Everything before that was clear, but nothing after. "No." I shook my head, trying once more. "I don't remember."

With his eyes softly on me, he explained how I'd called him in the early hours of the morning, and how I'd gotten sick on the phone. When I told him I needed to wash it off but hadn't hung up, he became concerned. I just disappeared. So he called Shane to find out where Caleb lived and came to get me.

"You left out the part about me being naked." It was kind of shitty of me to say.

He sighed and ran his hand over his cheek. That was when I noticed the cuts on his knuckles. They hadn't been there when I'd last seen him at the casino.

He caught me staring and put his hands behind his back. "When I found you at Caleb's, you were in the bathtub."

Fearing what he was about to tell me, I pulled the blanket up to my mouth and bit the edge. "What was I doing in there?"

This was the reason I almost always just stuck with weed. I didn't black out when I smoked, or make stupid decisions. I knew better than this. I knew what could happen when I lost control, and I knew what men were capable of. Not just strangers, but the ones who were supposed to love me, too.

"You were sleeping. Or more like passed out." The muscles in his jaw clenched and his eyelids narrowed. "There was some guy in the bathroom with you and...shit." He breathed again. This time it wasn't a sigh. It was deep, pained. "He was watching you. I don't know long he'd been in there...he promised me he hadn't touched you."

I felt the water and pills start to move back up my throat. "Who was it?"

"I don't know."

"And yet you trusted him when he 'promised' he hadn't touched me?"

"He promised me more than that, actually." The intensity on his face was almost frightening as he spoke through gritted teeth. Slowly, almost as though he wasn't aware of his movements, his hands found their way back to his lap. They looked even worse than they had a few minutes ago. The knuckles on his right hand were raw, the skin missing on several of them. It appeared like he had tried to wash off some of the blood. It was still there, circling several of the open scrapes.

"Does it hurt?" I asked.

"I'm fine. It's nothing."

"What's his face look like?"

He shook his head and shifted on the bed. "Not good." I silently reminded myself to ask Caleb who the guy was. Hart wouldn't be the only one to hit him. I had plenty to lay on him, too. "After I took care of him, I took care of you. I dried you off and carried you to your room. I didn't want to spend time looking for something to dress you in. I just wanted to get you the fuck out of there, so I wrapped your bed sheet around you and drove you here."

I had told him on the phone that I was at Caleb's. Had I told him I was living there, too?

"How did you know it was my room?"

"Caleb and Jeremy told me. They had my back the whole time once they found out what was going on, but I didn't need their help...and neither did you." His eyes were looking through me again. "Do you know they're drug dealers?"

I gave him a look.

"Oh yeah, Brady's your best friend. Of course you know."

I hated what he was insinuating. I hated that he found out I was living at Caleb's. I hated that in the time he had been away from Bar Harbor, I hadn't grown up at all. I was supposed to have a good job and a nice apartment and not run out of gas…and not get stared at by some pervert while I was passed out naked in a tub.

But that had become my life.

"Hart, look—"

My legs were now stretched out to the side. His hand rose and landed on top of my foot. It was covered in a blanket, but I felt the emotion his fingers triggered as if they were against my bare skin. "I don't know anything that's happened to you since I've been gone." He scanned my face, completely avoiding my scar. "You've obviously been through some shit, and I don't expect you to open up right away and tell me everything, but I want you to know you can, whenever you want to."

That was it. I couldn't take any more.

"You want me to open up? You want me to tell you all the shit that's happened to me?" My voice was getting louder and I didn't stop it. "How about this: someone I really loved left in the middle of the night and made no contact whatsoever in the years that followed, and he still hasn't apologized for it."

His fingers tightened on my toes. "Apologize…" Shock covered his eyes and lips. It didn't sound like he was testing me. It sounded like he honestly had no idea what I was talking about.

"You skipped town, Hart, in the middle of everything. You hadn't even told me prep school was a possibility." The stabbing in my chest had nothing to do with being sick to my stomach, though it wasn't helping at all. "You broke my fucking heart. And now you're suddenly back, flirting with me at the casino and shoving poker chips and your phone number into my apron. You tell me all about why you left, but you never said you're sorry for doing it in the first place."

His eyes dropped to my feet, his hand reaching up and brushing through his hair. Back and forth.

Back and forth.

He tugged at the strands. "It had nothing to do with you. I promise."

He just didn't seem to get it. "That doesn't matter! You left and didn't say good-bye, and you never reached out again."

When he looked up, the pain on his face stabbed the anger that had been building in my chest. "You're right. I'm sorry, Rae." Finally, it was there...and yet, I didn't feel relieved like I thought I would. "I never would have hurt you intentionally; you have to believe me. I'm sorry for all of it—for leaving you, and for not telling you anything about it, and for not having the balls to reach out to you. I know how much I fucked up, and it kills me that I can't change that. You have to know how much I loved you." He paused, waiting for me to respond. I didn't. "I had every intention of finding you when I returned. I didn't know if you were dating or married, and I didn't know anything about your life. I figured I'd have to look for you, or at least ask someone about you. But on my second night here, I drove up to the casino to unwind a little after a stressful day, and there you were. It's like I was meant to find you. That's got to mean something."

That was so weak. "So you lucked out and happened to show up where I worked. That doesn't win you any points."

"In a casino, of all places? Somewhere neither of us would have just happened to be? Come on, Rae. That's pretty significant."

I wasn't convinced. "Why did you want to find me all of a sudden?" I asked quietly.

His teeth dug into his bottom lip, and he dragged it into his mouth. "I wanted to see who you'd become, what you looked like. I wondered if you were anything like I'd imagined over the years. I wasn't planning on anything other than seeing you with my own eyes, but when I saw you in the casino, the feelings I used to have came right back."

The blanket had slipped, so I pulled it right back up to my neck. I needed the coverage, the protection. "You thought of me?" That was hard to believe.

He rubbed his chin against the top of his arm and looked at me through his lashes. "All the time."

"Well, good for you. I'm not letting you hurt me again." The same feelings had come back to me when I first saw him, too. I couldn't deny that. But I was willing to force them aside for the sake of my well-being. There was no way I would go through that kind of hurt again. Not now.

Twenty-five days.

"You can trust me," he said softly.

A laugh burst through my lips. It was either laugh or cry... and laughing felt safer. "I did trust you, and you fucking broke me."

His gaze turned intense. "That was five years ago, Rae."

"Yeah. I know." It had been a long time that I'd held onto the pain. I couldn't let it go that easily. "I don't even know you anymore so why would I trust you?" He didn't answer. I swallowed the knot that was building in my throat. "What do you want from me, Hart?"

His hand traveled to my calf. He wrapped his fingers around the muscle and tried to pull me toward him. "A chance."

I yanked my leg away and tucked my knees against my chest, pulling the blanket around them. I could feel something inside me letting go...giving way. Tears. A whole day's worth had collected, and they were getting ready to release—not a downpour. Just a sprinkle.

Drop, drop, drop.

"And what would keep you from hurting me this time? You've said it yourself: you'll be leaving town once you finish the spa so you can build another one. We'll be right back to where we were the last time."

He pushed his way to the middle of the bed, his legs stretching over the side of the mattress, his hands on either side of me. "I'll be here for the whole build out of Bar Harbor and Bangor, and probably Portland. That's over a year away, Rae. So much can change in that time."

"Portland is a two-and-a-half hour drive. You're going to live here and work there?"

A sly smile covered his mouth and lit his eyes. "You're looking for excuses."

I glanced at his hands. "I'm...protecting myself."

"You don't have to. I know the mistake I made, and I'm truly sorry for it. And I'm not just saying that because you told me you expected an apology. I'm saying it because you *deserve* one." He rested his hands on my knees and waited for me to meet his gaze. "I think we're destined for another chance. You can't stop what's going to happen, but you have to go in knowing that you're going to give it everything you have." His chin rested on his hands. "I can't guarantee the future will be happy for us, and neither can you. But I'm certain about my feelings for you. Tomorrow can always be taken away from us. What are you going to do right now?"

He really could pull thoughts out of my head.

I knew all about tomorrow being taken away from me. I knew regret. I knew what it was like to want something so badly, and to not be able to have it.

I knew what it was like to wake up and be alone, and then to never feel happiness happy again.

I opened my mouth to give him an answer, just as my cell began to ring from the nightstand. Mom's number appeared on the screen. Her timing couldn't have been worse.

His eyes jumped to my phone. "Why don't you answer that," he said. "Take a shower, even a nap if you think it will make you feel better. I'll be here when you're ready to talk again."

I didn't agree or disagree. I just locked eyes with him and watched him walk out of the room as I swiped my finger across the screen. "Mom—"

"I really wish you wouldn't make it so difficult to get in touch with you. You should answer your phone when I call you, at least."

I exhaled a long, aching breath. "What's up, Mom?" I didn't

have to ask; I already knew what she wanted. It was why I hadn't answered any of her calls lately or returned her voicemails. At least this conversation would buy me a few days.

"I'd like you to come over for your brother's birthday," she said.

I stood up and shuffled into the bathroom. What stared back at me from the mirror was so horrifying, I almost dropped the phone. Yesterday's makeup was caked and crusted under my eyelids. Bits of mascara and liner added to the black mess; smeared streaks of brown and gray sparkle that had once been the two-toned shadow I'd worn to work. I moistened my fingers under the faucet and tried to scrub it off.

"If you want to see me," I counter-offered, "I'll meet you for coffee…or something. But I'm not coming to the house."

"Why do you—"

"You know the deal, Mom. It hasn't changed since last year or the year before."

"Jesus, Rae."

I could picture the look on her face…all the pain, and the feelings that ate at her stomach. They were the same feelings that gnawed at mine. But that didn't mean I would change my mind. She knew how it was: I was never going back to that house.

Ever.

I was surprised she could even live in that damn place knowing everything that happened there.

"Maybe you can't do it for me," she said, her voice pleading, "but can you try to do it for your brother's sake?"

The reason I was staying away actually was for my brother's sake. I knew by now she wouldn't understand that.

"I've got to go," I said. "Shoot me a text if you want to get coffee and we can plan a time when we're both free."

"Rae—"

"Bye, Mom."

I hung up and placed the phone on the countertop. Water alone wasn't taking off any of the black; it was only smudging further. So

I squirted some soap onto my fingers and lathered until my hands filled with foam. The suds were able to soften the layers, and soon my face was clean, and all the makeup was off. It didn't matter so much for my eyes; they stood out pretty well on their own. But the darker tones that swirled through my scar were even more notice- able now that they weren't covered. And I had nothing with me that I could use to cover them back up.

I grabbed the tube of toothpaste that was sitting in a holder next to the sink, squirted a thick line onto my finger, and rubbed it over my teeth. It barely dented the furry coating that covered them. I needed a brush for that, but it didn't look like there was a spare one in here. So I spat out the rest of the minty paste and moved deeper into the bathroom. There was a closet next to the shower that held towels in all different sizes. I grabbed one that was big enough to wrap around my body, and one I could wash with. Everything else I needed—shampoo, conditioner and body wash—were sitting on a tiled shelf inside the shower. There was quite a difference between this tub and the one at Caleb and Jere- my's house.

I was grateful for that, at least.

Before going into the kitchen, I dressed in a pair of Hart's sweat- pants, double knotting the drawstring and folding the waist until they were the right length. I put on a fresh T-shirt that had also appeared on the bed while I'd been in the shower. As soon as he saw me, he moved over to the coffeemaker. Setting a mug under- neath the mouth, he hit a button for it to begin to brew. Once the cup was full, he poured in a splash of flavored creamer and handed it to me. "Hopefully you still drink your coffee the same way."

I leaned into the center island and moaned as I took my first sip. "It's perfect."

He slipped two pieces of bread into the toaster, setting a plate in front of it along with some butter. "The toast will help with your hangover, too."

"I thought grease was supposed to do that?"

"You need something light first to help settle your stomach. I'll feed you grease in a little while."

My free hand gripped the edge of the counter. "There's going to be another meal after this one?"

"Call it the main course. Toast is the appetizer." It popped up, as if on cue. He buttered both pieces and slid the plate over to me. "Do you have to work tonight?"

"No. It's my first night off." I took a bite and washed it down with coffee.

"Then why don't you just stay here?"

"You mean, overnight?"

He nodded. His gray gaze demanded an answer from me.

I set the coffee on the counter. Both hands now clutched the stone. "I don't know, Hart." I'd only gotten down a half a piece of toast, but my stomach already felt stronger.

He moved over to my side of the counter. I turned around to face him, keeping my hands behind me. I didn't want to reach for him, but my fingers were close to doing just that. "You never answered my question before your phone rang. You staying here could answer both at the same time."

This was the closest I'd been to him all morning. Even though my stomach was feeling better, I couldn't say the same for my chest. Something was happening inside of it—the same thing I felt whenever I was around him, only more intense this time. Maybe because he had told me how he felt, and what he wanted from me. Maybe because he'd finally apologized, and I could see that he was actually sorry for leaving me behind. Or maybe I was just seeing in him what I wanted to see.

That alone told me I might need to try.

"A chance?" I asked. "That's it?"

His hand reached toward me. With every inch that it drew closer, my muscles tightened a little bit more. My nails tapped underneath the counter, and there was a hesitation in my breath. I shifted out of the way just before he touched my face. It didn't matter how much of my body he had seen. There was no way he was touching my cheek.

"Sorry...I was just going to brush the crumbs off your lips." His hand hung in the air. His brows stayed perched, questions filled his eyes. "But yes, all I want is a chance. The rest is up to you." His gaze dove straight into mine. When I didn't look away, his hand fell to my waist. I felt it around the elastic that held up the sweats.

I hadn't ruined the moment; I'd changed it. His fingers were demons I would have to conquer. In the meantime, they wouldn't be allowed near my face...not until I was comfortable with it. I would be the one to place them there. For now, that distance was a good thing.

"Okay."

His hands tightened. "Okay? That's a yes?"

I smiled. It was genuine. "Yes."

THIRTEEN

I couldn't remember the last time I'd sat in front of a TV all day and watched movies. Maybe because it hadn't happened since Darren and I were kids. This time, I did it with Hart.

And he fed me the whole time.

There was a banquet constantly surrounding us. He made mozzarella cheese sticks, potato skins and deep-fried Oreos for our grease-filled lunch. During the movies, it was popcorn and candy…somehow he'd remembered that my favorite was anything gummy. He'd purchased every shape and flavor they sold—multiple bags of each. The final course was ribs, corn on the cob and potatoes that he'd grilled.

It was more than I had eaten all month.

Oddly—and thankfully—my stomach was keeping it down.

I set aside my last plate and leaned back into the couch. My legs rested on the ottoman, and my hands held my belly. I was so full, it was hard to breathe. It looked like Hart was having a hard time finishing what was on his plate. But my attention had drifted away from him, to the wall of windows just to the side of us. His place sat directly on the water with a full beach; glass panes ran the whole back length of the house, revealing a sky that was just starting to darken, and a sun getting ready to dip below the ocean.

"Move in with me."

He just said it out of nowhere while I was watching the horizon. My head snapped around. "What?"

"We don't have to call it a 'move-in' if that makes you uncomfortable. Think of it more like you're just staying with me for a while."

My hands reached between the cracks of the couch, gripping the cushions. "I can't do that."

"But you can live with a drug dealer?"

I wasn't sure if he was talking about Brady, Caleb or Jeremy.

"I've known those guys forever, and they're my friends. I'm only at Caleb's until I can afford my own place. That should be soon—real soon, actually."

He glanced at the TV. By giving me his profile, it highlighted the angles of his chin. He hadn't shaved for at least a few days; he didn't have a full beard quite yet, but his whiskers were thick and rough. There wasn't any scruff on his neck. It appeared as if he was intentionally growing it out. It looked good on him.

Anything looked good on him.

His stare returned and intensified. "Then stay here until you can afford something of your own," he insisted. "It's not safe for you to be there, especially after last night."

He had a point. I could imagine that creep hovering over me, and it made me feel ill. "I don't know."

"Are you using his drugs? Is that why you're not saying yes to me?"

"No!" It came out much louder than I'd intended, but my point needed to be made. "I don't do any of that shit. I just smoke weed." That was a weak follow-up. "But I do a lot less of that than I used to." I realized that he hadn't been around when I'd started smoking, so I understood why he would ask. It still sucked that he had thought that. "I'm just not sure that staying here is the right thing to do. It's a whole lot of *you* all at once."

He laughed, his eyelids closing down to a squint. He dropped his hand in my lap. "Still honest as hell, I see." His thumb traced a circle over my thigh. "We work opposite hours, so you wouldn't be seeing a whole lot of me. You would be in my house, and there would be a lot of my things around, and I'd make sure you got your fill of me. But I'd give you your space."

There was no question that "your fill" had a double meaning.

"I can't make this decision right now," I told him.

"Sure. Just think about it, please."

My fingers pulled out of the couch and rested on my stomach. They itched to touch his skin. His abs and his biceps had always been the most defined parts of his body. From the way his T-shirt clung to him, it looked like that hadn't changed.

"That guy who called you last night…will he be showing up at my door to check on you?"

It suddenly felt like his hands were on my throat, squeezing all the air out of me. There was nothing for me to hide behind. No blanket…no umbrella. I wanted one, at least. Or both. "What guy?"

He shrugged. "Before you got sick, you told me someone called you and didn't leave a message. You never said his name."

Fucking alcohol. I never would have said that to him if I hadn't been drinking. The only person I would have told that to was Brady.

"Did I say anything else?" I asked casually.

He was reading me again. If he had seen the truth of my past, he would have been perfectly justified in dragging me off the couch and shutting the front door in my face and never speaking to me again.

That was what I honestly deserved.

"No," he said. "You didn't say anything else."

A little relief came when his words sank in. But now he had reminded me of the phone call, which was something I had forgotten about. The call was part of the reason I had slammed so much beer last night. I was trying to bury it.

To bury him...Gerald.

To bury those years of my life.

And the closer I got to December, the worse it haunted me.

I shook my head, trying to push out the thoughts and return to Hart's question. "He won't be showing up here. He's just someone I used to know. That's all."

That was all he was getting out of me. There was no way I was going to discuss who Gerald was, or why he would have been calling me. I didn't even know if it was him. I just had a feeling. But my feelings were usually right.

His thumb was tracing larger circles now, and deep rectangles that almost reached my hip. "And there isn't anyone else?"

"No." I spoke so softly. "There isn't anyone who would show up unexpectedly, here or anywhere else. Don't worry, you can put your fists away."

He smiled. "As long as you're with me, I can never put them away. I have to protect you."

I had felt secure whenever I'd been with Saint or Brady, but my relationship with them wasn't about that. It was about caring for them. The feeling I had with Hart was deeper than just a sense of security or not having to worry about anyone harming me. He had already proven how far he would go to keep me safe by rescuing me from Caleb and Jeremy's horrible party. It made me want to trust him.

Even more, it made me feel like I actually could.

I turned my head and watched the TV screen. If I hadn't dragged my eyes away, I didn't know if I would have been able to stop myself from leaning forward and kissing him.

The thoughts in my head were so fucked up.

For years, I'd been running from my past, and Hart was such a huge part of that. Yet there I was, heading right toward him. I was giving him a chance, even though I'd sworn to myself that he'd never get another one. He was proving himself worthy. And I wanted his lips on me...and his hands, as long as he kept them in the right places.

I wanted more.

"You're going to stay the night at least, aren't you?" he asked.

I hated that he knew my thoughts even when he wasn't reading my eyes.

"Yes." I slowly turned toward him again. He gawked back through hooded lids. And when his lips parted, I gazed between them until I saw his tongue. I wondered how fast he could flick it now, how flat he could make the tip, and how pointed. I swallowed, trying to settle the tingling between my legs. "But I'm sleeping in the guest room."

"No hands," he whispered, carefully leaning closer to me. I wasn't sure what he meant until his nose landed on the side of my jaw, rubbing its entire length and across my chin. I could almost taste his gummy worm-scented breath. His exhale spread over my chest like a thick, hazy fog. "Though I'm sure I can get you to change your mind."

The deep breaths weren't helping. I squeezed my nails into my palm, trying to concentrate on the pain rather than the feelings exploding inside me. That didn't do anything for me, either. "Not tonight, you can't." I turned from him and reached for the remote. "Now play another movie, before I make you take me to Caleb's."

He kissed just below my ear. "You know I won't take you back there."

"What if I beg?"

"Fuck, Rae. If you start begging, I'm going to slide off this couch and get on my knees...and the place I head to won't be Caleb's." His fingers crawled over my stomach, his palm finally resting just under my ribs. The pad of his thumb continued to graze, this time over my belly button piercing. "Beg me to kiss you."

I knew what his mouth could do to me. I pushed off the couch, trying to stand up, but he stopped me just as I rose from the cushion and pulled me back down. With his fingers now wrapped around my hand, he guided me to him. Our faces were aligned, only inches from each other.

"Beg me," he repeated.

Whatever air he breathed out, I sucked into my mouth and swallowed like smoke. I was melting beside him, and there was nothing I could do to stop it.

"Beg…" His voice was soft and deep and so demanding. It triggered the wetness between my legs. My stomach jittered.

I pressed my fingers onto his lips, tracing their outline. I wanted to feel his unmarred skin, to be reminded of its texture. His thick, coarse stubble pricked my flesh. I covered both sides, wandering down to his chin and over his jaw.

I could feel him looking at me without meeting his gaze.

I passed over his lips again on the way to his other cheek. He kissed behind my knuckle. He gripped my waist even tighter, drawing me to him without actually moving me.

He was demanding me to beg for his mouth, and my submission would confirm his control. But there was no way I was going to bend so easily. I was going to give him the best part of me…the part that hadn't been broken or abused. The part that wasn't scarred. And for that, I needed to take my time.

I moved closer, my breathing becoming more rapid. The pulsing in my chest shivered through my stomach and settled in the spot between my legs. There were inches between my mouth and his…and I stopped. My eyelids shut. Air came through my nostrils, hit his face and bounced back. He was breathing just as hard as I was. His fingers would leave a bruise on my side, but I didn't care. I wanted the pain. I wanted the mark. I wanted to look at the imprint of his desire like ink across my skin and remember this moment in the morning.

I slid another inch closer.

I knew once I tasted him, everything between us was going to change. I would move into his house. I would eventually open up, share the past that I kept so tightly bound. I knew it would be a struggle to reveal those secrets, but it didn't seem important with his face so close to mine.

What I wanted was overcoming what I feared most.

It pushed me to press my lips to his. I thought once I gave him what he wanted, his touch would lighten. I thought everything within me would begin to unwind. I thought I'd be filled with a sense of calm, having let go of the tension that was building. None of that happened. The noise of our mouths merging, the feel of his scruff spreading over my face, the taste of his tongue—it all built up a tingling surge within me. I wasn't leading this kiss, and I wasn't leading the buzzing that was happening inside me.

I'd given him complete control, and it was exactly what I wanted.

What I needed.

First, his lips caressed my top one...then the bottom...then his tongue circled mine, and he pulled me close. I was being drawn into his storm.

And yet, I wasn't close enough.

My hands gripped the bottom of his T-shirt. It was so tempting to rip it off, to eliminate everything that separated us, to inspect him, to relearn every line and mark and ridge on his body. To become acquainted with how it had grown from a boy's body into a man's.

I wanted to hear the stories behind whatever scars he'd collected.

But I couldn't have that tonight. Tonight was about my lips, and he had those in his possession. They were sore and swollen, and his whiskers had brushed over my face so much I could feel the redness on my skin. Tonight, the pain wasn't something I resisted. He had saved me, and my pain was part of that exchange.

I placed both hands on his cheeks and after one final breath together, I pulled my face away. My eyes opened at the same time his did. He leaned forward and gently kissed the tip of my nose, leaving me again almost immediately. It was such a cute gesture after the intensity that had just passed between us.

"I'm going to have a hard time keeping my mouth off you."

I smiled, feeling my skin turn even redder. "You'll get only what I decide to give you." That was almost laughable. It had taken every bit of strength I had to pull away from him. I doubted I'd be able to do it again. But I didn't want him believing he had all the control.

"You've got it all wrong, baby." His stare moved down to my lips, pausing for several seconds before it moved back up. "I'm the giver here. And when it comes to your body, I want to give constantly. The only decisions that need to be made are which parts of *my* body I'm going to use when I please you, and how many orgasms I'm going to let you have."

I could tell that he saw in my eyes the effect his words were having. Knowing how well he read me, he probably saw the wetness coating my inner thighs.

"Does that smile mean you're begging for one of them tonight?" he asked.

Yes.

The remote was on the couch between us. I picked it up and handed it to him. "Movie. Now."

His laugher spread through me like thunder. It was such a sexy sound. "I didn't think so."

FOURTEEN

The bed in Hart's guest room was king-sized, wrapped in soft white sheets and an overly fluffy down comforter. It felt like I had been sleeping in a cotton ball. I hated to climb out of it, but I'd been awakened by a text from my mom. She had listed her schedule for the whole week; if we were going to have coffee, today was the only day that would work. My reply told her I'd meet her in an hour.

I showered quickly and used the hair dryer that I found under the sink. It was too cold now to go out with wet hair. I didn't have any cosmetics, so I finished my morning routine by using the toothbrush Hart had given me and dressing in the sweats, T-shirt and hoodie I had worn last night. His scent on the clothes had faded a bit since yesterday, but I could still smell hints of him everywhere.

When it was finally time to go to sleep, he'd walked me to the guest room, and I'd closed my door without kissing him good-night. It was safer that way. I knew his lips would only lead me straight to his bed. Then I'd leaned against the back of the door, listening to him move down the hallway and close his.

Now as I stood outside his room, I wondered what would happen after I knocked. I lifted my hand and tapped gently.

"Come in," he said.

I cracked open his door and peeked inside.

He smiled. "Seeing you in my clothes never gets old."

There were sheer white panels covering the windows, but they let in enough light that I could see every detail of his room. It took up the entire back corner of the house, with two full walls of glass that showed the most spectacular view of the ocean. The posters and the video games and the light wood furniture that had once been in here had all been replaced. The bed sat under the slanted roof, the bedding in mid-gray tones. Bold lighting fixtures hung from the ceiling, and all the furniture was now in chocolate-stained wood. It had a quiet elegance and a grown-up masculinity.

But the room was only a cloud-filled backdrop.

What held my attention like a searing sun—what I couldn't drag my eyes away from even if I'd tried—was Hart. He was sitting up, leaning against his headboard, with the sheets resting across his waist. He had no tattoos or visible scars. He was perfect, with the build of an athlete, muscles so defined I could rest my finger in the valleys between his abs. My vision traced the trail of hair that started at his belly button and disappeared beneath the sheet. From the way it rested over his lower half, it didn't look like he was wearing anything underneath.

It wasn't as if I'd forgotten how beautiful the shape of him was, but the image of him wasn't as crisp in my mind as my feelings for him. After this stunning reminder, I couldn't believe any of those details had ever left me.

My pain made me forget as many things as it made me remember.

His eyes gleamed. "Do you want to get in?"

My skin was already flushed from seeing his body lounging in bed. His invitation only made it worse. My eyes slowly drifted up his chest, past his neck, stopping when they reached his stare. I *did* want to get in. I wanted to do more than that, really. But it was still a huge step to take, and it was too late to cancel the plans I'd made with my mom. "Actually, I was hoping you could give me a ride to my car."

He lifted his arm, his bicep flexing as he ran his fingers through his messy hair. "You're going somewhere? Before I've gotten a chance to touch you?" It looked like he was trying to flatten his bed head. He didn't need to. His messiness was as sexy as his voice.

"I have to." He already knew I didn't have to go to work until later today. Before I could explain further, I noticed his eyes were no longer watching mine. They had wandered to my braless chest. My nipples were so hard, they poked through the thin cotton of his T-shirt. I zipped up the hoodie I wore over it.

"Why cover them?" he asked. "I've already seen them. I dreamed about them last night."

I chose not to respond to that. "I'm meeting my mom for coffee."

His eyes lit up. "Maybe I could join you before I head to the work site..." He paused, waiting for more of a reaction or waiting for me to change my plans. I was too frozen to do either. It was only a matter of time before he started asking about my family. I wanted to avoid that conversation for as long as I could. "Or maybe that's not a good idea," he said finally. "I'll take you to your car, then. But only if you promise to come back tonight."

My back pressed against the doorframe, and my hands reached behind me and squeezed the wood. The longer his naked body teased me, the harder it was to restrain myself. "I won't get off until—"

"Won't 'get off'?" he said, laughing his throaty, thunderous laugh. "Just because you didn't want to sleep in my bed last night doesn't mean I don't want to wake up to you tomorrow morning."

The way he wanted me—the way he was pursuing me—was enticing. It wasn't just our prior sexual chemistry that drew me closer. His hands were already inspiring feelings stronger than any orgasm his fingers could ever produce. Hands like Hart's should brush toast crumbs from my lips every morning and tuck my hair behind my ear before I left for work. Hands like his should provide comfort and safety.

If I could only get to a place where I could tolerate that kind of touch again.

"I'll text you before I leave Bangor," I confirmed.

He reached for the edge of the sheet and pushed himself off the headboard. "Then I guess I'd better get dressed." One of his legs stretched out from beneath the covering, and his foot landed on the floor. "Unless you want to watch me do that, you'll want to close that door. You're about to get an eyeful...we'll see if you won't 'get off' then." He winked.

It was so fucking tempting.

I hesitated, but finally stepped out of the room and shut the door behind me. Then I went into the kitchen to wait for him.

My mom was sitting at a table by the front window when I came into the coffee shop. I took a seat, and she pushed a paper to-go cup toward me. "Your outfit is so cute, Rae." I couldn't tell if her tone was sarcastic or sincere.

I glanced down, forgetting that I was still wearing Hart's clothes. I was already late when he dropped me at my car; I didn't have time to go into Caleb's house and put on something else. It also meant I still wasn't wearing a bra...not that my chest was big enough for it to matter. Still, I felt a little half-finished.

"I was in kind of a hurry," I said. I didn't see her too often, and because of this, I always noticed immediately if something about her had changed. Today it was her hair. Her long locks, the same shade of blonde as mine, had been chopped to her chin, and she'd added darker lowlights. It drew out her eyes.

"You look good," she told me. I saw her eyeing my thinness, the slight hollowing of my face that pulled my scar inward.

"I like your hair," I replied, trying to keep things balanced between us as I pulled the coffee closer.

She ran her fingers through the front of it, twirling the strands when she reached the ends. "Thanks...I think I like it. Not quite sure yet." She sounded so defeated still, so lost. I wondered if this was how I sounded to other people, too. "Irving tells me you stopped by looking for a job. What happened?"

I shrugged. "Things didn't work out with Saint. I needed hours."

"No, I mean, why is it that I had to hear it from your uncle and not you?"

The interrogation had begun. Whether or not she meant it that way, it was how I took it. "Saint and I broke up. He found someone else, and I'm not working for him anymore. End of story." Her eyes told me she didn't believe it was that simple. "I didn't want to make a big deal out of it, so I didn't tell you."

I never told her much about what was going on in my life. I didn't know why she would be surprised that I hadn't called her about this. We hadn't had that kind of relationship in a long time.

"Oh...okay."

"You don't believe me."

Her brows rose. "I didn't say that, Rae."

I stared as hard and as directly as I could into her dark choco-late irises. We both knew the implications of truth-telling in our lives. "Believe whatever you want."

"So you've moved on, then?" Her eyes dropped to my outfit.

I took a deep breath, trying to calm the anger that was building. "Why don't we just talk about why we're here." I took a sip of the coffee... it was black. No flavored creamer. No added sweetness. She didn't even know how I took my damn coffee.

Considering that I'd moved out of her house when I was sixteen, it would've been ridiculous for me to think she knew anything about me anymore.

"I've missed my daughter. That's all."

That's all? When it came to us, there was no such thing. There was always something more lingering below the surface.

"You only ever seem to miss me around the month leading up to Darren's birthday," I told her.

"I miss you all the time, Rae," she sighed. "But you know how difficult it gets around this time of the year." She reached across the table, her fingers circling my wrist. Her thumb and middle finger overlapped each other. "Looks like you've been feeling it, too."

She was measuring me.

I rolled my eyes and pulled out of her grasp. "Don't pretend you know how I feel."

"Rae, I don't—"

"And don't pretend you know my pain, either. You have no idea what I've gone through, or what I continue to go through every day."

Her gaze turned steely. "I know more than you give me credit for."

Even after all this time, we still hadn't dealt with our emotions concerning everything that had gone down—especially not about the events that had led up to the night I'd gotten my scar. It never took long before one of us got to this point, and it was almost always me. We allowed our emotions to build, even though they never spilled. Tears threatened to drizzle, but they never approached a downpour, or even came close. There wouldn't be one today, either. I needed to get out of there before I really lost my cool.

I lifted the coffee off the table and pushed my chair back. "Listen, it was nice to see you. You look good. I've got to go now."

"Wait, Rae." I halted while she gathered her nerve. "Will you at least think about coming over for your brother's birthday? It would be nice if we were together on that day." She didn't look at me. She watched her cup instead, wrapping her fingers around the lid, her chest rising and falling much faster than it needed to.

"There's nothing to think about. The answer is no."

Her eyes filled with tears. "You know Gerald—"

"I'm not talking about him."

"But he's—"

"I'm. Not. Talking. About. Him."

I used to hate her for everything that had happened. I realized then that my hatred had turned into pity. She couldn't seem to move forward. Then again, neither could I.

Maybe I pitied us both.

With everything that was already going through my head, Gerald was the last thing I wanted to think about. I stood and moved to her side, glaring down at the top of her bob. "Bye, Mom." I didn't give her a chance to respond.

I dropped the coffee in the trash can by the door and headed out onto the sidewalk. She'd chosen to meet at the only café on Main Street. It was the start of everyone's workday; there was a line all the way to the end of the block. I kept my eyes on the ground, held the collar of the sweatshirt just under my chin and began to walk. I didn't want anyone to recognize me. I wasn't exactly dressed for meeting people. I had no makeup on, and the cold air would only intensify the colors in my scar.

After only a few steps, I realized avoiding contact would be impossible.

A golden-haired dog had come rushing out of line, greeting me with squinty eyes and a wagging tail. Her tongue licked the tips of my fingers.

Bella.

As much as I couldn't stand Drew, I adored her yellow Lab. She was too cute to ignore, and she made it nearly impossible, swishing all around my legs as I tried to take a step. "Hi, girl," I said, scratching behind her ears while she reached up to kiss me.

"Keep walking, Rae."

I froze when I heard Saint's voice. The last time I had seen him was when he'd fired me. Had it been Drew in line to get coffee, she probably wouldn't have said anything to me at all. She was too polite to call me out, too reserved to cause a scene. But Saint wasn't afraid of anyone, especially me. I wondered why I hadn't felt his stare. I usually knew when he was nearby; as strange as it was, my chest would start to tingle in his presence.

That hadn't happened this time.

"I'm just petting her," I said. I finally looked up and found him on the sidewalk, his arm around Drew's waist. She held Bella's leash. His black jeans, black button-down shirt and loosely-laced black boots only emphasized his seductiveness. The hints of pain I still saw in his honey-colored eyes added to it as well. But none of it triggered anything within me anymore. I remembered our connection; I just didn't miss it.

I was curious if Drew ever noticed the scars I had left on his body. The ones on his shoulders, places where my nails had dragged across his flesh. I hadn't done it to hurt him; he'd *begged* me to make him bleed, to open his skin and release the demons that gnawed at him. So while he was ravaging me and giving me my release, my fingers were giving him his.

Those moments were long gone.

"Keep your fucking hands to yourself," he said, "and that includes keeping them away from my girl."

I didn't know which girl he was referring to. I lifted my fingers off Bella and shoved them in the pockets of Hart's sweatshirt. "Wasn't planning on touching her again."

Even when I'd made him bleed, I never felt any relief come from him. He'd been so wounded, and because I was so focused on mending him, I didn't respond to what he had really been asking for. He'd wanted to see my scars—the ones that existed underneath my skin rather than on its surface. I couldn't show him. I hadn't even tried. Our relationship wasn't about my scars. It was about caring for him in a way I hadn't been able to care for others in my life when they'd really needed me to.

It didn't matter anymore.

Now he just hated me. He couldn't have made it more obvious, inspecting me with such contempt, like I was a wad of gum stuck on the bottom of his boot. I wished we could be friends—that I'd been a little more composed when he'd finally ended things and kicked me out. That I hadn't lashed out at Drew like I did.

"If you do it again, Rae, we're going to have problems," he told me. "I don't even want you talking to her. Got it?"

My eyes finally moved to Drew. I envied her ability to care for him, since she was obviously better at it than me. But Saint's warnings weren't a joke, and really I had no reason to touch her again. From what Brady had told me, she'd been through a lot of shit, too. That alone made me regret hitting her. But I also regretted it because whatever I'd felt for Saint wasn't there anymore. My urge to heal him was gone. I'd wasted my energy being violent over something that ended up being insignificant.

My gaze slowly shifted back to him. "Got it."

"Now start walking."

I didn't even try to give Bella a final pat. I just shouted *"Screw you"* in my head and continued on to my car.

FIFTEEN

"It's always so nice to see you, Rae," Mary said from behind the counter. "Are you here for your usual deposit?"

Mary had been waiting on me since I'd opened my accounts at Bar Harbor Savings Bank five years ago. Over the years, I'd learned that she had started working here right out of high school. She was in her sixties now.

Bar Harbor may have been a town that held many secrets, but it didn't like change.

Neither did I.

"Thanks, Mary. I am." I pushed the white envelope across the counter. It held five hundred in cash. The same amount I always deposited.

"Missed you last month, dear. First time you skipped a deposit since I can remember. I was worried about you. I'm glad to see things are all right."

Last month was the only one I'd ever missed. I wouldn't let that happen again. And after a few more shifts, I hoped to be able to make up for it.

"Lost my job…it took me a few weeks to find a new one, but I did. I'm back on track now."

I had no idea why I told her that. Mary knew nothing about me other than I came in once a month and handed her an envelope filled with cash. But I was proud of myself for finally finding a job, and Brady hadn't been around to share the happiness. Maybe I wanted someone else to be proud of me, too.

"Of course you did, dear. Smart girls like you always find a way to land on your feet." She opened the envelope and pulled out the wad of bills, placing it all in the cash machine to be counted. She began to fill out a deposit slip while the bills riffled through the machine. "Savings?"

I smiled, keeping my face pointed directly at her. She never looked at my scar, so there was no reason to give her the good cheek. "Always."

"Still, got to ask." She gave me her full denture grin and wrote my account number on the top of the slip. "Getting a good little nest egg here. Someone taught you right. Must have been your mama."

My mom was the reason I wanted to save, not the person who had taught me to do it. That wasn't something I could share with Mary. I just continued to smile.

A text came through on my phone. It was Shane, wanting to know if I was free for an early lunch. I wrote back asking where he wanted to meet.

"Can you sign this for me, dear?"

I glanced up, gently accepting the pen from her delicate, aged hands and signed the bottom of the slip.

"See you next month," she said. It wasn't a question. She knew it didn't need to be.

"Yes, you will." I took the receipt, waved good-bye and turned for the door. Before I'd even gotten outside, Shane had sent another text with the name of the diner just down the street. I let him know I'd be there in a few minutes. The spa was just as close to the diner as the bank was; I knew I wouldn't have to wait long for him.

And I didn't.

He opened my car door before I even had it in park. As I stepped out, he opened his arms to give me a hug, keeping one hand on my shoulder and the other in the middle of my back. He knew the proper touch. Whenever he embraced me, I breathed differently. My eyes closed. My face tucked into his neck. I could completely relax.

This was how a parent's embrace was supposed to feel.

"Let's get you some food, and you can tell me all about your night with Hart." His eyes widened. "Not in *that kind* of detail, of course...just in general."

He kept his hand on my shoulder as we walked toward the entrance. I glanced at him, noticing how his lips had spread into a smile and his ocean-colored eyes were completely avoiding me. "How did you know I was with Hart?" I hadn't told him.

It had to have been Hart.

I wasn't sure how I felt about that.

Shane laughed. "He came to work this morning with the same look you're wearing right now."

"That's impossible," I laughed, although half of me liked that thought. "I just saw Drew and Saint a little while ago, so the look you're seeing isn't related to Hart."

"No?" He let out a deep chuckle and squeezed my shoulder a little harder. "I beg to differ. Knowing how you feel about Drew and Saint, you're looking way too happy for this to be about them. Besides, if it wasn't for your expression, the sweatshirt is a dead giveaway...and the sweats."

Shit.

I kept forgetting that I was still dressed in Hart's clothes. I'd left the coffee shop, paid my cell phone bill, made my car payment and headed straight to the bank. I really needed to get back to Caleb's to change or grab all my stuff...or whatever it was that I planned on doing. I still wasn't sure if I was going to move into Hart's.

"Just so you know, I slept in the guest room." Since my clothes confirmed I had stayed at his place, I felt like I needed to explain myself. If there was anyone in the world I wanted to think decently of me, it was Shane.

"You know, Rae, I always want to know when you're happy. And if you're not, I want to know that too, so I can help fix it."

I wrapped my hand around his fingers and gently tugged on them. "You do that, even if you don't realize it."

He opened the door for me, and we walked inside the diner and seated ourselves.

"Have you heard from Brady?" I asked, opening the menu the waitress handed to me.

"Before we get into that," he said gravely, "I need to know what happened to you the night Hart asked for Caleb's address. The mystery of it all has been haunting me."

I couldn't lie to Shane. I had to explain things. But I didn't have to tell him every detail of what had happened. I didn't want him worrying, or knowing what kind of position I'd put myself in. And he didn't need to go ballistic and end up in jail over something stupid. He hated Caleb enough for the influence he'd had on Brady. This would send him over the edge.

"I'm fine. Promise."

He leaned into the table, running his hands over the stubble on his chin that would soon turn into a beard. The guys in Bar Harbor got lazier in the winter and hardly ever shaved. It was something I liked, actually. "Are you living with Caleb?"

I hesitated, but nodded eventually.

"Had I known that was your plan, I would have tried to talk you out of it. Is that why you didn't tell me?"

"No. It was just going to be for a few weeks until I saved up some cash."

"You can take care of yourself, I know that. But it's November...and then it'll be December...and you don't need this added shit right now."

Twenty-four days.

I shut the menu and crossed my hands over my stomach. "I had coffee with Mom today, so add her into the mix, too."

"Your mom, Saint and Drew all in one day? Christ."

The waitress stood at the end of our table with a pad in her hand. She looked at me first to take my order. "Full stack of pancakes with a side of extra crispy French fries, and a Coke." I glanced at Shane, a smile lighting up his cheeks. He knew how my stomach was during this time of the year, which was probably the cause of his expression. "Hell, if it's going to force its way up later, at least I'm going to enjoy it while it goes down," I told him.

He peered up at the waitress. "I'll have the same thing." She collected our menus and left our table. His hands folded together, and he picked at his cuticles. There was dried glue on his thumbs.

I made myself look away from his hands.

"Back to Brady," I said. "Have you heard from him?"

"Not yet, but he should be getting phone privileges real soon." He paused as the waitress dropped off our drinks, letting her pass before he continued. "I chatted with his counselor this morning: he's out of detox and doing okay. Things got pretty rough when he was going through withdrawal. The swelling in his face and the broken ribs they found didn't help matters, and he had a cracked tooth that they had to deal with, too. But the counselor said Brady's following all the rules, listening and participating. Can't ask for more than that, can we?" His smile was hopeful.

I felt a little relief from Shane's news, but not enough to relax entirely. Brady had only been in rehab for about a week. Now that he had finally detoxed, he'd have to deal with his demons. That was going to be the hardest part, made worse by the fact that I couldn't be there with him while he was doing it. When I'd lived with him and Shane, there had been so many nights when he'd held my hand as I'd sobbed out my fears and memories.

I wanted to do the same for him.

It killed me that it wouldn't be possible.

SIXTEEN

"The way Hart hauled you out of here, we weren't sure when we'd be seeing you again," Jeremy said after he opened the door. He acted as if he hadn't spoken to me in days, which wasn't true at all.

"I sent you a text while I was at work to let you know I was coming over as soon as I got back to Bar Harbor...and you responded and you said that was fine," I told him.

His eyes practically popped out of their sockets. His arms wouldn't stop swinging back and forth, his feet taking turns to kick some invisible ball into the air. "Oh yeah...yeah. *Yeahhhhhh*."

I shadowed him to the living room and took my usual place on the couch, which put Caleb in between us. "Is he okay?" I whispered to Caleb.

"Been at it all day...and night. Ignore him. He's long gone."

"Shut it," Jeremy yelled. "I ain't gone, I'm...*goooooone*."

He was so fucking high.

So high that he'd also forgotten that he and Caleb had been texting me since the previous day. They wanted to know if I was all right after the peep show, and to let me know they hadn't heard anything from Gary—the peeper.

Caleb handed me the blunt he'd been puffing on. After the missed *unknown* call I'd received while I was at work—the one that left no voicemail—I really wanted this weed. A part of me wondered what Hart would think about that. We hadn't really discussed whether he smoked or not. Regardless, I filled my lungs and watched Jeremy pull a white rock out of his pocket. He used his knife to shave it into powder. The glass coffee table was already covered in dust from whatever he'd snorted earlier. He used a credit card to scrape up those specks, too.

"Hart fucked him up real good," Jeremy said, pulling the dollar bill out of his nose and lifting his head from the table. He ran the back of his hand underneath each nostril. When his darting eyes finally found me, I saw how blown his pupils were. I couldn't see his irises at all, and he had non-stop facial tics. The inside of his nose looked raw, and it only got worse when he snorted another line. "Fucker will be eating through a straw for the next couple months."

"He's talking about Gary," Caleb said.

I blew out a stream of smoke. "I figured."

Gary was one of the few guys at the house that night who I didn't really know. He lived a few towns over and only showed up once in a while—usually when Caleb decided to splurge on a keg and hire some strippers from Bangor. I remembered the keg from that night, but I couldn't recall any strippers. Maybe that was a good thing.

"Fat-ass won't be coming here no mo'," Jeremy said.

Caleb took the blunt from my hand and held it up to his lips. "Not just here at this house. That punk won't be stepping foot in Bar Harbor ever again. We don't put up with that kinda shit around here. Sent a few of my boys to relay that message to him." I didn't ask for any more details. The whole thing made me really uncomfortable. I was just glad it was over.

"Thanks for having my back, guys," I said.

Jeremy nodded, although it was more like a drugged-out

double-bob. He'd slid off the couch and was kneeling on the wood floor, running his fingers up and down the sticky panels. His shoulders swayed to a silent beat.

The doorbell rang. Caleb gave the blunt back to me and got up to answer it.

"Do you hear that?" Jeremy asked.

I coughed out the smoke. "Hear what?"

"That noise. It's a siren. A cop siren." He scurried over to the front window, hiding under the ledge with only the top of his head peeking out. It was covered with a long set of blinds and curtains on both sides. I imagined Caleb's parents had put those up when they'd lived there, and somehow they had survived all the chaos that had erupted. Jeremy lifted one of the slats, lowering his ass, bending his knees and extending his hands forward. "Do you see a light?"

It was impossible to see anything. The slat was only open enough for him to look out. "I'm sure it's the headlights from whoever just rang the bell."

"The bell rang?"

I took another long drag. "Yeah, just a minute ago. Caleb answered it."

"Stop him." He reminded me of a grasshopper as he looked over his shoulder to speak. "Stop him right now. Tell him to back away from the door. Slowly...so fucking slowly. And close it. Close it *haaaaard*. They're coming, Rae...they're coming for me!"

This wasn't the first time I'd seen someone act this way. I'd been around drugs and their users so much over the years, behavior like his was almost expected at times. It had never really bothered me. Maybe because the weed had given me a nice calm buzz, and I was able to tune it out. Or maybe because all my friends were druggies; if I wasn't hanging with them, listening to shit like this, I'd have been completely alone. Or maybe because this had become somewhat normal for me, and nothing—not even Jeremy acting like a squirrel and thinking there were imaginary people coming to get him—could have been more fucked up then the events that had led to my scar.

But some of that was no longer true. I was reconnecting with Hart, and he didn't use. And I wasn't nearly high enough to ignore Jeremy's tweaking side. And almost every time I'd been in this house, something happened…something that just wasn't right.

I really shouldn't have been taking this so lightly, but I needed something to alleviate the storm of pain roiling inside me.

"*Raaaaae*, you're ignoring me. Have they gotten to you, too, Rae? Have they taken over your body?"

"No, Jeremy, they haven't *taken over my body*." I stuck the tip of the blunt back in my mouth and sucked in another hit.

"Go get Caleb. *Noooow*." His eyes had moved back to the window. Tremors made his hands shake even harder than before. "Tell him to close the door."

"Tell me yourself," Caleb said, joining us in the living room. "Dude, you've got to lay off that shit. You're making less sense than you usually do." He stopped in front of me to pick up the blunt. When he saw the size of it, he walked away without it. "Keep it. I'll roll another."

"Caleb, we're surrounded!" Jeremy said, still staring out the window. "I'm telling you, they're penetrating."

"You mean infiltrating?" Caleb asked, breaking up a bud on the table.

"Same shit," Jeremy said. "I can see 'em. They're everywhere. Wearing black or some color like that. Holy fuck, did you see that one? It just jumped, Caleb! It fucking *jumped*!"

I kept puffing on the blunt until it was finally down to a roach. Caleb kept all the roaches—whether they were the very ends of joints or blunts—in a jar under the coffee table. When the jar got full every few weeks, he'd dump all the ends together, sprinkle in some resin and roll a massive godfather that was at least three papers wide. The last time I'd attended one of those epic smoking sessions was just before Brady had taken off. The jar was almost full; there would be another one coming up soon.

I wouldn't be here for that one.

I stubbed out the blunt, dropped it in the jar, put the lid back, and stood from the couch. "I'll see you guys in a little bit."

"Don't go out there," Jeremy yelled. "They'll get you. They'll—"

"I'm just going to my room," I said as I passed him. "Relax." I knew without checking that it was well past four in the morning. I needed to charge my phone for a bit and get all my clothes together. Hart would be getting up soon for work, if he wasn't already awake, and I didn't want to miss him.

My room was exactly as I'd left it, but the mattress was now bare. I didn't see the trash bag of puke anywhere. Thankfully, it seemed the boys had cleaned it up for me.

I was still dressed in Hart's sweatpants and hoodie as I took a seat on the floor next to the bed. The stains on the mattress looked worse than they had before. I couldn't tell if they were from piss or blood—most likely both. I imagined someone had crashed here after Hart had carried me out. The new splatter marks on the wall were probably from them, too…and the smell.

This place was just nasty.

The blunt was making me lazy. I wanted to get the hell out of there, but I just didn't have the energy after working all night and driving back to Bar Harbor. I leaned against the wall, trying to avoid the stains and crossed my legs. I pulled out the elastic that held my ponytail, letting the strands fall around my face and over my shoulders. My fingers ran through it, picking out the knots, smoothing down the soft waves.

I felt sleep coming. My lids were heavy, my mouth dry from the weed. My body was supported by the wall as my chin found a comfortable spot on my shoulder.

When my eyes closed, I saw Gerald's hands. They were in the middle of all the blackness.

My eyes burst open, but they were too heavy to remain that way and immediately shut again. And I was too tired to fight it.

To fight him.

He was there, waiting for me…

"You're such a sweet girl," he whispered. He was so close, his breath felt like a feather on my cheek. Or like the stuffing that came out of my doll when Darren ripped the head off. My brother said the doll was creepy-looking… maybe it was.

His warm hand rested on my back and began rubbing circles between my shoulder blades. After a few seconds, he moved up slowly until he reached the bare skin on my neck, the spot between the collar of my T-shirt and my hair.

"Do you like being a good girl…for me?"

I nodded. "Yes."

I liked to make him happy. When I did, he gave me presents or candy. Mommy worked nights, so she didn't know what he fed me. He liked it that way…and I think I did, too.

"To help you fall asleep, I want you to think about one of your favorite places. Will you do that for me?"

I nodded again.

That favorite place was Mommy's bed on Sunday mornings. She never worked on Sundays. Darren and I would crawl in on both sides of her and fall asleep against her arms. When we would wake up, she'd be gone. She was usually in the kitchen making us breakfast. Sometimes he'd be out there with her, and they'd fight about money.

Then later in the morning, while Darren and I were watching cartoons on the couch, she'd go into her room and lock the door. I'd lean against it and listen to her. She'd be crying. That was as close as she'd let me get, so that's where I'd stay. I usually fell asleep there.

One time she forgot to lock her door. It was after one of their money fights. I brought in my piggy bank and set it on her big bed. She wouldn't take it, so I emptied it on top of her blanket and told her to keep all the quarters. It had taken me so long to save them, but I wanted her to have it all.

Mommy needed my money more than I did.

"Close your eyes for me, sweetheart," he said.

I did as he said and curled my arms around my pillow.

His hand moved a little higher as he brushed over my hair. His fingers were like the comb Mommy used on me sometimes when she helped me get ready for school, sliding back and forth between each strand. Every couple of passes, he'd sweep the hair out of my eyes or tuck it behind my ear. Then he'd start again, brush, brush, sweep.

Brush, brush, sweep.

Back and forth...back and forth.

His skin was so warm, and even though it was rough, it didn't hurt when he brushed. The dryness on his fingers would often make my forehead sore, or my cheek, or my neck. But the sweep was quickly followed by two brushes and I loved those.

Brush, brush, sweep.

"Good night, Rae," he said.

Brush, brush, sweep.

His lips kissed the middle of my cheek. His mouth was always wet enough to leave a mark on my skin. Sometimes it took minutes for it to dry. But I didn't concentrate on that. I concentrated on my Mommy.

Brush, brush, sweep.

Back and forth.

***

I woke to the scream that tore from my lips, and I tucked my legs against my chest. My arms clasped around my knees as I rocked.

Back and forth.

Twenty-three days.

My ass swayed over the crunchy carpet, and goose bumps covered my entire body. I had a similar reaction when Hart touched me, but for completely different reasons. This time, it was the same as when I thought about Gary, the fucking peeper. How I'd been completely naked. Totally vulnerable.

Open for his touch without even knowing it.

Considering the missed call and the so-called meeting with my mom, I wasn't surprised he'd popped into my dream.

Not my dream. My *nightmare.*

Those hands...I couldn't get them out of my head.

Every time I swallowed, more saliva shot into my mouth. It was my stomach's way of responding to the feel of his fingers, and the meaning behind them. It was also a warning, telling me I needed to head to a bathroom and that I didn't have much time.

I rose quickly and sprinted out of my room, my stomach heaving before I even got to the hallway. The door to the bathroom was open. Jeremy was kneeling in front of the toilet, so I went straight to the sink. I'd told Shane earlier that the pancakes had tasted so good going down. They didn't hold any of their fluffy buttery goodness when they came back up. The small piece of chicken and two sodas that I'd had at work only made it worse.

When my stomach finally felt empty and I'd stopped dry heaving, I turned on the faucet to wash everything down the drain. The basin was half-full; the added water filled it even higher. I glanced at Jeremy while I waited for it to drain. His finger was down his throat as he gagged over the toilet, but nothing solid came out. His face turned redder with each heave.

"Not feeling so hot?" I asked.

It was a stupid question. He was trying to make himself sick; obviously, he wasn't feeling good. But something seemed off. I stared for a second, realizing the hand that wasn't down his throat had slid past the elastic waist of his sweats. He was jerking off... and whimpering. I couldn't tell if his noises were from how good it felt or if the fingers hitting the back of his throat were causing him pain.

The combination of the two was way too fucking bizarre.

"Jeremy," I barked, "what the hell?"

His hand poked into the fabric of his sweats on the upstroke and disappeared during the downstroke. It began to move faster, his breath quickened. "I'm...getting...them...out." He gagged again, shoving his other fingers even deeper down his throat. Not even saliva came, or bile. He was as empty as I was.

I glanced back at the sink. The puke was floating on the top of the water, which had now pooled and almost filled the entire bowl. I needed to stick my fingers in the drain to unclog it or get a plunger. Something.

But I was too distracted by the asshole masturbating and heaving next to me.

"They penetrated me," he said. "I need to get them out."

He hadn't sobered up at all. He'd probably taken even more shit, and this was just the start of his psychosis.

I wasn't going to stick around to watch the middle...or the end.

Or any more of the beginning.

His jerking filled the silence as I looked under the sink for a plunger. There was nothing there, so I checked the bathroom closet.

"*Ahhhhh!*" he yelled. A gag followed. "*Get. The. Fuck. Out. Of. Me!*" Each word came out of his mouth in the same beat that he pumped his fist. "*Get. The. Fuck. Out. Of. Me!*"

Someone else could clean up the sink and the puke water.

I needed to get the hell out of there.

I tore off to the kitchen, searching through the cabinets for a trash bag. The only one I could find was on the floor of the pantry, covered in dust and hairballs. I picked it up, opened it and shook it out as I rushed back into my room. I didn't fold my clothes or put them in any kind of order. I just shoved them into the bag. This was the second time I'd done this—cramming my whole wardrobe into plastic, unfolded and probably even a little damp and stained from whatever was musty on the carpet. It didn't matter.

After I collected all my stuff, I shut the bedroom door behind me. Jeremy was still in the bathroom, his sounds growing louder as I approached. Skin rubbing on raw flesh. Gagging on his own fingers. He was unfazed as I stood in the doorway watching him. The crank had made him like that. Most of Brady's boys had been on it at some point over the years. It made them do some insane things.

Even Saint.

He was such a straightedge now, but he'd earned his nickname years ago when his grandmother had dragged him to church early one Sunday morning after a party. Mid-sermon, Saint tried to get up from the pew to make a run for the bathroom. He didn't make it. He ended up hurling all over his grandmother. Jeremy's parents had been sitting in the pew behind them and his dad shouted, "That boy ain't no fuckin' saint."

The name just stuck after that.

There were a few times Saint had completely freaked out on meth, so he ended up switching to opiates. He thought those would give him more control over his mind. So instead of tweaking, he nodded out. That phase didn't last long. And afterward, he quit using everything. He didn't even drink anymore.

I hoped Brady could do that.

I hoped he'd never come back to this house after he got out of rehab. I hoped I'd never see him bent over a toilet, dry heaving and jerking off at the same time.

I hoped he'd leave his demons behind without having them follow him home.

I didn't bother saying good-bye to Jeremy; I figured he was occupied enough as it was. I didn't see Caleb in the living room or kitchen, so I didn't say bye to him either. I went straight out to my car, threw my bag in the passenger seat and pulled out my phone to send them both texts. The screen was black. I'd forgotten to charge it before my nap.

I couldn't call Hart and let him know I was on my way over.

He'd know soon enough when I showed up.

But that also meant I couldn't see if there were any other calls from *unknown* since the last time I'd checked. The thought made my heart shudder.

Before I started the engine, before I even put on my seatbelt, I pressed my forehead against the steering wheel, wrapped my hands around it, closed my eyes and breathed. Shane was right: I didn't need any more shit right now.

Not with only *twenty-three days*.

Hart had asked me to move in, and I knew then that I would. I wasn't running to him as much as I was escaping the mess in Caleb's house. I didn't know how long I'd stay, or if it was even the right place for me to live.

But anything was better than Caleb's.

SEVENTEEN

I left my things on the passenger seat of the car and walked up the path to Hart's front door. My knuckles had barely touched the wood before it flew open. He stood on the other side, leaning into the frame with his feet crossed, wearing only a pair of jeans. He took a sip from the mug he held. "Where the hell have you been?"

I didn't realize how exhausted I was until that very moment. The last few hours had caught up to me; the sights, the sounds, the smells...I just wanted to sit somewhere clean.

"I...came. Like I said I would. Didn't you want me to?"

"It's seven in the morning. I haven't heard from you since I dropped you off at your car almost twenty-four hours ago." He didn't step back to let me in.

I pulled my phone from the pocket of the hoodie and held it up for him to see. "It's dead. I had no way to call you."

His face told me he wasn't convinced. "That's the best excuse you've got?"

I couldn't tell if he was more worried or angry. But I could tell he definitely cared about where I'd been.

"I have puke on my breath," I explained, "and probably on my face...and most definitely in my hair. I need a shower so badly... and I'm afraid to close my eyes." I didn't know why I included that last part. It would only lead to questions. There was no way I could tell him about my nightmares just yet.

But maybe I wanted him to ask why I was afraid.

"I should have called you, Hart. It was just...a mess."

"What was a mess, Rae?" His tone had softened.

"Nothing...everything. I'm sorry. I'm so fucking sorry."

I didn't know what was coming out of me, but I couldn't stop it. Hart didn't try to make me either. He set the mug on the floor and reached for me, gently slipping one arm around my waist and another behind my knees as he picked me up and carried me through the house. He took me into his bathroom and sat me on the edge of his jetted tub, turning the nozzle to fill it. He disappeared and returned with my toothbrush and toothpaste. I brushed my teeth at the sink.

His hands held my waist the whole time. When I was finished, he pulled me toward him. I smelled the scent of his skin. His flesh was smooth, almost glossy as it rounded the hard contours of his muscled chest. A simple silver rod ran horizontally through his nipple. I had stood as close as this when he'd gotten it pierced; he'd done the same only minutes later when my belly button was pierced. I remembered the look on his face when the needle punctured that sensitive spot, the breath he held in, the way his exhale blanketed me. I could feel that same breath now as his hand traveled up to the zipper of my hoodie and slowly pulled it down. I wore only a bra underneath. It was the one Christy had given me on my first night at the casino and it pushed my breasts high onto my chest.

They heaved as the sweatshirt fell open.

The sound of the heavy fabric hitting the tile floor was the only other noise besides the flow of water and the rush of our breath. His hands clasped my hips, pushing the sweatpants down my thighs and past my knees. I felt his air once more, a sharp, hot exhale that came when he realized I wasn't wearing any panties.

His eyes found mine again, and he unhooked the clasp of my bra, setting my breasts free. Then he carefully lifted me and placed me in the bubbling water. There were jets on both sides of the tub, behind me and all around. They massaged everything that hurt... on the outside, at least.

They weren't able to touch anything that hurt within.

Hart sat on the tile base that framed the tub. He squeezed a dab of soap over a coral-like sponge and mashed it between his hands until it was a sudsy ball. Starting at my feet, he rubbed the soft scrubber over my toes and up my calves, massaging with each pass. He moved to the outside of my thighs, slowly working his way to the inside before sliding back up.

He hovered over my navel and caressed the rod that hung from my belly button.

"It's even sexier now than when you first got it," he said.

The sound of him surprised me. It wasn't his usual tone. It was deeper, more seductive...a morning voice, a mix of coffee and need that translated all the way to his fingers.

He was caring for me, cleansing me, trying to help me close my eyes again. I couldn't concentrate on anything other than his voice...and his hands. They were everywhere, slowly moving closer to my neck.

My scar suddenly felt like it had ripped open, like rain was pouring out of its jagged edges. Ironically, my skin felt like it was on fire, a blaze that spread across the surface of my entire cheek.

I flinched.

"Rae, what's wrong?" Hart's voice took on a new tone. It was soft and tender, full of concern again. "Am I hurting you?"

I was holding my breath. My lids were squeezed shut; my stomach was queasy, even though there was nothing in it.

All I could picture were Gerald's hands.

I couldn't get them out of my head. What those hands had done... what they had taken from me. It was so fresh—too fresh from my nightmare. And yet, I knew the difference between his hands and Hart's. They weren't similar in any way, not their touch or their scent.

So why did I fear Hart touching my cheek, or my hair? Why was the thought of that making it so hard to find my breath again?

"Rae, talk to me."

My eyes burst open. I pulled my legs up to my chest and wrapped my arms around them. And I rocked.

Back and forth.

The waves I created splashed over the sides of the tub and soaked his jeans. He dropped the sponge in the water. It floated over the top of the pool as his hands moved up my arms and stopped at the base of my shoulders.

"Please," I begged, "don't go any higher." I tucked my chin against my chest, pressed my forehead to my knees and hid my face.

"I won't," he assured me.

"Keep your hands right there, okay?" It was softer than a whisper. A nearly-silent plea that I wasn't sure he heard, but I hoped he had.

I couldn't see what he was doing, but he made sure I felt his presence. The tips of his toes touched mine first, then his legs surrounded both sides of me. His arms slid around my back, the strength of them pulling me into his lap. He'd left his jeans on when he'd climbed into the tub. They rubbed over my ass as he hugged me.

I was still in a ball, pushed into his chest, and his lips pressed against my knees. "I want to help you."

"You can't."

"Yes, I can." His hands pressed harder. "But you have to let me. You have to tell me how I can make this better for you."

My arms carefully unfolded; my legs separated to spread over him. My fingers drew to his shoulders. The sun was rising, the added light glistening over his chest and neck and face. My eyes skimmed all of him as my fingers traced his shape. When I reached his shoulder, I felt something bumpy and slightly rough. I moved my hand away and felt the scar underneath, starting at the corner of his shoulder and stopping at the top of his bicep. With his skin still holding its summer tan, the white line was even more noticeable. It was thick and dotted on both sides where the stitches had once weaved through his flesh.

So similar to mine, and yet so different.

I met his stare as my fingers drew over his scar again. And again. "You're healed."

He searched my eyes. I knew it was impossible, but I could feel him looking inside me, into the space where I kept my fears and my past and my scars. They were all so deeply pulled within. He was trying his best to read them all and understand me. His face told me that suddenly he did.

"You can be healed, too," he said.

I wanted to believe him. I wanted to know that I could gaze at myself in the mirror and not think of that night in the storm, and of everything I had lost. With my scar, my memories and my nightmares unwilling to let go, I just didn't know how it would be possible.

"Is that what you really believe?" Maybe he knew something I didn't.

It probably meant I'd have to give him more...tell him more. I couldn't do that now.

Shit, I hadn't even been able to reply when he'd asked to have coffee with my mom and me. How much longer would I be able to avoid discussing my family?

And if I did finally tell him the truth, would he still look at me the way he did now?

"Of course I do," he said. "Everyone has a chance to heal. Some people choose to stay in the past and let their scars define them. Others choose to let it be nothing more than a mark on their body. That's what I've done. It doesn't define me. It sure as fuck doesn't determine where I'm going."

My scar had done just that. But his was hidden, and mine tattooed more than just my skin.

My scar was everywhere.

I broke away from his silvery gaze and tried to fill my lungs with air. He knew I'd needed his encouragement, and I knew I did, too. But it was all too real, too fast.

"Hey…come back to me." He wrapped me into his chest, his hands pressing even harder. "You're freezing. Let me get you out of here." He stood in the tub, my legs crossed around his waist, my arms clinging to his neck. I could hear the water falling from his jeans onto the tile when he stepped out.

It sounded like rain.

He reached for a towel and spread its soft warmth around me, tucking it into my chest and under my butt. I watched as he carefully kept away from my neck and anything above it without realizing how much that meant. "You'll be warm in a minute."

I wasn't shaking because of the air temperature, though I didn't tell him that.

He carried me into his room, pulling back the sheet and blankets as he placed me under both. Once I was settled, he went into his closet and returned wearing dry clothes. Then he sat next to me on the bed, rubbing my blanket-covered limbs as if he were trying to warm them.

"I know you have to go," I said. "Don't stay because of me. I'll be fine here alone." I tucked the blanket around my head. The only thing uncovered now was my face. The shaking was starting to settle down.

His fingers ran up and down my thigh, staying on the outside, never coming close to the inside. "There's nowhere I need to be. I just had to get out of those wet jeans."

I didn't want him to leave the house, necessarily. But I needed some time to clear my head of everything that had happened in the last few hours. And to do that, I needed his hands off me. "That's not true. I know you have to work today. You should have already been there."

His stare moved to my lips. "You need me more than my job does."

That was probably the truest thing he'd said.

"I do need you, but I'm willing to share you right now. I promise I'll be okay." My hand snuck out of the blanket. I clutched his fingers and pulled them to my lips. I kissed each one softly. "I need to get some sleep. If you're here, that won't happen." I nipped his knuckle.

His eyes narrowed, and the corners of his lips pointed upward. He enjoyed the sharp little blast of pain as much as I thought he would. "For wanting me gone, you're making it difficult for me to leave..."

I laughed, dropping his hand and covering mine with the blanket again. "Go," I teased. "Before I change my mind." His lips weren't far. It would have been so easy to lean forward and taste them. "You have to go." If he stayed one minute longer, I would be popping off every button on his shirt, and then there really would be nothing separating us. When he didn't budge, I tried again, "Hart, right now. I'm not kidding."

His grin dripped with as much seduction as concern. He stood from the bed. "Sleep here. I'll come back to check on you when the guys go to lunch." He leaned forward and pressed his lips against mine before he backed away. "I'm glad I made you smile...a real one, this time."

And then he was gone.

EIGHTEEN

When I finally woke, I was in the same position as when I'd fallen asleep. I didn't know what made my eyes open. I was comfortable; I wasn't too hot beneath the blankets, and I'd set the alarm on Hart's nightstand, but it hadn't gone off yet. Even though I'd only napped for a few hours, I felt surprisingly well-rested.

I slowly unfolded from the nest of blankets and pillows I had built around me. I was still wearing the towel he'd wrapped me in. I hadn't unpacked my clothes from the car, so I went into his closet to find something to wear. It was a walk-in with shelves and drawers and racks made of wood the same dark color as his furniture. All of them were full.

The tips of my fingers brushed over the sleeves of his shirts and the hems of his pants. It smelled like him in here. His cologne. His body wash. Those scents had haunted me years ago when my fingers had ached to touch him—when I'd stared at the empty space on my bed where he used to lay when he came over.

But there were no more empty spaces when it came to him.

He was here. He wanted me.

I didn't understand it...but I didn't feel as if I had to.

I chose one of the button-downs—a white one. He had plenty more just like it. Releasing the towel, I slid my arms into the silky material and buttoned the bottom, leaving the top two open.

I dropped the towel in the hamper and wandered out through the living room. As I passed the dining room, just before arriving at the kitchen, I heard a noise and froze.

"It's me," Hart said.

There was a wall between us. I held on to its edge with both hands and peeked around it. He was standing in front of the island with his hand inside a plastic bag. "Did I wake you?"

I shook my head.

"Come here," he commanded.

I moved my body out from behind the wall, my bare feet tapping on the wood floor.

"Stop," he said after only two steps. His exhale was loud. He removed his hand from the bag and placed both palms on the countertop. "Turn around."

The look on his face told me how serious he was. Was he pissed that I'd dressed in his clothes, or was he getting ready to hurdle the island?

I rose to my tiptoes and began to twirl.

"Slower."

I obeyed his order, gradually making my way around until I faced him again. His eyes almost felt like fingers and they were all over me—my legs, my breasts, my face. Maybe out of habit—or maybe because I wanted to keep my scar hidden from him more than anyone else—I tilted my unmarred cheek toward him.

"Get over here."

I felt the beat of those three little words shoot straight between my legs. That was all it took to get my feet moving again.

I reached the island, leaning my back into the countertop as he shifted in front of me. His hands gripped the stone on both sides of me. I touched the starched collar of my shirt. "My clothes are in my car." I felt the heat of his gaze, watching him eventually release his bottom lip, which he had been stabbing with his teeth.

"When you're in my house, I only want you wearing my clothes."

"Even your boxers?"

"If I tell you to, yes. Nothing of yours...not even panties." He bent his head, running his nose across my shoulder and to the opening of the shirt. "I want my scent to be on you—always."

The soft concern he had showed in the tub had been replaced with a vibrant urgency.

There were spots on my body that ached for him. He leaned over me, his hardness pressing against me. Even though I could feel how much he wanted me, Hart wasn't someone I could rush.

"I don't want my smell just *here*," he said, kissing down my chest and stopping at the first closed button. His lips sat directly between my breasts. "I want it *here*, too." The tip of his finger touched the middle of my thigh. "And *here*." It moved closer to where my legs met. "And *here*." Then it continued to slide up until it stopped on my clit. He only gave me the edge of his finger, and with hardly any pressure. It was enough to stop my breathing. "I want this spot to always smell like I've been here." My back arched as he licked across my collarbone. "And I don't think I can wait any longer to taste it."

I didn't think I could, either. Without the counter behind me, my body would have melted into the floor. He owned it now—every drop of moisture, every thought, every breath that came from my lips.

"Let me have it, Rae." His lips were pushing the shirt aside while he worked his way over to my nipple. "Let my tongue make you come."

I moaned into the air, and my eyes closed. I'd already given him control, but his words confirmed how deeply he was able to reach within me and the intensity of everything that swirled together now. "I'm yours."

His breath caressed my neck and wrapped around the base of my chin. "Fuck...I'm going to devour you." He exhaled, and the breeze rushed between my skin and the shirt, hardening my nipples even more. "What time do you have to leave for work?"

It was hard to bring myself back to the moment, to even know what time it was or where I had to be. His hands never stopped touching me, and his lips never stopped kissing my body while I thought about his question. "Not for a few hours, I think."

He nibbled on my bottom lip, sucking it into his mouth. He tasted like breakfast, sweet syrup and vanilla coffee. It was delicious. "I wish I could have you all night long." His hands traveled up my sides, bringing the button-down with them.

I couldn't imagine telling him to stop so I could go to work. But I also couldn't risk losing my job.

"I—"

His fingers brushed across my stomach and dipped between my legs again. I gasped.

"If you want me to stop, tell me now." He had only one finger on me, running over the length as it circled and spread my wetness. He gave just enough pressure to make me moan.

When his finger suddenly paused, I reached down and placed my hand on top of his. "Don't stop."

"Then tell me what I want to hear."

A wave quickly spread through me. "Hart," I groaned. I gripped his arm, sliding down just enough so that the back of my head rested on the countertop. My legs spread apart a little more. His lips brushed over my mouth while the pad of his thumb continued to graze my clit.

"Tell me," he demanded. "Tell me this is mine and no one else's."

"It's yours."

His thumb moved up, then slowly down, flicking from one side to the other like a tongue. I could feel my wetness on his skin—not just damp or slick. I was sopping.

"Now I want to hear you moan my name again."

My hips swiveled, urging him to push harder, to insert one, two of his fingers while he circled me at the same time. "*Hart…*"

The heat of his mouth turned to my nipple, sucking it through the fabric. "Yes. Now do it again."

My back arched. He knew from so many years ago how sensitive my breasts were, and how I would respond if he used his teeth, if he tugged the hardened tip into his mouth and bit down. But instead of going further, he moved his hands to my ass and lifted me into the air. My legs circled his waist, and I kissed him as he carried me. My fingers snaked through his hair, my toes linking together as I fed on his mouth.

I was starving for him.

He sat me on the edge of the dining room table with my legs still around him. The button-down had ridden up to my mid-thighs and bunched around my stomach. He glanced at the bottom of the shirt and back up at me. "Show it to me." The silver of his eyes had darkened to a deep, piercing gray. It stirred me almost as hard as his fingers gripped my skin.

My hands were behind me holding my weight. I lifted them and moved to the hem of the shirt. The slow reveal wasn't only for him. It was just as much for me.

"Lean back and show me what I want," he insisted.

The way my body responded to his demands just added to the build. But he wasn't nearly as patient as I was. He untangled my feet from behind him and pushed my thighs even farther apart, watching as the shirt rode up.

"Rae…show it to me."

There was only about an inch to go. I clipped the bottom of it between my fingers and gradually lifted. My eyes stayed on his face, watching his expression as I exposed myself. He'd seen it before—not just when we'd dated all those years ago, but when he'd found me in the bathtub at Caleb's and when he'd placed me in his own just several hours ago. And yet, the look that crossed his face didn't seem to show that. It was as if this was something he'd waited for, something he'd longed for.

Something he was going to savor, now that he finally had it again.

He dropped to his knees, hooked his arms around my thighs and brought me to his mouth. "This," and he licked the entire length of me, "is what I've wanted for so long." His tongue flattened as he ran it vertically and pointed when he swept from side to side. His fingers found a place too, giving me the feeling of fullness that I needed.

My hands moved behind me so I wouldn't fall. I rested a heel on the top of the nearest chair. It had been years since I'd been able to look down and see the top of Hart's head at my center. Though there had been changes for both of us, the man he'd grown to be only made me want him more. I'd been too young and too immature back then to understand what the future really meant, how satisfying it could be to give your body to someone who knew how to please it. If it wasn't for his absence and the other men I'd dated who only served as stand-ins, guys I tried to put back together from whatever pain they were feeling, I wouldn't have appreciated the man Hart had become. But I could do that now.

I completely surrendered to it.

I let my head fall back between my shoulders, allowing the sensation to build inside my body. The combination of his tongue and fingers brought me dangerously close to the edge.

"Don't come yet," he demanded as his movements slowed. My body and moans must have told him I was seconds away. "I'm not even close to being done with you."

"Hart," I breathed, my chest heaving, my hands reaching forward to grip his hair. I pulled as hard as I could. "Don't stop."

"I know how badly you want it." His chin glistened as he spoke. "But we're going at my pace, baby, not yours."

I released his hair and fell back against the table. My arms spread, and my fingers folded around the lip. The pressure of the wood felt good as it resisted my grasp, but not nearly as good as what his tongue was doing to me. "Please, Hart, let me come."

My request changed his speed. He started going even faster. That was what he wanted: for me to beg.

So I did.

"Right there, Hart, don't stop...please don't stop."

His tongue flicked even quicker; his fingers continued to fill me. When I got to the point where I was shuddering, he let me quiver through it. He didn't stop, and he didn't pause; he let my body feel each ripple, like thunder rolling across me.

When I'd finally stilled and settled, he crawled over my body and kissed his way up my chest until he reached my lips. "You gave me exactly what I asked for...and you were fucking delicious."

I swiped my finger over his mouth and around his scruff, sweeping off some of the wetness. He caught it between his lips and sucked it all off.

He had wanted his scent all over me.

But all I could smell was my scent all over him.

"You have to go back to work," I said. I didn't want the moment to turn awkward, so I gave him an out before it did. And I really had to get ready for work, too.

His hands moved around to my back as he lifted me off the table and carried me to one of the couches. "If I had my way, neither of us would be going anywhere."

"I know." I leaned up to brush my lips over his. "I'll wake you up when I get back."

"You're coming back after work?"

I nodded.

His brows furrowed. "What does that mean, Rae?"

"It means...I'm moving in. If you still want me to." His eyes caught fire. I didn't want to give him the wrong impression. "I can't say for how long. I'm still getting used to all this again, but if you'll have me, I'd like to stay."

He laughed, his tongue sweeping across his lip. "You're not going anywhere."

He was probably right. But I wasn't going to tell him that.

"At some point, we're going to have to talk about what happened in the bath."

I leaned forward and bit down gently on his lip. "Let's talk about us instead."

I'd made him comfortable enough to reach for my face. I knew it would happen sooner or later, I just wasn't prepared for it. His thumb slowly grazed my chin and crept to my lip, then his fingers cupped my cheek. I flinched and shuddered. It didn't matter that it was out of instinct and fear associated with someone other than Hart.

As soon as it happened, I regretted it.

His hand dropped, his eyes lingering on mine as they searched for answers they wouldn't find. He pulled away and shifted to the other side of the couch, but I grabbed his arm. I had to fill the gap somehow. "Please don't leave. I'm sorry."

His confusion was visible. "Are you scared of me?"

I pulled my legs up to my chest, my usual defensive position. "No, I'm not scared."

"Then why do you cringe whenever I try to touch your face or your hair?"

I wasn't ready to explain it to him. "I'm going to work on that."

The truth was I had no idea how to even begin working on it. I just didn't know what else to say to keep him from feeling like my fear had anything to do with him. There were moments in the past five years when someone had touched one of my restricted places and I hadn't freaked out—Saint, mostly, and usually when we were fucked up. But Saint knew the places he couldn't touch, and he never tried to push it. I suspected Hart would do just that. Not because he wanted to hurt me, but because he wanted to heal me.

I wasn't entirely sure I was ready for that.

Twenty-three days.

He started to speak and I cut him off, "I know you have questions— years' worth, I'm sure. I promise we'll talk about it. *All* of it. And soon. But not now. I need time, and you have to give me that."

His hand slid up and down my shin, and he pulled me closer to his body. I tucked my face into his neck and took in his warmth. "Whenever you're ready," he said, "I'll be ready, too."

NINETEEN

Shane had sent a text during my shift to let me know Brady was now allowed visitors in addition to phone calls. Since my work schedule took up my nights, he arranged for us to make a trip to the center early the next morning. It meant that I'd only get about two hours of sleep before I'd have to leave again. Shane's text apologized for that. My reply told him that when it came to Brady, I didn't care if I got any sleep at all.

I returned to Hart's place after work, letting myself in with the key he'd given me. It was immediately obvious that I wouldn't be crawling into bed to wake him. All the lights were on, and I smelled bacon and cinnamon as I moved inside. The table was fully set; he handed me a mug of coffee when I met him in the kitchen. I took a sip as his lips pressed into my neck.

"I missed this smell." His face dug into the collar of my jacket and kissed the spot next to my shoulder. "And this taste."

I smiled. I couldn't help it. "I missed your mouth."

"Oh yeah?" His brows rose. He pulled his lips away and lifted the mug out of my grasp, setting it on the counter next to us. "There's no reason you have to wait for it."

My stomach growled, as if on cue. I'd been so busy at work, I hadn't had a chance to take any of my breaks, let alone eat anything. It was still so sensitive, but I had to give it something.

He heard the grumble and laughed. His hands rubbed circles over my navel. "I think I'd better feed you first."

I didn't disagree.

I pulled the mug back into my hands. "What are you doing up this early?"

He returned to the stove, stirring the potatoes and flipping the strips of bacon and the two omelets he had frying in separate pans. "I like to go for a run before the sun comes up, when the road is dark and quiet. Then I head to the office before the guys so I can prepare for the disasters of the day."

I slid next to him and leaned my back into the countertop. "You have such a grown-up job managing all those people." There was only a two-year age difference between us. It suddenly felt like ten.

"I managed *you* just fine yesterday, didn't I?" He grinned, keeping his eyes on the eggs.

I laughed. "But I don't work for you."

"True. The guys respect me because I've earned it. I have a strict no-bullshit policy. They appreciate that."

I liked hearing about his professional life. "Does it get easier as you go?"

He shook his head. "Actually, the job gets more complex with each build-out. But I also become more knowledgeable. It works for now."

"For now?"

"You shouldn't be surprised to hear that spas really aren't my thing."

"The sports guy doesn't appreciate spa living?" I teased.

"Shocking, isn't it? I'm trying to figure out how to apply my business degree to that arena—something more athletics-based. In the meantime, this is affording me some time to think about it and come up with a solid plan."

If Brady were heading off to a construction site, he'd be dressed in a flannel and a pair of paint-covered jeans. Not Hart. He wore dark jeans that had small, fashionably-placed holes around the pockets. His shirt matched the color of his eyes and it was mostly hidden beneath a hoodie. It was different from the one he'd lent me; this one was fitted and had a brand logo I didn't recognize. His taste had a stylish edge that hinted at his power.

It didn't scream wealth.

It whispered it instead.

"Maine doesn't have any sports teams," I told him. "But you know that already."

He laughed as he lifted a spoonful of potato and held it up to my lips. "Blow…it's hot."

I knew whichever job he ended up with, the spa gig or something to do with sports, he'd have to leave Bar Harbor. Eventually, he'd share his plans and I'd reveal my secrets. That was the only way this would work.

Whatever *this* was.

I kept my eyes locked on his as I pressed my lips together and puffed out air to cool down the potatoes. I stopped, and he slowly slid the spoon inside my mouth. I licked the seasoning off my lips.

"I was going to ask you if it needed salt, but suddenly, I don't really care if it does." He leaned forward and devoured my mouth while I still had tiny pieces of food left in there.

The spatula and spoon both clunked against their pans as he dropped them to put his hands on my waist. His fingers traveled to the underwire of my bra, then down to the string of my panties.

Whenever I kissed him, his mouth always had a hint of sweetness to it. This morning, it was toothpaste and cinnamon rolls. He'd sampled whatever was baking in the oven. The dampness in his hair and the smell of his skin told me he'd finished his run and already showered before I had arrived. I wondered how his citrus-scented body wash would taste.

My hand reached underneath his layers, rubbing over his belt buckle and up over his stomach.

I bent at the knees, heading down for a taste of him, but he bit my bottom lip and stopped me. "Move over there." He motioned to the other side of the kitchen as he gently removed my hands from his stomach. "If you don't, I'll throw you across the countertop and take you right here."

My eyes glazed at the thought of it. "That would be giving me exactly what I want, Hart."

His silver eyes pierced me. A familiar throbbing started to pulse between my legs. "Get over there. Now." I smiled as I stepped away and moved around to the other end of the island. "When I fuck you, it isn't going to be on a counter...and it isn't going to be rushed like it would have to be now."

I licked what salt remained from my lips. "Okay."

He turned back to the stove. "Look in the bag over there."

I'd been so preoccupied with him, I hadn't even noticed the bag. When I reached inside, I found a phone charger. "Is this for me?"

He nodded. "Keep it in your car."

"So I won't ever have a dead phone again..."

That was his way of taking care of me. I was living with him and yet I hadn't paid for anything, which was something else we needed to talk about. And now, he was buying me things. Small things, but things nonetheless.

"How much do I owe you for it?"

He glanced over his shoulder. "It's a gift. I don't want your money; I just want you to be safe. You're driving back and forth from Bangor to Bar Harbor almost every day in the early hours of the morning. I want to make sure you can at least call for help if something happens."

"That's thoughtful of you." My voice softened as much as my posture.

"It's what people do when they care about someone."

I was learning that...slowly. And I was trying to accept it. I wasn't used to dating someone like grown-up Hart. I was used to high-school-junior Hart, and grown men who were nothing like him. There was quite a difference.

He walked past me, carrying the full plates of food to the table.

My mouth watered from their smells. I knew the pangs in my stomach weren't just from hunger. It was almost the end of November now. The days were ticking away. But there was no reason to dwell on the date, or wonder whether I'd throw up this food after I ate it. Whatever was happening here, at this moment, felt right.

He made one last trip to the table before clasping my hand in his and bringing me with him. We sat next to each other, and I dove right into my plate. The food tasted even better than it smelled. The cinnamon buns were gooey and oozed icing when I took a bite.

"You can cook," I said. "Like, *really* cook."

"Thanks. Can't you?"

"The basics, and I'm not even really good at that."

"How about baking? I remember Darren making us some mean chocolate chip cookies…"

A sharp pain stabbed at the back of my throat. I couldn't let it come through my voice. "I don't bake, either."

"I can teach you, if you want. It's something we can do together."

I finally looked up from my plate, trying to hide the pain in my eyes, too. "I like the way that sounds."

"Good. We can start with something simple, like cookies, and you can bring a batch over to your Mom's place. She still lives around here, doesn't she?"

"She does." I took a sip, washing down the food in my mouth before I choked on it. I needed to change the subject. "I have to work tonight, but I'm going to be swinging by the spa in a few hours."

His brows rose. "Coming by to bring me my…*lunch?*"

I laughed and blushed at the same time, the hurt finally starting to ease. I was thankful he hadn't waited for me to answer him about the cookies. "Not exactly. I'm meeting Shane and we're driving to Bangor together. Brady's finally allowed visitors."

He said nothing in response. He didn't even blink. He wiped

his mouth with a napkin, lifted his plate and walked it over to the sink. "That's what you're doing today? Visiting Brady?"

I didn't understand his sudden mood change.

"Why do you sound so surprised?" I asked.

"I just didn't realize he'd be allowed visitors so soon. That's all." He carried the frying pans over to the sink and dropped them in loudly.

"It's been almost two weeks, which isn't really all that soon considering rehab is only thirty days."

He turned to face me, his expression full of disapproval. We were only feet apart, but it suddenly felt like I was on the other side of town.

The wrong side.

"I've never known anyone who's gone to *rehab*, Rae, so I wouldn't know."

I stood from my chair, my heart pounding against my chest. "What's that supposed to mean?"

"Nothing. I just…" His voice trailed off, and he paused. "Does that mean I won't be seeing you when I come home for lunch?"

I nodded, holding tightly to the back of the chair. "I'm going to stay up there until I have to go to work."

He walked toward me, leaving me with a rough, insincere kiss that landed half on my lips and half on my chin. It was a careless attempt, and he didn't try to fix it. He just grabbed his jacket and continued to walk to the door. With his hand on the knob, he turned around. "I'll see you when I get home."

"I'll see you—"

I didn't get to finish before he walked out and shut the door.

When I got to the spa, Shane was waiting for me outside his truck. We were driving separately, though he wanted to follow me up to Bangor. I'd driven there and back every night since I'd started working at the casino, but in his eyes, I was still a kid. This was his way of watching out for me, to make sure I didn't get lost and that I arrived safely. It was a sweet gesture, and another reminder of how a parent was supposed to act.

"You ready?" he asked as I got out of my car and gave him a quick hug.

"Yeah, one second. I just want to say hello to Hart."

He stuck one foot inside his truck. "He's not here."

My heart skipped when I heard that. "Where did he go?"

"Don't know," he said. "A car pulled up here a few minutes ago and he hopped in. Not sure where they were going."

They?

I smiled and walked to my car. It was the most artificial grin; I was sure he knew that. "Then let's go."

"Okay," he said cautiously. He climbed all the way into his truck.

We both pulled out of the driveway and onto the main road. I let him lead the way—not because I didn't know how to get to Acadia; everyone in this town knew where the rehab center was. It was because I didn't want to really pay attention. Something felt off about Hart, in light of what Shane had just told me.

I didn't like it at all.

TWENTY

Shane and I sat a table in the rec room waiting for Brady to come out. The woman at the front desk where we'd signed in and had been patted down told us he was almost finished with his morning therapy session and would join us as soon as it was over.

Shane's nerves showed. He traced the grooves that had been dug into the table with his thumbnail, over and over again. I was nervous, too. The last time I'd seen my best friend, his whole face had been swollen, bruised, bloodied. When he hadn't been throwing up, he'd been screaming out in pain.

Sober Brady had a distinctly different look, of course. His skin had a youthful shine, his eyes were clear, almost radiant, and his laugh was carefree. He was sunshine. Sometimes, his demon would remain quiet for several months, allowing his light to linger. But inevitably, it rose and dragged him back down again.

Maybe that was because he'd never gotten help before.

I knew Shane was feeling the same thing, this blend of happiness and heartbreak. I saw the worry on his face, the fear that Brady would leave rehab before he was ready, or start using as soon as he got out. There was plenty of hope now, for both of us. But I didn't know if the underlying fear would ever go away, or if I would ever be completely certain that he wouldn't turn to drugs when the demons nipped at his heels again.

I wondered that for myself, too.

Would I ever not turn to weed to dull the pain of my own scars? Would I ever be able to keep my food down in the days that led to December seventeenth? Would I ever leave the nightmares behind?

"Brady," I whispered as my eyes drifted toward the doorway.

It was loud enough for Shane to hear. He lifted his head and glanced in the same direction. Then he looked back at me, and a thought passed between us. I'd seen Shane and Brady do something similar so many times before, and now I understood what it meant, what it felt like.

Without speaking, we knew we were in complete agreement.

"Hey," Brady said quietly. There was still a bit of bruising under his eye, and the stitches he'd gotten above his brow hadn't yet dissolved. The cuts around his lips were still healing. Regardless, it was impossible to miss the certainty in his movement, and the clarity in his eyes.

His mouth broke into a smile.

"Brady…" I said aloud.

Shane pushed his chair back and rushed to greet him, throwing his arms around his son's neck. He kissed the top of his head as Brady folded into his chest.

I'd seen them hug each other affectionately so many times. This was something entirely different. This was two people being reunited after spending years apart. This was a love so deep, so genuine, I knew I wouldn't feel anything like it until I had children of my own. It was overwhelming to see them together again.

They finally parted. Shane wiped the corners of his eyes and walked back to his chair.

"What?" Brady said, his arms open, the smile still on his face. "No hug for the asshole in rehab?"

I hurried over and curled into his chest, letting him take most of my weight. His chin rested on the top of my head. His hands ran a trail along my back, up to my neck and down to the middle of my spine.

"I missed you so much." My fingers clung to his shoulders; I didn't even try to stop my nails from digging into his skin.

I wanted him to stay like this forever.

"I missed you, too." His breath was clean and minty—no alcohol. His shirt smelled like fabric softener instead of smoke. He wasn't sniffing or wiping his nose.

He was clean.

I squeezed harder. "You look so good."

"You look tired...and way too fucking skinny."

I laughed at his honesty—another thing I missed. Besides Shane, Brady was the only person who could say something like that without offending me. I knew it came from a place of concern. He'd more than earned the right to call me on my shit. "I've been eating. A little."

"I know it's hard for you to keep it down, but Rae, you've got to try to eat more." He pressed his cheek against the side of my forehead. "Just twenty-two more days."

I couldn't stop the knot from lodging into my throat.

Even in rehab, he'd remembered my countdown.

"I know," I whispered. "I'm almost there." I gently pulled out of his arms, clasped onto his hand and brought him over to the table.

"You're looking so much healthier, son," Shane said once we both took a seat. "How do you feel?"

Brady didn't take his eyes off me. I knew he had questions—I could see them. He wanted to know everything he'd missed since he had been gone, how bad I was feeling, if my mom had been in touch. But Shane and I weren't here to talk about me. This visit was all about him.

"We'll catch up later," I promised him. "Tell us how you're doing."

He nodded, his pale blue stare finally shifting to his dad. "I'm good...*very* good, actually. I'm starting to sort shit out, you know, with my counselors. They're helping me find my triggers and teaching me about what I'll have to change when I get out of here."

Brady's childhood had been nothing like mine, but he understood what it felt like to be raised by a single parent and to have the other want nothing to do with him. His mom had re-married when we were in middle school; Brady had never gotten along with her new husband. He was loud and physically abusive, and he and Shane had gotten into it more than a few times over how he was treating Brady. When Brady's mom got pregnant, her husband didn't want him around anymore. It was ugly.

It was also the beginning of his storm.

"Everything is all ready for when you come home," Shane said. "Got your things all set up in your old room, and the rest of your stuff is in my garage. It'll be like old times for us."

I wished Shane hadn't brought that up. The second he'd mentioned it, I knew Brady was going to have a strong reaction. I also knew it would lead him to worry about my living situation.

The lines in Brady's forehead deepened. He looked at me intently, waiting for an explanation. I didn't say anything. He then looked at his dad. "What happened to my apartment?"

I would never lie to him. Rehab or not, he deserved the truth. "I lost your apartment, Brady. I couldn't afford it so the landlord evicted us…or me. I'm sorry." I wished I hadn't needed to admit how much I'd failed.

He shook his head. "You didn't lose anything. It's my fault for not paying and for leaving it all for you to handle." His hand rested on top of mine. There were still a few cuts on his knuckles, but his nails were now short and clean, and the calluses under his fingers had softened a little. "I hope it means you're living with my dad…that's where you are, right?"

Shane crossed his arms over the table. His thumb went back to tracing the grooves.

He realized his mistake, and everything that would follow now.

"I stayed with Caleb and Jeremy for a little bit," I said.

"A little bit?" I knew that tone. He was worried; he had every reason to be. "So you're not there anymore?"

I shook my head.

"What made you leave?"

I definitely wasn't getting into any of that now. Once Brady was out of rehab and able to keep his anger in check, I'd tell him everything that had happened at that house. But I couldn't take the chance of jeopardizing his stay there or his progress just to tell him about Gary, the peeping fuck.

"I'm staying at Hart's house now. He's back." It came out before I could consider what those words would mean to him.

"Hart?" He glanced at his dad, whose eyes were still pointed at the table, then back at me. "Hart Booker?"

We didn't know any other Hart. "Yes."

"You're *living* with *Hart Booker?*"

I couldn't fault him for his reaction. It was a name I hadn't thought I'd ever say again, either.

"I'm *staying* with him." I decided not to bring up that Hart was also Shane's boss, and it didn't seem like Shane was going to volunteer that information. It felt like this was all too much for him. Brady didn't like anyone who'd hurt me, and Hart had been on that list for quite some time. "Would you rather me stay at Caleb's?" I hadn't meant for so much attitude to rush out of me, but Hart had stormed out of the house when Brady's name had come up, and now Brady didn't look pleased that I was at Hart's.

Didn't anyone care about what *I* wanted?

"No, I'd rather you be at my dad's." He leaned back in his chair and fiddled with the bottom of his T-shirt. "I'm surprised he's back, and that you'd even let him talk to you after everything that went down between you two." I could feel his questions starting to mount. He was wondering if we were *together*, if my feelings for him were similar to the ones I'd had for Saint. What was developing between me and Hart was completely different from anything I'd had before—especially with Saint. There was no way Brady would know that, and this wasn't the right time to tell him.

"For what it's worth, I'm glad you're not at Caleb's," he said. He didn't look at me when he spoke, which told me he wasn't happy I was at Hart's.

Shane looked up from the table as soon as Brady paused. "Son, give us more details about the things you're discussing with your counselors. What are they teaching you?"

I silently thanked Shane for changing the topic. The attention should never have been on me. Brady needed to focus on himself and on staying clean.

I watched the way his mouth moved as he answered Shane's questions. How his pupils grew after each blink and stayed larger than the pinpoints I was used to staring at. The opiates he had always taken had kept them that way, and had given him his raw and often bloody nose, and his heavy lids, and his busy hands that were usually scratching some part of his body. His fingers didn't jitter now. They'd released the end of his shirt and rested on the table. They were crossed and relaxed.

Brady was back, and it sounded like he was finding himself within these walls. He told us about his daily schedule and how things had been since he'd checked in, how he was trying to find new habits to replace the old ones. He discussed the staff, the counselors he clicked with and the aids who were in recovery themselves. He was really learning how to cope and master the tools he would need to finally change his life and stay clean.

I envied him.

I envied that he was able to admit when he had reached rock bottom, and that he'd been able to ask for help. That he had finally faced his darkness and had stayed in rehab for this long already. He was conquering his demons with courage.

My demon was a man who haunted my dreams, my past. There was no way in hell I would ever submit to that sick bastard.

But how could I ever conquer him?

And what would it take for me to finally ask for help if I couldn't do it on my own?

Help wouldn't heal the scar on my face or what it represented, or the loss I felt because of it. It wouldn't erase the memories. It wouldn't heal me. It wasn't as if Hart could do that for me, either. And my brother certainly couldn't.

The only one who could do it was me.

"Brady," a man said from the doorway. "Lunch in three."

Brady sighed, one of his hands touching his dad's shoulder and the other resting on top of mine. "I've got to go. If we're late to anything, we get toilet duty and an even earlier bedtime."

Shane stood from the table and pulled Brady in for a hug. "I understand, son. Happy we got to see you for as long as we did. Keep doing good, you hear me?"

"I hear you, Dad."

"Got lots of things to tell you—*good* things—but they'll have to wait until you're healthy. Don't you worry about what's going on out there; Rae and I are handling that."

Brady finally pulled away from Shane, and he reached for me. I tucked myself into his chest again and buried my face in the crook of his neck. I loved his new smell. It reminded me of the earth after a heavy rain. "I'm so damn proud of you, Brady."

He squeezed tighter. "Yeah, well...I'm worried about you."

"Don't be. I'm fine."

"Twenty-two days. I don't know if I'll be out in time."

Save me, I screamed silently.

"I'll be okay," I lied.

He kissed the top of my head, gripped my arms and held me back a few inches, looking into my face. "Promise me that?"

I nodded. "Don't worry about me. Just concentrate on getting healthy so I can have my best friend back."

His lips softly touched my forehead. He was giving me whatever was in him—his strength, his warmth. His brotherly love.

I knew I depended on him and Shane. They had become my surrogate family, so having him back for the briefest moment only made me miss him more. I felt his absence in my bones. I felt it every time I took a breath.

Shane's arms circled around me, and together we watched

Brady walk through the door and away from us yet again. It closed completely and locked into place. We still hadn't moved. We just watched the space that had held him, and the door he'd disappeared behind.

"He's going to be just fine," Shane said softly, "and so are you." His grip tightened. I rested my head on his shoulder.

I wanted Brady to be in here, where he was safe. But part of me wanted to break him out and keep him with me for the next twenty-two days. He understood what I was going through, what happened within me every year at this time, and he had always given me exactly what I needed. It might not have been enough to fix what was broken, though it had been enough to get me past the seventeenth.

I needed my best friend back.

It was so selfish of me to want that now. I had Hart; my feelings for him were real, and he was good for me. I had Shane, too; he was the closest thing I had to a dad. As for my past, he knew almost as much as Brady. He just didn't know about those dark nights...the moments when I'd curled into a ball at the end of Brady's bed and sobbed until I couldn't breathe. I'd cried so hard I'd made myself sick. No matter how much of a mess I was or how many times I threw up, or how I couldn't stop my body from rocking back and forth, Brady still wouldn't let me go.

He was a real friend and a true part of my family. He didn't do my hair or paint makeup over my scar like a girlfriend would, and we didn't take pictures of each other and post them all over some bullshit website. He meant more to me than any of those things.

Besides the month he was gone, he never left me when I needed him, he never made promises he couldn't keep, and he always made me believe that someday there would be a safe harbor on the other side of my storm.

And now, he was finding that for himself, on the other side of his.

TWENTY-ONE

"Are you driving home?"

Hart's voice jumped through the phone as soon as I answered his call. I glanced at my dashboard to check the time. I had just clocked out and wasn't even at the Bangor city limits quite yet. I was actually surprised to be hearing from him. I'd sent him a text as I was leaving the rehab center; during my shift, sometime around ten, he'd finally replied, telling me to call when I was on my way home.

I hadn't done that.

"Yes, I'm driving," I said. "Do you want me there?"

"Why wouldn't I?" His words were clipped.

I rolled my eyes even though he couldn't see me. "Cut the bullshit, Hart. You had all day to reach out to me and you didn't. You weren't even at the spa when I went there to meet Shane, and now you suddenly want me at your house? Your words and your actions aren't lining up."

"It was a busy day."

He hadn't appreciated that dead phone excuse I'd used not that long ago. I felt the same about what he'd just said.

"Busy doesn't work for me," I told him rudely. "I need something better than that."

He was silent for a while. "It won't happen again, Rae." His tone was stern, business-like. I imagined this was how he addressed the guys who worked for him.

I adjusted the seatbelt a little and relaxed my grip on the steering wheel. "That's better." It didn't make up for the way he had acted earlier, but at least he recognized that ignoring me all day was wrong.

"I'll see you soon?"

I tried to match my tone to his. "Yes, you will."

And he did, but this time I didn't smell breakfast when I walked in the door, and he didn't hand me a mug of coffee when I got to the kitchen. He was freshly showered again, using the island as a desk and reading something on his laptop while he sipped a glass of juice. He had sprayed on too much cologne, and he looked tired. A little messy, even.

"How was your visit with Brady?" he asked, finally looking up to greet me as I walked past him.

I took a bottle of water from the fridge and gulped most of it down. "It was good. I think he's finding what he needs. Or learning to, at least."

He shut the screen of his laptop and straightened up. I stood in front of the coffeemaker, several feet separating us, and waited for him to speak. I wasn't able to dive into his eyes and read his thoughts like he could do with mine. Still, I could feel the tension crackling between us, like the charge in the air just before a lightning strike. "If you want to know something, ask me. I can't promise I'll answer, but I'll try."

"Brady..."

I stayed clear-eyed. "What about him?"

"There's more there than just a friendship. Tell me the truth, Rae. Whenever you talk about him, you get this look on your face. I don't like it."

I took a deep breath to calm the swirl of anger that was

building inside me. I'd had this same conversation with Saint, and I was tired of talking about it. I couldn't stand the automatic assumption made by the men in my life that two people of the opposite sex weren't capable of being friends. I didn't feel the need to justify my relationship with Brady. But for Hart's sake, I would explain it. "Brady and I were already best friends when you and I dated in high school. Nothing more has ever happened between us, and it never will. He's like family to me. Shane, too." I moved to the island and stood directly across from him, not dropping my gaze for even a second. "I haven't lied to you, Hart. You have no reason not to believe me."

His shoulders relaxed. His stare lost its intensity. "You're right."

I wasn't used to hearing that from a man. "If you want to be in my life, you're going to have to accept that Brady is a part of me, and he always will be. I won't choose you over him just because you don't understand what he means to me. So don't ever ask me to."

"I can accept that." He glanced down at his fingers, the tips turning white from his grip. "What bothers me about your relationship is that I can't touch your face...and he knows why that is. That I see pain in your eyes and I don't know what caused it, but he does. He has the answers to all my questions, and it doesn't feel like you're getting any closer to telling me what they are."

I held the bottle of water against the counter to steady my hands. "You're wrong. I *am* getting closer. But Brady has earned those answers; he's been with me since the beginning, and he's never left my side."

"You're still punishing me because I left Bar Harbor." It wasn't a question, and he didn't phrase it as one.

As soon as the words hit me, I recognized the sadness in his eyes, the regret. He hadn't been given a choice to stay; I understood that, and I wasn't blaming him for that anymore. But there was no way I could reach down into my memory and pull out every storm-darkened moment that had happened between the time he left and when he returned.

It was too much pain to relive.

"No," I whispered, "I'm not. I'm just protecting myself."

"You don't have to." He moved to my side of the island, reaching for my shoulders and slowly pulling me closer. "I'm not going to hurt you, Rae, but you've got to let me in. You've got to show me the girl behind the smile I keep seeing. She's the one I'm after."

I looked away, filling my lungs with air and rubbing my stomach to calm it. Slowly, I met his steely gaze, blinking away whatever was clouding my vision. "I'm going to give you exactly what you're asking for, but you've got to give me something first."

He kept his hands on my waist as he kissed my eyelids. "Anything."

He may not have intended on hurting me, but digging up the truth again would do just that. I had to know that I was ready. "Time. That's all I'm asking for."

I needed to get through the next *twenty-one days*.

He smiled, the thickness of his lips covering only the edges of his teeth, so straight and white. It was the first time he had done that since I'd gotten to the house. It was so warm as it shone on me. "You got it."

I pushed myself up on my toes and brushed my lips over his smile. "I have tonight off."

His fingers tightened and his breathing sped up. "Mmm...finally." He checked his watch without letting me go. I saw the corners of his smile drop. "I don't know what time I'll be home."

I ran my tongue over his lips. "Doesn't matter," I told him. "I'll be up whenever you get back."

TWENTY-TWO

I t was the first day off I'd had during which Hart wasn't at the
house, so I only rested for a few hours. I needed to get my
things organized. All of my clothes had to be washed, and most of
my cosmetics were close to being empty. I made a quick trip into
town to restock everything, and then began setting up my things
in the guest room. I had no intention of sleeping in there, but it
gave me a place to spread out. It was almost like my own little
apartment, which was something I'd never had before but had
always wanted.

Instead of being crammed into trash bags, my clothes were
now either hung neatly on different racks in the closet, or folded
inside the dresser. My new cosmetics were in a single row next to
the sink. None of the plastic bottles had a filmy haze over them,
and there wasn't thick, curly black hair on the counter or inside the
shower...or used condoms in the trash.

Most of the guys I'd lived with were about as grimy as Jeremy
and Caleb. Saint had been much better. But Hart's house was spot-
less. His housekeeper kept it that way and made sure the fridge
and pantry were stocked. He also had a gardener, and someone

who shoveled his snow. He even had a service that delivered his dry cleaning.

He was on a whole different level than what I was used to.

I was so far from reaching the things he had accomplished. Still, I was proud of the job I'd gotten; it afforded me to start making my monthly deposits again. I just knew at some point my lack of success would matter to him. It was important to be proud of the person you chose to be with; maybe that was part of the reason my relationships in the past hadn't lasted. Saint couldn't be proud of someone who worked for him. And there was no way Hart would be proud of the girl who served him drinks at the casino.

A better career was waiting for me.

I knew what I wanted it to be, too.

I knew reaching for it would require me to go back to school. But first, I had to establish a permanent place to live. Portland was really too far of a commute regardless of what Hart had said, therefore I knew he'd be leaving after he finished the Bar Harbor and Bangor spas. I didn't want to go back to Caleb's, and although I had always liked staying with Brady, I couldn't crash on his couch when he got out of rehab. It would be especially awkward if he started dating someone, which I really hoped would happen. All that really meant was I needed to get my own place. If I continued making the money I was, I'd probably be able to afford something fairly soon. I needed to start thinking about that option.

I had about an hour before Hart left work, so I stepped into the shower. The showerhead had multiple settings, which was something I wasn't used to. I tried each one and stopped when the water began to pulse and massage. For once, I wasn't in a rush. The tub was clean; my feet didn't stick to the bottom. There wasn't anyone waiting to use the bathroom, or any drugged-out peepers lurking around. It was a welcome change.

The scent of the shampoo mixed with the steam. It smelled like the beach on a day with a perfectly clear sky and the warmest water. I moved under the stream to wash out the suds and closed my eyes. My hands pushed against the wall in front of me. My hair fell around my face, clinging to my cheeks. The scent passed through me, relaxed me; it washed me clean in a way I hadn't been before. Slowly, I was letting go of it all—every thought, every memory, every scar. I was letting them be cleansed from my skin and my soul, and allowing the water to bring me to a place of peace, of total white.

Cloud white.

It didn't last long.

Strong, determined hands had found their way to my sides, rubbing up to my ribs and down to the base of my ass. Soft, firm lips pressed into the back of my neck. My breathing sped up in response. The wetness that covered me from within thickened, especially when his fingers grazed my nipples.

"Finding you naked in the shower is even better than finding you in my clothes." His breath licked my shoulders, and a shiver trickled down toward my navel.

"I didn't expect you back so soon."

I tried to turn around. He wouldn't let me. "That was my plan." His arms pressed harder against me; his mouth turned hungrier. My head tilted back into his chest and I leaned into him, feeling his nakedness behind me. His hand crawled down between my inner thighs and pushed them apart. He stopped me before I shifted. "Don't move. Just take everything I'm about to give you."

Since the moment he'd come back into my life, all I had done was take from him. He was completely in control. He was practically all I thought about. My body responded to him. It became more evident each day that he really did own it, so I didn't try to dissuade him or promise him things in return for what he gave.

If he wanted something from me, it sounded like he would take that, too.

The water pounded over my head. I closed my eyes and focused on his fingers as they traveled around my breasts. They rubbed in circles and tugged at the sensitive mounds rising beneath his touch. His free hand spread over my stomach. Every reaction that came from me started in my core—the quivering, the shuddering, the goose bumps. The tightness that gripped me as I waited for his next move. If he was testing how far he could take me, I made sure to show him it was working. I bucked when he pinched; I arched my back when he used the pad of his finger. I ground into him when he lowered his hand to my inner thighs.

"Breathe," he whispered into my neck.

I pulled my face out of the water and flipped my hair back. It fell over his chest and down the top of his abs. His nipple piercing peeked through my locks and pushed against my shoulder. The metal wasn't cold like I expected it to be. The shower had warmed it along with his skin.

"Mmm," he groaned. "You keep pushing into me like that, and I'm going to punish you. I'm going to make you beg for it." His lips closed around the bottom of my earlobe; his hand was once again between my legs. It came from underneath and cupped me. "Is this what you want?"

I looked down to see the tips of his fingers. "Yes…"

"Like this?" His skin, so hot and wet, almost felt like a tongue. He used his fingers to draw a line that ran down the middle of me, passing over the exact spot that was throbbing for his touch.

My back jerked against him; my legs spread farther apart. "Just like that. Now give me more."

The arm that was on my breast moved up and tightened around my neck. His thumb rubbed over my lips, pressing into my mouth. I sucked his fingertip, my teeth gently dragging over his knuckle while my tongue circled it.

"Your mouth is going to get you in trouble," he panted, "but that's what you want, isn't it?"

"I just want—" His fingers entered me, and my words morphed into a moan. My hands flattened against the wall to bear my weight.

"Fuck my fingers," he ordered.

I moved my hips back and forth, grinding them in a circle so I could feel his fingertips twist inside me. The wall had become too slippery, so I reached behind me and surrounded his neck the same way he had surrounded mine. I ran my hands through his hair and pulled as hard as I could.

"Fuck them harder, Rae."

His arm left my neck, and I felt another finger touching me, pressing on my clit and circling while I moved against him. With all his attention on my body, on the spots that could bring me to that place, I could focus on nothing other than getting there. I pumped faster as the build began to spark. My hands fell from his hair. The intensity in my stomach increased. I knew it would only take a few more passes before it would peak.

"You're tightening around me, baby. I can feel how close you are...but you're not going to come on my fingers."

His hands left me completely.

The heat from him standing behind me was gone. Then his arms bent under my knees and around my waist as he picked me up. I flew through the cold air, this new sensation floating over my skin as we moved hurriedly into the bedroom. He tossed me onto the bed, the comforter turning damp from my hair and the drops rolling off my skin.

Hart disappeared briefly and returned with a small foil packet, licking between my legs as he put it on. "I can taste how close you were."

My legs spread even wider. "Don't stop." I gripped the blanket between my fingers, the build once again threatening to peak. "Please... don't stop."

"You taste so fucking good."

I ran my other hand through his hair, the strands slick from the shower. When I pulled them, he looked up at me with his piercing metallic gaze. His fingers were inside me; his tongue was flat against me, slowly moving up and dipping down before starting to climb again.

The ache was a teasing torture.

His fingers moved out and up to my navel, lightly pressing to feel how hard he was making me quiver. "Are you happy with just my tongue inside you...or do you want more?"

"More," I breathed. "I want more."

He climbed up my body, my legs automatically straddled his waist, his fingers pressing into the bed next to my neck and he filled me. Completely. Then he stayed still while I stretched to accommodate his size. With his mouth on my lips, his tongue delicately circled mine.

"I forgot how good this felt with you."

This wasn't the rushed, urgent grinding I had done to tease him in the shower. This was a slower, much more erotic pace. We flowed in and out of each other like water. His movements were all about pleasuring me, figuring out what he could do to drive me further. It was more than what he did between my legs; it was how he kissed me, how his hands navigated my body, how his mouth triggered passion in the same places his fingers drove out the pain.

"You're so tight, I can feel you pulsing around my cock," he said, pulling away from my lips. My back arched and his mouth dipped to my nipples just long enough for him to flick both. "I want you to come—now. For me."

My body had already been so close so many times.

Those words were all I needed.

I felt the jolt as it built and exploded within my stomach, the rest of my body turning completely numb.

"*Fuck, Rae...Fuck!*" he screamed. As his thrusting quickened, his teeth nipped my bottom lip, and he sucked it into his mouth. He shuddered against me before he fell completely. Slowly unraveling from my body, he slid next to me on the bed and pulled me onto his chest.

I gently pushed down on his nipple, in the spot where I could feel the metal underneath. I remembered how the ends of each puncture spread to hold the rod. Those used to be some of his most sensitive spots.

"You used to love to bite on it," he said, "especially when it was healing." He was inside my head again. "Do you remember what our bet was?"

"Holy shit, that's right." The reason we had gotten the piercings was all over a bet. Once mine was done, Hart had decided to get one, too. He let me choose the spot, so I chose his nipple, out of spite. I didn't expect to like it as much as I had. "I don't remember what it was," I said. I was sure it was over something silly, something that didn't even matter from a time that had been so carefree. "But I'm glad I won."

He lifted my hand and held the tips of my fingers against his lips. The warmth from his breath heated them. "You didn't win."

"Yes, I did."

"No way," he laughed, kissing the tops of my nails. "I never would have let you win. That doesn't sound like me at all." I nuzzled my face against his arm. His scar was just a few inches above my eyes. "My plan was to have more than just your belly button pierced. Had things lasted, you'd probably have holes all over your body."

He could have punched rods through every part of me if that had meant he would have stayed in Bar Harbor.

But things hadn't lasted.

And he'd broken my fucking heart. No piercing required.

My hand slowly crawled up his arm, resting on the thick white line that I traced back and forth.

Back and forth.

It somewhat resembled mine, though they felt nothing alike. Mine wasn't a straight line; it was jagged and circular, rougher in the center where the skin had broken open and healed savagely.

"It was shoulder surgery," he said, finally addressing it.

"I thought so." It sounded like it was still painful for him. "We don't have to talk about it." I figured if we didn't talk about his, I wouldn't have to talk about mine.

"No, you should know." He blew out a burst of air. It wasn't a sigh. This was deeper, more emotional. "There was separation, complete tearing throughout. I dislocated my elbow, too. A whole bunch of damage. Four surgeries, and the end of a career that hadn't even started."

"And now?" I asked.

"It hurts worse when it rains."

Scars and rain. We were more similar than I'd thought. Mine also hurt worse when it rained, but for much different reasons. Hart didn't know anything about my fear of an angry sky dropping its fury down on me. I hated to think what would happen when we finally discussed it.

"It also hurts when I think about what could have been," he said.

I wasn't going to try to spin that into something positive. My mom had done that when I'd been in the hospital, with my face and body trying to heal from everything that had happened. She kept telling me the stitches and scars would give me character. Yeah...real fucking character. Every time she spoke, I gave the narcotics pump a squeeze, hoping the dose would make me pass out so I wouldn't have to listen to her anymore.

"My dad's favorite quote is that everything happens for a reason," he said.

It sounded stale and hollow. "Do you really believe that?"

He thought for a second. "Not until now. Had I gotten into the league, I wouldn't be partners with my parents. I wouldn't have purchased their house." He rolled to his side so we faced each other. "I wouldn't have come back to Bar Harbor. And I don't mean that in the way it sounds."

I knew what he meant.

"I think it's all happened like it was supposed to. I want to be here, Rae. With you." He reached forward to brush the hair from my eye, but I stopped him, holding his hand in mine and looking down at his knuckles. "Sorry," he whispered. "I forget sometimes."

It felt ridiculous: his hand had been all over my body—his fingers had been *inside* me. But when it came to my cheeks or my hair, I still wasn't ready for him to touch me.

Twenty-one days.

I kissed his palm, wondering how he could forget things I hadn't even told him about. "I know. Soon." That was probably a lie, but I didn't know what else to say. I released his hand and traced his piercing again. "You didn't give me a chance to bite it, you know."

"Mmm." His bottom lip brushed the edge of my ear. "I can't help it. All I think about is your body. I don't want to be distracted while I'm taking what I've been dreaming about for so long."

I laughed...or maybe it was more of a sigh. I couldn't tell, I had lost control again. "You've been dreaming about this?"

His hands clamped my sides. He rolled onto his back and brought me on top of him. "I never stopped. Especially after I hurt my shoulder."

"Is that why you're *really* here?"

The way he looked at me changed. It was as though he was about to admit something for the first time. "It's one of the reasons."

He had come here knowing I could have been dating someone —or married, even, and not wanting to even speak to him after all our years apart. Still, he'd taken the chance.

I didn't know how I felt about that.

"When we dated," he told me, "you said you only wanted one thing from me. No one else I've been with has ever wanted something so pure, so simple from me."

"I did?" I asked him.

"Yes. You did."

I honestly didn't recall. "What was it?"

"My love." He kissed my lips. "Just my love."

"Your—" I didn't get a chance to finish. His mouth had covered mine while he flipped me onto my back. He was rubbing the spot between my legs again, and his teeth were biting my nipples. I sank deeper into the mattress.

The only sound I could produce was a moan.

TWENTY-THREE

Hart and I developed a routine. On my days off, I got everything done that I needed to before he got home from work, so we could spend every minute together until he had to leave the next morning. When I came home from my night shifts, we ate breakfast together, and sometimes lunch if I woke up in time. The hours I worked weren't ideal, but we weren't after something perfect. Perfection didn't suit me, and he never tried to push me in that direction.

I continued to keep my things in the guest room, though I slept in his bed—even if he wasn't in it. His smell lulled me to sleep, and the comfort of that suited me in a way that no other place could. I'd taken on more shifts and was really able to start saving some decent money. Still, I didn't expect anything for free...and that was exactly what his hospitality was.

It wasn't long before I brought up the subject of paying him rent.

"No way," he said over lunch one day, "there's no way I'm taking your money." He opened the fridge, which was completely stocked with groceries I hadn't paid for. I wasn't able to eat much, and what little I did eat was staying down for the most part. It didn't matter. Whatever I put in my mouth was his food, not something I'd picked up on the road. And it wasn't right.

"It's not fair for me to live here for free, Hart."

"Not fair to whom?" He twisted the cap off his water bottle. "You do my laundry. That makes things pretty even."

"I did it *once*, and only because you left clothes in the dryer and I needed to use it."

He took a huge swig. I could tell he was searching for excuses. "You clean up. That's something."

"I wipe down the counters and do the dishes after *you make us breakfast*. I wouldn't exactly call that 'cleaning up'. You have a housekeeper who does that, and everything else."

He walked over to me and leaned against my body. "I don't want your money. I just want you."

"But I need to give you something—the electric bill, water, your car payment, whatever. Just let me help out."

Did he even have a car payment? I knew I couldn't afford to make a mortgage payment on a place like this, but I could at least contribute something—the utilities, if nothing else.

His cloud-gray eyes darkened, as if a storm had descended in their reflection. "If you want to give me something," he said calmly and firmly, "then stop working at the casino."

He was serious. This was the first time he had ever mentioned my job and not wanting me to work there. We'd finally reached the pride stage. He was ashamed of what I did for a living, and he wanted me to stop.

"It's because I'm cocktailing, right?" It was easier not to make eye contact. So I stared at the divot between his throat and his chest. "It bothers you."

"Nothing about what you do bothers me, Rae, except the hours you work. I never see you, and I hate it."

I rubbed my hands over his stomach and up to his neck. "I don't like that my hours take time away from you. But it's winter. Off-season. No one in Bar Harbor is hiring."

"Then work for me."

So that's where this was headed. "No way." I slid out from between his arms and moved to the other side of the counter. My whole body went slack from his words. There was no way I was going to sleep with my boss again, or take any money from him. My relationship and job needed to stay separate. One month of being unemployed had lost me Brady's apartment and prevented me from making my deposit. I could never let that happen again. Not for anyone.

"Rae, just hear me out." I refused to look at him. "I have tons of admin work that I don't have time for—filing, emailing, organizing...things like that. You'd get to be with Shane, and you and I would have so much time together. You'd be working normal hours again."

He made points that were difficult to deny. I'd gotten used to my schedule, but I didn't enjoy all the driving. Christy had been my only friend at work, and she and pink streaks had taken off to New Orleans. There wasn't anyone else there who I even spoke to. The money was the only reason I stayed.

"I'll pay you whatever you're making at the casino, plus another fifteen percent on top of that." He waited for me to look at him, to signal my agreement. "I'll give you benefits, too, which I doubt they're giving you there."

He was right; I didn't have benefits. Saint hadn't even given me those.

"Sounds like a little too much to be paying your assistant." But not his girlfriend...

I didn't like the feel of it.

He smirked. "Good help doesn't come cheap."

I wasn't amused by any of this. "What happens in a few weeks when I've gotten you all caught up and you don't have any more work to give me? It will be the middle of the winter, and I won't be able to get another job."

"That won't happen." He leaned across the counter to get closer. He sounded so sure of himself. "This isn't something I just thought of. I've needed an admin for a while, and once we finish the job here, you can come with me to the Bangor location."

He hadn't mentioned anything about the Portland spa, which meant I'd have a job for as long as he was in the area, but not forever...unless I was willing to relocate. The same was true for my relationship.

Both would expire within a year.

But from the moment I'd gotten my scar, I'd learned that nothing else lasted. Not relationships, not family—not life. Was that a good enough reason not to try? I wasn't sure.

I also wasn't sure I was ready to work for another boyfriend.

"I'll think about it," I said.

"I expected you to say that." He came around the counter and held me again, leaning down to kiss my neck. Then his lips moved up and stopped beside my mouth, grazing the smooth skin of my unscarred cheek. His breath floated like mist around me; my eyes closed and my body relaxed. I reached for the bottom of his shirt. It was the safest place for my hands to be. If I were to touch any part of him, I'd want to rub my fingers over his skin...and then his muscles beneath.

He didn't have time for being naked, or that kind of sexual insanity before he had to go back to work.

"I'll see you in the morning," he said. He kissed me one last time.

He wasn't out the door for more than a few seconds before my cell started ringing. I pulled it out of my back pocket and stared at the screen. It was a Bar Harbor number, one that I didn't recognize.

But it was safe to answer.

Because Gerald wasn't in Bar Harbor.

Fourteen days.

"Hello?"

"Hi Rae. It's Mom."

She must have been calling from the hospital. She probably figured calling from a number I didn't recognize would be her best chance of getting me to answer. It made sense; she'd been calling for the last few days, and I hadn't picked up or returned any of her voicemails.

"What's up, Mom?"

"Just a few weeks until your brother's birthday," she continued. "You know how much I'd like for you to be here. Tell me you plan on coming."

She already knew what my answer was going to be. It hadn't changed since the last time she asked and it was always the same. "I have something going on that day...I can't."

"That doesn't sound like the truth to me."

I understood why she had a hard time believing what I said. Even before the incident that led to my scar, I hadn't been the best daughter in the world. I'd snuck out of the house and gotten shitty grades and smoked pot when I should have been doing my homework. But I was just a fucking kid, doing the things that all my friends were doing.

It hadn't meant I was a complete liar.

But when I'd needed her to really believe me for the most important thing I had ever told her, she'd already made up her mind that my word couldn't be trusted.

"Yeah, well...you don't seem to recognize the truth much, so..." I said, knowing how biting that would be to her.

"Rae..." Instead of the hard edge she usually used with me, her voice was becoming raspy. She was breaking down, finally showing a bit of emotion. "I need you there. Please."

She needed me? I'd needed *her* to be there, a long time ago. I'd needed *her* to believe me, and she hadn't.

I'd needed *her* to be my mom, and she couldn't.

I felt like I should be the one begging. But I was too angry for that. "I can't, Mom," I said.

I hung up without letting her say another word.

TWENTY-FOUR

My belly was so full. He'd cooked me exactly what I'd asked for: macaroni with an extra big squirt of ketchup, a big tablespoon of butter and just a little pepper. Mommy wouldn't cook that for me. She said putting ketchup on pasta was gross. How did she know if she wouldn't even try it?

Mommy was so silly sometimes.

I curled up in the corner of the couch and rested my arm on the side cushion. It would be bed time soon, but I didn't want to go to bed. "Wanna play a game?" I asked him. My cheek pressed into the cushion when I looked over at him. It smelled flowery, like Mommy's perfume.

"Let's just rest here a minute. Then I'll play a game with you." He gently tugged on the corner of the blanket that I had wrapped around me. "Share this with me, won't you, sweetheart?"

I only shared with Darren. I hated sharing with everyone else. But he'd cooked me macaroni and ketchup and he'd made it wicked buttery, which was my favorite way to eat it, so I unwrapped a little and let him cover himself. Of course, the piece he'd taken was too small to reach his super long legs. I moved closer to give him a bit more. This new spot was the worst part of the couch because it was in between the cushions, so I sagged into the crack.

I wished I hadn't given him any of the blanket.

"Why don't you come sit on my lap so you're more comfortable?" he asked.

His lap would be more comfy than the couch crack, I guess. And he had cooked me what I'd wanted so I could at least do what he asked.

Mom had defrosted venison for us to eat. Deer was just icky.

Whenever he asked me to sit on his lap, I always fell asleep early and he carried me to my bed. Maybe he wanted me to fall asleep so he wouldn't have to play a game with me. Whatever. I didn't want to play anyway. He always let me win, so it wasn't all that fun.

I crawled up onto his long legs and fell back on his chest. Then he covered us both in the blanket. The scruffiness on the side of his face poked into the top of my head.

I hated it.

I didn't like what he was watching on TV, so I made up my own game: I only breathed when he did, but not as loud. And when the air came through my nose, it didn't whistle like his. He needed to blow his nose.

But I didn't tell him that.

Breathe, whistle, breathe.

"Raaaaaee," Darren called from his room.

"Whaaaaat?" I yelled back.

Instead of answering, he came out into the living room to look for me. His eyes went wide when he saw me. Wide like my favorite cartoon. That crazy rabbit always made me laugh with those eyes of his.

"Come hang out with me," Darren said.

Breathe, whistle, breathe. Breathe, whistle, breathe. Breathe, whistle, breathe.

He was breathing way too fast for me. I couldn't keep up.

"Go back to your room, Darren. Your sister needs to go to bed. So do you."

"Can't she hang out with me until—"

"No!" he yelled, cutting Darren off. "Go to your room! Now!"

Darren stormed off. My brother was always getting in trouble with him.

When it was just us again, his hand went to my cheek, the one that wasn't resting on his chest. His skin was so rough. Sandpaper rough. He brushed it over my cheek and into my hair, tucking the loose strands behind my ear.

Now that Darren was gone, his breathing went back to normal.

Breathe, whistle, brush, breathe.

"You're such a good girl," he said.

I knew I was. I mean, I didn't do anything bad. Except for eating the macaroni and ketchup when Mommy wanted us to have venison. She knew I hated that kind of meat, so it was really her fault that I had asked him to make me something else.

Breathe, whistle, brush, breathe.

"Such a good girl," he repeated.

His hand stopped moving every few minutes, then started up again, rubbing over my cheek and straight up into my hair. Sometimes his thumb would just draw circles over my skin. Maybe he'd gotten tired.

I knew I had.

With such a full belly and all the brushing and breathing, my eyes were heavy.

"My Rae is always such a good girl," he said.

Breathe, whistle, rub, breathe.

"Rae, wake up…you're having a bad dream."

My eyelids shot open and widened, searching the room. There was a face so close to mine as I gasped for breath. It wasn't him… Gerald. It was Hart.

"I came home from lunch, and I heard you screaming," he said. He sat on the bed and rubbed my stomach over the blanket. His fingers were spread out, each of his nails cut short. There was nothing rough about his skin, I reminded myself.

Breathe.

His hands had already been on my body. They had filled me. They had loved me.

Breathe.

They were gentle. Harmless. They were even a little pretty.

Breathe.

"You have tears," he said. "I want to wipe them away, but…"

He knew he couldn't touch me there.

I used the back of my hand to dry them, then I pulled the blanket up past my nose, hiding everything but my eyes.

"What were you dreaming about?" he asked.

It wasn't a dream. It was a fucking nightmare, and there was no way I was going to tell him about it. Not until I absolutely had to.

And at that moment, I didn't.

"It must have been something really scary," I said, my voice muffled from behind the blanket. "But I don't remember."

The silver of his eyes had changed to a sky blue that matched his shirt. "I never remember my dreams either…unless they involve you."

I remembered all of mine. At least the ones that included Gerald. They weren't scenarios that my mind had created. They were moments that had actually taken place. Memories of a past that I would do anything to forget.

"You haven't slept this late in a while. Are you feeling okay?" he asked.

My eyes glanced to the nightstand, but I wasn't able to see my phone. "What time is it?"

"Almost one."

I'd slept for nine straight hours. I hadn't done that in months.

"Just tired, I guess."

"It's because of your schedule. You're working all those hours, not taking any breaks, then driving over an hour home. Your body is going to shut down if you keep this up." His hand moved down to my thigh and started to massage the muscle. "Trust me, I know what I'm talking about."

I had been much more tired lately, especially since I'd started working at the casino. I'd gotten more used to the odd hours, but I knew I wasn't getting enough sleep. It was so hard to close my eyes and relax when the room was filled with light—even when the blinds were closed. I also hadn't been eating enough. I didn't think I'd gotten any thinner, but I hadn't gained any weight, either. *Thirteen days.*

"I worry about you."

I stuck my hand out of the blanket and rested it on his cheek, rubbing my thumb over his lips. His beard was growing out, and the messiness of his facial hair with his dark, edgy style was such a sexy combination. "I know."

"Take the job I'm offering you, Rae. It's been over a week since we talked about it, and you still haven't said anything. Your concerns are valid, but I promise what you fear isn't going to happen."

"You don't understand. I've worked for my boyfriend before. It didn't work out—it was a disaster, actually."

"Yes," he kissed my thumb, "I do understand. I'm not some asshole who would ask you to quit a good job, then leave you unemployed in a few months. Give me a little credit here."

I'd thought about working for him while I had been driving home early this morning. What it would feel like to have a normal job with regular hours. It wasn't the kind of work that I really wanted to be doing at a spa, but it was for a company that built them. Without any schooling, I probably couldn't get much closer than that and get paid the amount he was offering.

"I have to give them at least two weeks' notice," I said.

He smiled and leaned down, his lips drifting onto mine. His body followed, hovering directly over me. I used his fabric softener, but it smelled different on him, mixed with his cologne and the scent of his skin. I wanted to eat both smells constantly.

"Even your sleep tastes delicious," he said, his mouth finally pulling away.

I'd showered before I had gotten into his bed, but after nine hours of sleep, a flood of tears, and even a little screaming, I couldn't imagine that I tasted very good.

I ran my hands over his chest, down his abs and slipped them under the waist of his jeans. I met the elastic of his boxer briefs and started to move even lower. "How much time do I have?"

He gave me a quick peck. "Not nearly enough...not for what I want to do to you."

"This isn't about me. It's about you."

"Mmm." His lips ran over my neck before he moved off me and stood next to the bed. Though he no longer touched me, I was still covered in goose bumps. "You know the second one of your fingers comes near me, it will become about you. But time isn't going to be an issue anymore, is it?"

I shook my head.

"I promise you won't regret your decision." I hoped he was right. "I'll see you in the morning, baby." He kissed me one more time before he left the room.

I heard the front door close and got out of bed, heading for the guest room. There was only one thing I'd hidden in there. I couldn't even call it hiding—I'd stuck the box in the last drawer of the dresser and covered it with a sweatshirt. If he looked, he'd find it easily.

I took it out of the drawer, grabbed my purse and sat on the floor. With my legs crossed under me, I removed the envelope from my bag. I'd already written *Darren Ryan* on the front cover, and Mom's address.

I love you.
—Rae

Those were the only words I had written on his birthday card. The only words I ever wrote to him. The things I needed to say couldn't be written down; they had to be said out loud, screamed and sobbed in order for him to truly understand how sorry I really was.

I held the card up to my lips and kissed his name.

I'm so fucking sorry, Darren.

Then I opened the top of the box. Inside were four other

envelopes, one for each of the birthdays I had missed. I placed the one for his nineteenth on top of the pile and shut the lid.

I hadn't missed his birthdays.

Not even close.

But I hadn't mailed the cards...because he wasn't there. Not at Mom's, not in Bar Harbor. Not even in the rain.

Darren wasn't anywhere anymore.

He was dead. He had been for the last five years.

TWENTY-FIVE

"I hate that I have to wait an hour to have you."

Hart's voice was deep and filled with longing, and it intensified the tingling in my lower stomach. I was leaning against my car in the parking lot of the casino; he was standing in front of me. His hands had crawled underneath my jacket, his fingers drawing lines around my navel.

I'd given the manager my two-week notice a few days before. The waitlist to work there had become so lengthy, he only needed me to stay long enough to train a new waitress. Tonight was my last shift, and Hart had come up to play poker. I knew he was really just there to see me.

"Sixty minutes, then we'll be at the house. I know you can make it." I didn't really mean that. I was having just as hard of a time waiting so long to touch him. His lips alone hadn't given me enough satisfaction, even as I wiped my gloss off them now.

I wanted more.

I'd been wet practically from the moment he'd arrived at the casino. It was from the way he'd looked at me, the way his fingers had grazed my skin throughout the night, how his hand had found its way under the front of my skirt. Knowing that my smell and my wetness were all over him while he had played was such a turn on.

He opened my car door, and I climbed inside. "One hour—not a minute more." He said it through gritted teeth, his eyes hungrily devouring my body. Frustrated sighs came out of him as he restrained himself from touching me.

I wasn't sure if he was going to close the door and let me drive off, or if he was going to rip my clothes off and take me in the front seat. I made the decision for him, shutting the door and watching as he turned slowly and walked across the lot. As soon as I saw his headlights flip on, I drove onto the main road.

We weren't even out of Bangor before my phone rang.

"I'm only a few feet in front of you and…" I glanced at the gas gauge, "I have a full tank of gas, so don't worry…"

"I want you to take your left leg and push it against the door. Make sure it's locked." The intensity in his voice was almost startling. He was demanding without being intimidating.

I pressed the lock, lifted my leg, and pushed it against the door. I couldn't imagine why he wanted me to do that. "Done."

"Now take your fingers and gently touch the inside of your right thigh. Just the inside, don't go any farther." A smile spread over my lips as I realized where this was going and what he was actually asking me to do. "I know what you're wearing, which means I know how far you can spread your legs, and what that fabric is going to feel like when you rub your fingers over it."

I was in leggings; spreading my thighs wouldn't be a problem. And he was right: the softness of the fabric was going to feel amazing against my skin…*too* amazing while I was driving.

I glanced in my rearview mirror as my left hand moved off the steering wheel. The thought of him giving me orders from the vehicle behind me in total darkness, where I couldn't see his face or know what he was doing with his hands, was so sexy.

"I'll know if you touched yourself from your breathing. So just your thighs, Rae, and do it slowly."

My fingers moved down my jacket. I ran them over the hem of

the pants, stopping before they came too close to the throbbing spot.

"That's it." His voice had deepened and become raspy. "It feels good, doesn't it, baby?"

My right hand squeezed the steering wheel as if it were trying to slip away. "I want more." Heat blasted through the vents of my freezing car. I switched it to air conditioning and loosened my scarf and the top buttons of my jacket. I wasn't cold anymore.

"Now brush your fingers over your pussy—don't linger there, just touch it. Gently. If you want permission to slide under the fabric, I need to hear how much you want it."

The guy I had dated before Saint was the biggest freak I'd ever been with. Before him, I hadn't ever explored the darker side of sex. He was into wax, matches, lighters...he had a thing for heat and how it could add to our pleasure. That, I could handle. But I reached my limit when he asked me to try snowballing. It was then that I immediately left him. I couldn't heal someone who didn't want to get better even if his wounds were attractive. I was all for trying new shit; having him squirt his man juice into my mouth and then for me to dump it into his wasn't erotic. It was fucking gross.

Fortunately, Hart was nothing like him. His commands were forceful and naughty, and seductive. He wasn't doing things just to experiment or shock me. And it wasn't only his words that were persuasive; it was just as much my desire to please him, knowing how good that would make me feel, that he would reward me in orgasms that truly made my body buck to his commands.

"*Ahhhh...*" I moaned.

"I can just imagine how wet you're getting. Now I want to hear it. But first, I need you to slow the car down." I took my foot off the gas and let it coast. "Good. Now push your pants all the way down to your ankles."

I had to arch my back and thrust my butt off the seat to slide the leggings down to my knees. I sat back down and used the heel of my boot to bring them to my ankles. "Okay, they're there."

"Are your panties wet?"

I didn't even have to touch them to know. The wetness had seeped through the fabric. "Yes. Sopping."

"I want you to keep them on, but move them to the side so your fingertips have plenty of room to explore."

The material wasn't really meant for coverage; they were really made for looks, so it was easy to push the flimsy piece aside. "Done."

"Now touch yourself, Rae. Just the outside. I don't want anything inside you yet."

Holding them aside with the edge of my hand, I pushed my head back against the seat and sucked in my breath as my skin landed on the sensitive spot. There was so much heat, so much wetness. A flood shuddered from within me. "I wish this was your hand instead of mine."

"Soon, baby," he said. "Do you know how hot it is to see the silhouette of your body through the back of your car, knowing you're touching yourself exactly the way I want you to?"

"It feels…" I was rubbing just the outside, the tops of my lips, teasing the center. "…so good." There was nothing in front of me to look at except the road and trees and an occasional sign that told me how many more miles until Bar Harbor. And the red lights from the dashboard that reflected on the top of my hand.

"Now I want you to put your cell on speaker mode and rest it on the seat between your legs."

I lifted my hand just long enough to take the phone off my shoulder, hit the button he had requested and place it on the seat. "It's there."

"I can hear it…and the difference in your voice."

I was now rubbing circles over my clit. My back wouldn't keep still, or my legs, or my right hand as it slid over the top and bottom of the steering wheel. I wasn't sure if it was the position I was in, or if it was from driving and trying to keep my focus on the road while all this was happening, but the build was coming much faster than normal. "I'm close. So *fucking* close."

"Finger-fuck yourself now. Let me hear just how wet you really are."

My ass moved down the seat, and I leaned back a little to give me more room. My finger slowly entered—just one. I didn't try to quiet my breathing or soften the moans. Hart needed to hear exactly what he was doing to me.

"Shit...you're so fucking wet," he said. "That sounds so goddamn good."

It was getting harder to concentrate on the road. We weren't far from town; the street was beginning to weave and climb, unlike the straight drive that had led us here.

"Hart..."

"I can hear how close you are. Add another finger."

I inserted a second one, my slickness allowing it to pass in and out so easily. I could feel it dripping on my inner thighs and on the seat underneath me. I kept my eyes open, but it was hard. "Tell me I can come."

My own fingers didn't usually turn me on this much. They were mostly orgasms out of need; I wasn't sopping, my back wasn't arching, I wasn't moaning so loud the back of my throat hurt...but all of that was happening right now. My body was on the verge. I had reached the place where I'd lost control of the build. I couldn't feel my toes or the pedal beneath them; my hands were numb; my legs tingled...

"Come for me..."

That was all I needed to hear.

Hart's command brought out a spark that coursed through my whole body like a lightning strike, starting in my lower half and climbing all the way to my fingers. It jerked me forward, my face looming near the steering wheel, then it shot back down into my feet.

"Wow." The word sounded like a moan.

I wasn't sure if that had come out of my mouth or his. Maybe both.

I caught my breath and put the car in park. We had reached his house.

I felt the chilly rush of air as he opened my door, reached inside, and pulled me out. My leggings were still around my ankles; my fingers hadn't even dried yet. Hart plunged them into his mouth and sucked my wetness off them while he ripped away my pants and carried me in with my legs straddling him.

We got only as far as the foyer before he pressed my back against the wall. My pussy ground against his jeans as my lips crushed his mouth. There wasn't anything gentle about either of our movements. He held me with one hand, cradling me in his arm as he reached down with the other to unbuckle his belt and drop his pants. I stayed just as busy, sliding out of my jacket and yanking off my scarf and sweater.

"I don't have a condom," he breathed into my neck. "We'll have to go into the bedroom to get one."

"Don't use one," I whispered.

His body stilled. He pulled his face out of my neck to look up at me. "Are you sure?"

"I've never been so sure."

He smiled, and then he entered me. I slammed against the wall and screamed out in surprise, even though I had been anticipating it. His size was something I was still getting used to again, but his power was something entirely new. He'd been much more gentle and reserved all those years ago when we were learning each other's bodies. What he was capable of now was much more intense than anything I'd ever had. Not just in the physical sense, though his strength and endurance were more than evident. It was an emotional intensity as well—the way his hands gripped me as if slipping through his fingers would cause him the greatest ache, the way he kissed me with so much passion. The sounds he made weren't just moans of pleasure; they were cries filled with the deepest longing, the most gripping desire.

It made me believe no one had ever wanted me more than he did.

"You were so submissive in your car, listening to every command I gave you, and coming with your fingers. Now I want to feel you do it all again, but on my dick this time."

My shoulder blades rubbed against the wall, chafing like it was carpet. It wasn't painful. It couldn't have been.

Nothing about this moment could ever feel bad.

"I'm so close again." I pressed my head into the wall and released everything in my mind, in my body. The tension within me slackened, and I fell straight into the movement.

"Ah, shit...I just felt you tighten around me," he said.

My hands were the only part of me that hadn't relaxed. They gripped his neck, feeling the muscles and the strain as he plunged his body into mine. His fingers roamed my skin, pinching my nipples, then rubbing my clit with such speed that I melted into him.

"I can't stop what's happening," I breathed. "I can't control it."

His lips pressed against my ear. "Then don't. Let me feel you. Let me hear that fucking voice of yours."

I gave him my voice, like thunder, letting the sounds match the feelings that were building inside me. And when they reached the absolute peak of pleasure, my body began to shudder and shake. I came down from a place I didn't think I could reach again so intensely, or so soon, after what had just happened in my car.

Hart had given that to me.

His body slowed, though his thrust lost none of its power. I could feel how close he was by the way he kissed me, how his muscles tightened and wracked with spasms just like mine had. His pounding slowly wound to a complete stop. He didn't slide out of me or pull me off of him. We stayed just the way we were, limp against each other. His breath blanketed me, warming me as I glowed within his touch.

We were the calm after a beautiful storm that I never wanted to end.

TWENTY-SIX

Working for Hart was much different than I'd thought it would be. From the moment I arrived at the spa, people asked me questions; they depended on me, they relied on my knowledge to make their jobs easier and to help the construction progress. I wasn't just holding Jack and Coke on a tray, smiling so people would drop more dollars in my apron.

I was someone who was trusted to have answers.

Being on the jobsite meant I also got to spend more time with Shane. We had coffee together every morning as we talked about the timeline for the day, and he popped into my office whenever he had a chance. I shared a workspace with Hart, so Shane was always careful to wait until we were alone before he brought up something personal. It was usually when he wanted to discuss Brady, to hear how I was doing, and to find out if I was staying on track with my deposits. With Hart paying me even more than I had made at the casino, I was able to increase the amount I put in the bank. But as proud as I was for building my savings, the high quickly wore off when I would remind Shane of the countdown.

Nine days.

He knew I was holding myself together and it was probably only because of Hart.

And Hart wasn't just dominating my thoughts and body; I was also consumed with maintaining his work schedule. That was why it seemed really strange the morning he kissed me good-bye and said he'd be gone all day for a meeting. His calendar completely disagreed with that; he was supposed to be on-site all day. It was even stranger when he left his keys on his desk, and a white Lexus picked him up at the end of the driveway. I asked Shane about it. All he knew was the same car had picked up Hart the last time he'd disappeared for the day.

I needed to talk to Hart.

Hart sent a text later, saying he'd be home around eight. It was well past ten before he walked through the door. I was on the couch, and the TV was on, but I had no clue what was showing on the screen. I hadn't been able to concentrate on it. Too many things were running through my head, my thoughts rushing back and forth.

Back and forth.

"Do I need to worry about where you've been?" I blurted out. He hadn't even set down his messenger bag or taken off his jacket. I didn't care. The fear and anxiety had been eating away at me for hours, and I couldn't hold it in any longer.

He looked surprised. "Why would you worry?"

I'd been cheated on before by that freaky fuck I'd dated, though I hadn't learned about the other girl until after I had already dumped him. Apparently my level of freaky hadn't been enough for him. There had been signs, which I'd ignored. I wasn't going to do that again. Not when there was so much strangeness about today. Hart hadn't told me who he was leaving with, or that he was leaving with anyone at all. He hadn't even called to say he was going to be back later than eight. The fact that he could stand just a few feet away and glare at me like I was the crazy one for thinking this only got me more worked up.

"Don't make me feel stupid, Hart. You were gone all day when there was *nothing on your schedule*. You didn't answer your phone when I called you at lunch, and you never bothered to call me back. And according to your text, you should have been home over two hours ago. So where the hell have you been?" If he made me ask the obvious question, I would hate him for it.

He moved over to the back of the couch, clutching the edge. "I was in a meeting, Rae. The only events I put in my work calendar are things that are related to the spa."

A meeting that wasn't work-related...

"So why didn't you tell me about it?"

He sighed. I could see how tired he was, the way his body slouched and his eyelids drooped. I didn't care. I needed answers before I'd even consider letting up.

"I didn't have time," he said. "It was scheduled at the last minute."

"No, it was scheduled at the *first* minute...you left before I even had a sip of my coffee."

He walked to my side of the couch and sat in the spot next to me. I could tell he wanted to pull me into his arms. He didn't, which was smart of him since it wouldn't have gone over well. "You're making a bigger deal out of this then there needs to be."

My thoughts began flowing onto my tongue. They were going to be heard at some point, anyway. There was no reason to keep holding them in. "Please don't lie to me. If there's someone else, just tell me and I'll pack my things and get out. I have nothing to offer you—I don't have money like you, I don't have your education or your career. I don't—"

"Hey..." He reached forward, and I flinched. He kept moving slowly. Carefully. "I'm going to wipe the tears from your eyes—just your eyes, nowhere else." Ever so softly, the tips of his fingers landed on the bottom of my lids and caught the drops before they fell.

His warning suddenly filled me with sadness. I hated that he had to tell me before he touched any part of my face. And that he touched me cautiously, like I was some damaged, wilted girl, rocking herself in a corner while a pair of clean, safe hands dragged her out into the sun.

Back and forth.

I guess I really was that girl.

What I wanted to blurt out, to scream, to sob until he understood was that there were only *nine days* left until my brother's birthday. But I couldn't tell him that. He'd look at me like I was vile and disgusting.

I'd rather he consider me broken than repulsive.

"There isn't anyone else, Rae," he assured me. "You should already know that and be able to feel it. I haven't been able to keep my hands off you since you came back into my life." He kissed below each eye where it was still damp. "You have nothing to worry about. I'm so crazy about you."

I didn't know if I was truly acting nuts and overreacting over nothing or if my overly-emotional state was entirely related to the next *nine days*. It was likely I was taking my terror out on him. It horrified me that I couldn't tell the difference.

His hands moved to my knees, and he leaned close to my face. I tried my best not to flinch or pull away. "As for everything else you listed off," he said, his tone soft and even, "do you really think I care whether or not you have money? Or if you went to college? Those are superficial things that have nothing to do with how I *feel* about you." His lips brushed over mine. "I'm following my feelings, and I'm happiest when I'm with you. I always was...I always am."

The tears only flowed faster; I couldn't stop them. His honesty was just what I needed to hear. It took me by surprise and made me wonder how I could possibly deserve someone like Hart.

"I understand why you were upset," he continued, "but there are just some business things I can't tell you yet. Things that need to remain confidential for now. They aren't bad, and they have nothing to do with us. I promise."

Business matters that didn't involve me or my position in his company had to remain separate from our relationship. I knew then that it wasn't because he didn't trust me; he just wasn't in a position to discuss them.

I was doing the same thing.

There were subjects that, if I could, I'd never tell him.

"Yes, of course." I smiled, though it was weak.

"Good." He pecked my lips. "I'm happy to hear that, because I would never do anything to hurt you."

I believed him.

TWENTY-SEVEN

The tears I'd shed that night on the couch changed things between us. Hart became even more attentive to my needs, more sensitive to my triggers. He spent additional time at the office training me on other aspects of the business—things I didn't necessarily need to know in order to do my job, like the stages of construction and the operating procedures. He even showed me things that business owners didn't typically share with general employees, things like the financial statements, prospective expenses, budgets and projected income. Saint had never discussed those things with me. Shane hadn't either, so I had no real understanding of what the majority of it meant. I still knew how much money I was looking at, and how much the spa was expected to make. Bar Harbor and its tourists were wealthier than I had realized.

Which meant Hart's family was, too.

Based on his budgets, my job was more than secure while the Bar Harbor and Bangor locations were being built. But every time I reviewed the numbers—like I was doing for the second time that morning—I was reminded of how different we really were. It wasn't as if my mom was poor; we'd never had our electric shut off like some of the kids I knew, and there had always been food in the fridge. Maybe that was because she hadn't done it all by herself.

Gerald had lived with us to help with the bills.

I still never had the extras that Hart had. I didn't have a three-story house that overlooked the ocean. I didn't have an expensive car.

I didn't have a home, in the truest sense of the word.

I didn't think I ever would again.

"Let's go out to lunch," Hart said. "I think we could both use a break from this place."

I jumped from the sound of his voice, not realizing he had come into the office. "Let me clean up some things and I'll meet you outside," I told him, pulling the budget spreadsheets against my chest. He'd given me my own copy, but I didn't want him to see that I'd been staring at them. I had so much work that needed to be done. Gazing at his financials wasn't part of that.

He grabbed his jacket and smiled. "Don't take too long."

Once he was gone, I tucked the papers into a folder and hid it in the bottom of my desk drawer. Then I bundled up for the weather.

Hart was standing in front of his Range Rover talking to Shane when I got outside, discussing the tile that was going to be placed under the shampoo basins. He looked troubled. "Last purchase order I saw said the basins were due to be delivered a few days ago."

"Josh said the silver sinks never came in," Shane informed him. "They've been back-ordered for at least two months."

"We can't wait two months," Hart said. "We'll have to go with whatever color they have in stock, which means we'll also have to change the color of the tile. Those one-by-ones were chosen to match the silver." I could hear his frustration.

"No need to change anything," I said. Both of them looked at me. "The silver sinks are scheduled to be here at the end of the week."

"They're not back-ordered?" Hart asked.

"They were, but I found another distributor who had them in stock. I told them I'd cancel my other order and give them the business if they threw in freight. So they did." My eyes bounced from Hart to Shane. I couldn't tell what either of them was thinking. "I hope that's okay? I know I didn't get permission, but I figured since I was saving you money it wouldn't be a problem."

Hart laughed and gripped the bottom of my scarf to pull me in closer. "Aren't you just a little negotiator." He kissed my forehead. "What gave you the idea to have them throw in the shipping?"

I blushed as his mouth left me. No one had ever kissed me in front of Shane before. Even though it was only my forehead, it still felt a little wrong. "I figured the worst they could say was no." Calling the second distributor—or any distributor, really—wasn't part of my job. But based on the schedule, I knew if they didn't arrive quickly, they would have held up production. So I'd made a judgment call.

But maybe it hadn't been the right thing to do…

"I'm sorry—"

"No," Hart said, shaking his head. "You have nothing to be sorry for. You did good."

I smiled shyly.

Shane had been concerned when I told him I'd be working for Hart. Among his many worries, he believed my relationship with Hart would get in the way of my new responsibilities, and either the job or the relationship would suffer. His concerns were valid. Though it only made me want to work harder…and it looked like my efforts had paid off. The smile on his face told me he felt the same.

"Hart, when a woman saves you money instead of spending it," Shane said, "she deserves a raise."

This was the first time I'd ever been recognized for doing a good job—anywhere. Saint had never said anything about the way I worked. At the casino, I was just another serving girl in a short skirt. Shane and Brady were the only people who'd ever complimented me, but it was always for my appearance. I'd wanted someone to do more than tell me I looked pretty to compensate for having the scar on my face. I needed my efforts recognized, too.

"I think you might be right," Hart said. His arm went around my shoulders. "If anyone needs us, tell them I'm taking our negotiator out to lunch. We'll be gone a while."

Shane squeezed my hand through my mitten. "I think that's an excellent start."

Hart led me to the passenger side of his SUV and helped me get settled before jumping in next to me. His hand rested on my thigh as he backed out of the long driveway and onto the main road. Despite how sexual he normally was, this touch wasn't erotic. It was emotional, an expression of his feelings, not just his attraction.

"I know you were hesitant about working for me," he said quietly. "I hope today showed you it was a good decision."

"It did." I turned toward him and crossed my legs. His hand remained where it was. "But I also really like the job. I've always wanted to work at a spa. I feel like this is allowing me to do that, in a way."

His eyebrows rose. I think my confession had surprised him. "What do you see yourself doing there?"

I didn't have to think about it. "Skin, for sure. I'd love to do hair, too. I just want to make women feel as beautiful as they really are."

"There's a school in Bangor," he said. "You should apply."

I liked the way he thought. "I plan to."

He squinted at me, scanning my eyes. He was reading me again. "I'm happy to hear that." His stare moved back to the road; his hand slid to my knee.

I loved his touch as much as I loved his faith in me.

We were on Main Street, passing the rows of restaurants and pubs and boutiques that lined both sides of the road. He pointed at one of the shops. I already knew which one it was; I knew them all by heart. It was the one place I wished he hadn't seen—the one I'd distracted him from every time we'd passed it in the last few weeks because I didn't want it to spark a memory.

A memory I wasn't ready to discuss.

"That's the ice cream place we used to take your brother to, remember?" He was still pointing at it, and my stomach began to churn. "He used to order some crazy flavor. Wasn't it lobster-something?"

It was vanilla lobster, actually.

Seven days.

I nodded.

"Then he'd put those gummy things on top. The same gummies you love," he said. "Worms or bears...one of those."

They were gummy bears.

Seven days.

I nodded again.

I pushed back against the seat, hoping to still the trembling that had risen in my body. My hands gripped the safety bar above the window, but it did nothing to calm them. And it didn't matter how many times I swallowed; I couldn't get rid of the dryness in my throat.

"I know I've asked you before, but I don't think you ever answered me. How's Darren doing?"

He'd asked twice before—once over dinner a few days ago and the other last week while we were getting ready for bed—and I'd changed the subject both times. I could have avoided it again, or I could have lied to keep the conversation moving. Neither of those felt right, especially lying. Telling him Darren was still alive would have been more painful than telling him he was dead.

I stared at the side of his face, watching his eyes shift from side to side as they took in every car that passed. It was time. "He's..."

"I'm trying to remember, he's a baseball player, right?" *Was* a baseball player. "He's got to be a senior by now, or did he already graduate?" He looked at me again. I glanced away. "If he's around, I'd like to see him. You should bring him by the jobsite."

225

"He's…not around." I tried so hard to make my voice louder than a whisper. I couldn't.

"Did he go to college out of state?"

I shook my head. "No, nothing like that."

The SUV came to a stop. We were parked outside the diner that Shane usually took me to. Hart turned in his seat to face me. When he saw me avoiding his gaze, he gently pressed his hand to my neck and turned me toward him. "You're pale, Rae." I felt his stare inside me. "What happened? Did I say something wrong?"

I clutched my stomach with both arms, my typical position for whenever I shut down. "I don't talk about my brother that often."

"Why? You two used to be so close. I could barely get alone time with you because he always tagged along."

For the briefest of seconds, the memory made me smile. It was so true. Every time I had left the house, Darren had wanted to come with me. I almost always let him. I knew now why he never wanted to be home, but I didn't understand back then.

I should have always taken him with me.

I should have never left him alone.

I should have done so many things that I didn't.

"We were close…so close," I said. "He was my best friend."

"Something happened?"

I couldn't swallow. I couldn't take in any air. I couldn't calm anything inside me. I would deal with the consequences of the truth later, but I couldn't drag this out any longer. "He's dead, Hart. Darren died five years ago."

Died.

It was a word I'd never gotten used to, a sound that had a strange, disconnected meaning. The same sensation came from the word *home.*

I hated both words equally.

He shook his head, as if he couldn't believe what I was saying. I almost couldn't believe it, either. "I had no idea, Rae. I hadn't heard anything about it until now." It was strange that Shane hadn't mentioned it to him. Although knowing Shane, he wouldn't want to be the one to share that kind of news "Was he sick or…?"

The details of that night flashed in front of me, a downpour of images that closed in around my vision and choked me senseless.

It was a flood of pain that I couldn't hold back, couldn't relive or rearrange no matter how much I wished I could. I'd seen what I'd seen, then I'd fled my mom's house, running out of one storm and straight into another. Thinking of it reminded me how much I wanted him back.

And looking directly into the memory of that night reminded me that I never would.

"He killed himself."

His reached for my hand and squeezed until it hurt. I normally would have cried out in pain. Today, I needed it. "Why would he ever do that?" That made me wince. "Oh shit, that wasn't the right thing to say. I'm just…stunned, really."

"He didn't leave a note." He hadn't needed to. I knew the reason he'd done it. That was another storm entirely, one I wasn't ready to discuss.

Though Hart was silent, his grip remained firm. "I'm so sorry, Rae." Everyone was sorry. Nobody more than me. "I wish I'd known. I wish I'd been there for you, to help you."

I turned my head and gazed out the window. "There was nothing you could have done."

The pain of losing Darren was something I felt every day. It hadn't faded or dimmed. It had become a permanent feature of my emotional landscape. Sometimes all it took was an expression to remind me of him—a scent, or the weather…days with rain, in particular. It was raining when he did it. It was raining when I got my scar.

He lifted my hand and pressed his lips against it. "Can I do anything now?"

I tried to smile, but it didn't work. "You're here. That helps."

Seven days.

He looked toward the ice cream parlor, which was several

blocks from the diner, and he seemed to recognize how heavy the image was for me. "Do you even feel like eating?" I shrugged. "We can go grab coffee instead, head to some place that's quiet."

"No. Let's eat." I didn't know if the food would stay down, but at least there would be something distracting, hopefully to keep him from asking a lot more questions.

He reached forward to hug me, and my body stiffened. So he backed away a bit and kept his hands low, rubbing circles along my back. I kept waiting for them to move, for him to reach for my face. I didn't need any more reminders of my scars.

I wished I could have convinced my brain that hands weren't to be feared—especially Hart's. The part of me that felt strongly for him wanted to take his palm and press it against my cheek so I could smell his scent and feel his warmth against my mangled skin.

But the part of me that knew how much it would hurt kept that from happening.

As I was heading back to the trailer where our office was located, I noticed a white car parked at the bottom of the driveway—a Lexus. It was the same one Hart had climbed into a few days before. I moved carefully to the side of the trailer, hidden and out of sight from anyone who walked by, and I tried to peek through the windshield. The tint on the windows was too dark to see inside.

I heard the door of the trailer open.

"No, no…don't come up," Hart said, as he climbed down the front steps. He was putting on his jacket, shouldering his phone as he spoke. "I'm coming out right now."

I watched him rush to the passenger door and open it. A woman's hand reached across the center console to move a purse off the seat. Her nails were painted dark red.

The car drove away, and I felt my phone vibrate in my back pocket.

Another unscheduled meeting came up. Probably be home late.

Something crawled into my stomach as I re-read Hart's text and it churned the food around like debris in a windstorm. Hart was only partly to blame for the way I was feeling.

Seven days.

Even though I hadn't reacted well when Saint had chosen to be with Drew, I really wasn't a jealous bitch. With Saint, it wasn't about loving him or if he loved me. It was feeling like I had failed him. With Hart, I was allowing him to see the deepest part of me, showing him the depth of my pain, and he hadn't returned the trust. He hadn't told me what these mysterious meetings were about, or the woman they were with. They couldn't have been any more personal than what I had shared, yet his text was so cold. That made it difficult to believe they were truly only business meetings.

I felt like an idiot for trusting him.

I had another choice, but now that I'd reached this place with him, I hated the thought of it.

TWENTY-EIGHT

K nowing Hart's version of coming home *late* meant sometime after ten, I stopped at Caleb's after work to buy a dime bag. I hadn't smoked since I'd moved in with Hart, but tonight I wanted a buzz, like the glass or two of wine people drank with dinner to take the edge off. Something that would let the clouds drift over my body and keep the claws and fangs of the day from doing any more damage than they already had.

I sat in one of the two Adirondack chairs on the back porch. Hart had already cleared out and stored all the rest of the furniture for winter. The arms were just wide enough to hold the plastic cup that I'd use as an ashtray, the pack of rolling papers and the small sack of weed.

I listened to the quiet and broke up the bud.

Some people used dollar bills or rolling machines. Not me. My fingers pushed the paper up the back side of my hand in one fluid motion. The result was a perfect joint. It wasn't a quality everyone would find attractive, though most of the guys I'd dated had been impressed. I couldn't imagine Hart would have been. It was probably best he never see that part of me.

I lit the end of the joint and relaxed into the chair, resting my feet on the handrail of the deck. It really felt like December; the sky had been dark for hours already, and the air was crisp and sharp. Endless fog poured from my mouth as I exhaled, warming the chill. Everything around me was frozen, but heat had entered my chest. Subtle at first, then stronger as it spread, like a new spring day.

I took another drag, just as my phone vibrated. Hoping it was Hart, I pulled it out of my jacket pocket. *Unknown.* Over the past several weeks, that word had appeared many times on the screen.

Too many, actually.

Considering the timing of the calls, there was no chance the caller was truly unknown.

Seven days.

I couldn't confirm that it was Gerald, but I had this strong feeling it was him. I didn't understand what he could possibly want to say to me, or why he hadn't just left a message by now. Nothing he could say would bring my brother back, or make me forgive what he'd done. His words couldn't make me whole again.

Fuck him for even trying, and for thinking I would listen.

I hit *ignore* and dropped the phone on the armrest. The weed helped a bit to settle the storm inside me, but things still churned. The more I thought about him, the queasier my stomach turned. All I could see were his hands.

His fingers.

His touch.

It would have been easy for him to get my new number; small towns never held secrets for very long, especially when other family members still lived there. I wondered what else he knew about me…where I was living, or working, or my relationship with Hart. Did it really matter if he knew any of those things, anyway?

Part of me wished I had answered his call so I wouldn't have to question this anymore.

Part of me didn't want to waste another minute thinking about it.

The phone vibrated against the chair, and I jumped from the sound. I almost dropped the joint on my lap.

New voicemail.

I took a deep breath and swiped my finger over the screen.

Eighteen seconds. That was how long the message was. It was more than just a hang-up. It was his words.

His voice.

I filled my mouth, then swallowed the smoke into my lungs while still holding the joint to my lips. I didn't want that little sliver of weed to be too far away from me...not when it was the only calm within my reach. The only thing his presence on my phone couldn't take away from me.

After a few more hits, it was down to a roach. I set it next to my phone and stared at the screen. There was always a chance it wasn't him, that it was some pesky telemarketer or one of the guys who blocked their caller ID, or a wrong number.

The gnawing in my stomach told me otherwise.

I could delete the message without listening to it. Then I'd wonder even more about what he wanted to say to me. I could wait and listen to it later, when I'd had time to work up the courage. Really, there was no reason for me to do that. Courage wasn't going to be found, especially when it came to him. As much as I didn't want to hear it, I had to.

I had to know.

I sucked in a mouthful of air and held the phone up to my ear as I hit the button to play the message. My free hand slid under my knees and I rocked in the chair, slamming my back against the wood, then folding forward to help alleviate the pain in my stomach.

Back and forth.

"Rae..."

The sound of his voice saying my name held me still.

"I've been trying to get in touch with you." His tone hadn't changed at all; it was still raspy from years of smoking, like he was always on the verge of a cough. His sound was almost as rough as his skin. "Since you never answer, I figured a message might get you to call me back. Darren's birthday is coming up…"

The ache in my stomach shot to my chest when he said my brother's name.

He had no fucking right to speak that word.

I began rocking again, faster, though I knew it would only help my dinner work its way up my throat. "I need to talk to you. Call me back, please." He said his phone number, which meant I now had a way to reach him, a connection I'd severed so long ago. I tried swallowing the surge of saliva that filled my mouth. It was a warning, a rush before the flood. I needed to get to the bathroom. "And Rae? Don't make me keep calling."

I dropped the phone and ran inside, heading for the nearest toilet. I gripped the edge of the porcelain as my mind wandered past my retching stomach and my heaving chest. It wandered to thoughts of his hands—the hands that had touched me until I was sixteen years old. Hands that had stroked my head and brushed my hair, fingers that were meant to soothe me, to express love, to keep me safe and sound. All they ended up doing was hurting me. They hurt everyone who came into contact with them.

No one had known that better than Darren.

"It's Mom's birthday," I said. "I want to wear something really special. Not just jeans and a fancy shirt." I left the rack of tops and moved over to the display of dresses.

We'd driven all the way up to Bangor—which had the nearest mall—and had made our way through one of the two department stores. We'd started in the boy's section to get Darren a nice button-down and a pair of jeans that didn't have holes. Boys were so rough with their clothes. Still, he was pretty excited to buy some new stuff.

But now that the three of us were in the girl's section, Darren was hanging back several racks behind us, leaning on the clothes like they were a pillow. "I'm bored," he said. "I'm gonna go to the arcade. I'll catch up with you guys in a while." Darren didn't wait for permission. He just left.

Shopping was one of the few times when Darren didn't like to hang out with me. I didn't blame him; he was an all-black-and-holes boy. Being surrounded by all the frilly stuff made him anxious and uncomfortable, even though he knew pink wasn't my favorite color. That color was worn by the girls who liked the sun to shine directly on their faces, who smiled as they stood on their toes and twirled in a circle for everyone to watch. Everyone always clapped for pink.

That was why purple was my favorite. It was for the girls who liked the shadows.

I didn't need the sun in order to sparkle.

My hands ran over the row of blue dresses, the red ones and the dark lavender. They weren't wicked girly like the pastel colored ones and decorated with lots of fluff. They were fitted, tight through the stomach and chest, widening a little at the waist. They were all sleeveless and perfect for dinner.

"Aren't those a little old for you?" he asked.

Whenever I left the house, he would look over my outfit to make sure I didn't look too old—whatever that meant. I was twelve. I was still in a training bra and had acne on my forehead. It was impossible for me to look old.

"We're in the teen section," I said. "And I'm a teen, so these are my kind of clothes."

He stood at my side, his glare as stern as his voice. "Sweet girl, the teen section is for high school. You're in middle school."

"I'm going to be with you and Mom and Darren, so it doesn't matter what school I'm in."

"Rae..."

"This isn't fair," I stomped. "Mom gave me money to find something to wear, and this is where I want to shop, and you're—"

"How about you buy any dress you want, but I get to pick out the sweater that you're going to wear over it? Deal?"

I could take off the sweater when I got to dinner. It was Mom's birthday, so I knew he wouldn't fight with me in front of her about doing that, especially if I told him I was hot. I wondered what he'd say about the eyeliner and mascara I planned on wearing. Maybe I'd do it in the car, so he wouldn't be able to tell me to wash it off before we left the house.

"Okay," I said, finding my size in each color. "I'll wear a sweater."

He lifted the hangers out of my hand. "Good girl. Now...are these the ones you want to try on?"

I nodded. I'd only looked through one rack, but the colors were cool, and one of the dresses would look good enough.

"Then let's get you in a dressing room," he said.

I followed him to the back of the store and over to one of the registers. He stopped along the way to pick up a long-sleeved cardigan that would match any of the dresses.

"Can you please get her a dressing room?" he asked the woman who stood behind the register.

"Follow me," she said, taking the dresses from him. She walked past the entrance of the dressing room and over to a side door. "This is our family dressing room..." She placed the dresses inside. "...and this is the waiting area."

He nodded and took a seat in one of the chairs. "You can do a little fashion show for me, Rae," he said.

I didn't think he cared which dress I bought, as long as I was wearing a sweater. But if he wanted to watch me twirl in anything but pink, I guess that was okay.

I shut the door behind me, undid the button on my shorts and lifted the tank over my head, wiggling out of both as they dropped to the floor. Unzipping the back of the red dress, I stepped into it, shimming it up my stomach and placing my arms through the holes.

I hadn't been in there for more than three minutes when I heard him call out, "Rae, let's hurry this up. I'm worried about your brother."

Darren was at the arcade. Really, there was no need to be worried about him. The only trouble he'd find there would be if he ran out of quarters or threw a fit if he didn't beat his top score. But whatever...I really didn't have to try on any of the others. The red dress was my favorite anyway.

I walked out of the dressing room and stood in front of him. "You like this one?"

His hand dropped from his mouth. He'd been biting the skin around one of his nails. I did the same thing when I was nervous, like before I took a test I hadn't studied for. "Turn around."

"I didn't zip it." I twirled. "Wanna do it for me real quick so I can make sure it fits?"

His hands pressed on my bare back. I could feel the wetness from where he'd been biting as his fingers moved to the zipper. When the dress was fastened, I walked over to the full-length mirror. It fit perfectly.

I usually didn't wear red; my skin was too pale for that color. But this shade looked really good. It matched the little circles on my cheeks. It was so hot in this store.

"Put on the sweater," he said.

To quiet him down, I went back inside the dressing room and yanked the sweater over my shoulders. "Better?"

He nodded.

I took it off again and turned around. "Unzip me, please?" When I felt the dress loosen in the back, I shut the door behind me. Then I put on my own clothes. "So it's cool if I get this one?" I called over the door.

"If that's what you want, sweet girl."

I exited the dressing room and stood beside his chair as I waited for him to get to his feet. He slowly pushed himself up using the arms. His hand was suddenly on my cheek, the tips of his fingers brushing the edge of my hair. "You're such a good girl, you know that?" He paused to take a raspy breath. "Rae, my sweet, sweet, Rae."

"Rae...Rae?" Hart squeezed my arm to get my attention. "Rae, are you okay?"

I squinted from the brightness of the lamp that glowed directly in my face and slung my arm over my forehead to block out the light. "I'm okay."

"You had another one of those dreams, baby. You were screaming."

I didn't even remember getting into bed. The last thing I recalled was cleaning up outside to hide the evidence of my smoking and cuddling up on the couch with a mug of tea. He must have carried me in here when he'd gotten home.

I didn't want him to see my tears. I had no strength to explain them, so I rolled over and turned my back to him. "I was watching something scary before I fell asleep. It must have worked its way into my dream."

I instantly regretted lying to him.

"Do you want me to get you anything? Some water or—"

"No, I'm good. Thanks." I pulled the blanket up to my neck and tucked my head between the pillows.

As much as he wanted to help me, he couldn't. Not knowing where he'd been tonight didn't help things. I wondered what time he'd gotten back, and what time it was now. I was almost afraid to ask.

"Rae, are you sure I can't—"

"I just want to go back to sleep, Hart. I'm really tired."

Several seconds of silence passed before he finally turned off the light and moved closer. "I'm here if you need me." He didn't touch me, but I could feel the heat from his body. It wasn't enough to put me to sleep, though he had no trouble passing out. I heard his breathing change, and the rhythm of his chest grew slow and steady. I even heard him dream.

There was no chance of my eyes closing again tonight.

TWENTY-NINE

I didn't know why there was so much light around me. It was never this bright when I got up for work. It was usually pitch black until I turned on the hallway light and tiptoed into the kitchen to make my first cup of coffee. I'd sip the hot brew, and the sun would begin to peek over the water, the soft rays spilling through the window and washing over the counters.

Not this time.

I reached blindly for my cell on the nightstand and held it above my face. My eyes slowly opened to find 9:48 on the screen. It was almost ten in the morning?

"Shit!"

I sat up as fast as I could, threw the blanket off and swung my feet to the floor. Then I saw the note on the nightstand, next to the space where my phone had been. Hart's penmanship covered the paper.

You hardly slept last night. I want you to take your time coming into work.
I left you breakfast in the fridge.
Don't rush...I mean it.

239

I set the note back on the nightstand and stretched my legs into the air, pushing back on my hands to hold my weight. I didn't know how I'd slept through his alarm, or the sound of the water running while he'd taken a shower, or him moving through the room while he'd gotten dressed. It hadn't been easy falling back to sleep. I was surprised it had even happened. But I was glad it had lasted as long as it did.

Slipping into the guest room closet, I grabbed a sweater to put over my white cotton tank and shorts and went into the kitchen to brew a cup of coffee. The liquid dripped steadily into the cup as I checked the fridge to see what he'd made for breakfast. I found a burrito with eggs, cheese, onions and bacon rolled up tightly inside. I didn't bother heating it up; I just grabbed it and took a bite. Even cold, it tasted good. Hart could cook better than anyone I knew—even better than my mom when she'd actually taken the time to fix us a proper meal.

I finished and wiped off the counter with a cloth, brushing the crumbs into the sink. That was when I heard the back door open. I wondered what had brought Hart home so early. "I'm fine," I said, finally looking over my shoulder. "I told you I—" I dropped the cloth and nervously clutched the edges of my sweater, crossing them over my braless chest. "Mrs. Booker...I wasn't expecting you." Why hadn't Hart warned me that she was coming over? He had told me they were in Vermont.

He really had lied to me.

"Don't stop cleaning on my account," she said. Her tone was cold and clipped. Her long dark hair was curled and set, and it didn't move at all when she walked. Her breasts didn't either. She opened her jacket and rested her hands on her hips. "It's what we pay you to do after all, isn't it?"

My eyes widened. I tried desperately to control the sarcasm that threatened to erupt from me. "Not exactly. You pay me to do administrative work, though I do tend to keep things pretty clean."

"Wait a minute..." She pointed her finger at me, long and thin, with perfectly manicured nails. "You were at the spa the other day, weren't you? You were standing outside the office trailer." She appeared to be thinking, but her forehead didn't move.

My forehead must have been moving all over the place because I was thinking, too. I was sure I'd have remembered seeing her there.

"Yes, it was you," she decided. "I didn't realize Hart had hired the maid to be his assistant, too." Her eyes moved to my legs and slid slowly back up to my face. "He's undoubtedly given you quite the promotion, Maria. With the salary increase, I'd hope you'd be able to buy some clothing that covers a little more than these do."

What the hell was she talking about?

I took a deep breath and tried to calm my nerves. She was Hart's mom, I reminded myself. She'd never been this windy when I'd known her before, not so long ago. It seemed that her face and breasts weren't the only things about her that had changed. "My name isn't Maria."

She shrugged. "Maria, Mary, close enough."

"It isn't Mary, either."

"Look *sweetie*, I have many houses, all over the country. You'll forgive me if I can't keep all the names of my maids straight."

She thought I was Hart's housekeeper, Marlene—not Maria *or* Mary—and that he had promoted me to be his assistant in addition to being his maid?

That didn't make any sense.

"I'm not *your* maid, and I'm not *Hart's* maid, either," I said, my tone as sharp as my words. "I live here…*with your son*."

"You *what?*" She spun to face the back of the house where Hart's bedroom was located. "That's impossible. Hart? Hart, honey? Come explain to me who this *woman* is…" Her voice trailed off as she wove around the couches and end tables, toward the hallway and bedrooms. Her walk was more of a march as she returned alone. Her hair didn't move, no matter what she did.

"He isn't here," I told her.

She didn't even acknowledge my comment. "Why in hell would you be living here with my son?"

Apparently, Hart hadn't told her anything about me—not that he and I were together again, not that I was working for him at the spa. Nothing. I hadn't told my mom about us either, so I had no right to be upset with him for that. But he was only a partner for their business, which meant, technically, I also worked for his parents. That made things completely different.

And so fucking messy all of a sudden.

I waited for some recognition to appear in her eyes, for a memory of me to spark a light in her somewhere. But the surgeries and injections had removed all the emotion from her face.

I was glad I only had a scar to deal with.

"You don't recognize me, do you?" I asked finally.

Her hard gaze ran the length of me again. Her tongue wet her lips—lips that were far too plump to be natural. "Should I?" she asked.

"I would hope so. I'm Rae." I paused, waiting for a reaction from the sound of my name. It hadn't been all that long ago. Had I really changed that much? "Rae Ryan. I dated Hart before he left for prep school."

She gasped. Finally, she knew me. "Oh dear God, child!" Her hand covered her nose and mouth, as if she smelled something rancid. "What on earth happened to your face?"

The question shocked me. No one had ever been this straight forward. Everyone in town knew the story, and the strangers I waited on may have let their eyes linger a bit too long, but they weren't rude enough to ask me about my scar.

The circular lines in my marred skin burned from the heat of her stare. "I was in an accident." I refused to say any more.

"Don't you know there are doctors who can fix scars?" She sucked in her cheeks, and her chin tilted up so her gaze pointed down at me. "No need to keep walking around with it ruining your face like that."

Screw you, I thought, as loudly as I could.

Not everyone had her kind of money to just throw at a surgeon. Insurance didn't cover cosmetic corrections, which was what a procedure like mine would be considered. I had looked into it a long time ago. The cost was so much more than I'd ever been able to afford.

Her eyes dipped to the plate I had left on the counter. *Sleet.* That was what they reminded me of—cold and gray and miserable, their impact capable of great damage. "So, *Rae*," she said pointedly, as if she were trying to blend me together with Mary, Maria and Marlene, "you eat his food, and you process his paperwork at the spa, and you occupy his home. My son has become quite the philanthropist." I opened my mouth, but was quickly cut off before I could say a word. "I wondered why he was having me meet him at the jobsite and not here. I thought there must have been something wrong with the house that he didn't want me to see, or that he'd redecorated it in a manner I wouldn't approve of." Her eyes slipped up my neck and rested on my scar again. "I suppose, in a way, he did, though he kept you particularly well-hidden. Until now."

I gripped the edge of the granite and leaned my stomach into the stone. It didn't matter if my sweater fell open and revealed my see-thru tank; she could stare at my tits for all I cared. They were as real as the rest of me. "I don't believe he's *hiding* me just because he hasn't told you about us."

"Then you're deluding yourself." Her tone was so condescending. "If my son were proud of the woman he's invited into his life, he certainly would have shown her off to his parents—or at the very least, alerted them to the fact that she's living in his home." Her back straightened. "I'm afraid you and your scar simply don't fit into his clean, perfect world. Hart knows it. I know it." Her eyes narrowed. "And now, you know it, too."

I was so tempted to reach over the counter and whip my fingers across her plumped-up face, or allow all the churning emotions inside me to blast out at her in a hurricane of words. But she was Hart's mom. I didn't care if she was hurt by me, but I cared if he was.

That made it worth getting past the anger.

So I released my grip on the counter, tucked my hands into the pockets of the sweater and walked into the guest room. My messenger bag was on the floor of the closet. I shoved a pair of jeans, a second sweater, boots and a few cosmetics into the bag and walked back into the kitchen. I didn't say anything as I passed her.

I didn't even look at her.

But I did notice her white Lexus as I moved down the driveway to get into my car. It was parked on the side of the house, leaving me plenty of room to get out.

I was glad for that.

She didn't have to like me, and she didn't have to approve of our relationship. Parental approval was the last thing I was after. But there was a reason Hart hadn't told her that I was his assistant and living at his house.

She was right: he'd kept me hidden.

And if he couldn't share me with his family now, how would he ever be comfortable with me at all? I was someone to hide, the girl who would never measure up to his family's level of success, with the mystery scar that covered half her face.

The girl who rocked back and forth for no apparent reason.

The girl who had nightmares she couldn't explain to him, and who wouldn't let him touch her cheek no matter how tender he was.

How would he ever be able to truly accept the girl in the never-ending storm?

THIRTY

I needed my best friend. His understanding voice, his non-judgmental gaze watching over me as I spilled my soul. His kind, patient hands rubbing my back while I vented everything I had pent up inside. But today wasn't a visitation day at the rehab center, which meant Brady wasn't available. So I drove to Shane's house. It was the closest thing I'd had to a home since Darren had died. Feeling like this, it was also the only place I wanted to be. It wasn't even noon yet. I knew Shane would still be at work because I should have been there, too. There was no chance of that happening today.

I took my cell phone out of my jacket pocket to send him a text.

Me: I'm outside your house. Do you care if I hang inside for a while?
Shane: Why aren't you at work?
Me: Looong story.
Shane: We'll talk about it when I get home.
Me: Ok. Don't tell him I'm here.
Shane: Now we definitely need to talk. Stay put until I get there.

I slung my bag over my shoulder and let myself in through the front door using the key Shane had given me years ago. It was the first time I'd used it since I had moved out.

His place was so different from Hart's. It was cozy and felt like someone actually lived in it instead of having the model home feel where nothing was ever out of place. It wasn't normal for a house to constantly smell like lavender and be dust-free all the time. Shane's house smelled like pine and tree bark, with a touch of sport-scented deodorant. And it was worn-in: the couch sagged in the middle in the spot where he sat, and the coffee table showed marks where his feet rested. There were newspapers on the counter and dishes in the sink. It was more of a home than anyplace I knew.

I dropped my bag on one of the chairs and curled up in the corner of the couch cushions, breathing it all in. There should have been more life in the house than there was. Brady's absence felt so obvious. I fingered my phone in my pocket. I wasn't able to see him, but that didn't mean I couldn't talk to him.

I dialed the rehab center. It was the direct line to the phone in the common room. No one had ever answered whenever I'd called before. I had no other way to contact him, so I tried again.

Someone picked up after the third ring. "Rec room." It was a male voice.

"Is Brady there?" I pulled a pillow against my chest.

Please. Please say yes.

"Brady who?"

"Brady Lucas," I clarified.

"Oooh, yeah…him. Let me check. Hang on." I heard him place the phone down. His feet pounded over the floor. There was laugher in the background or yelling. I couldn't tell which.

I busied myself by brushing my fingers through the long strings that hung from each side of the square pillow. I stopped when I felt something weird. It was a little piece of a potato chip. I smiled as I set it on the coffee table.

"Hello?" His voice came through the phone like sunshine.

"Brady?" I sat up sharply. "It's Rae."

"Hey, good timing! I just got out of my one-on-one."
I tried not to let my voice quiver. "I'm so glad you answered."
"Is everything okay?"

I couldn't bitch about Hart not telling his family about me, or what had happened with his mom. Brady wasn't a big fan of Hart to begin with. But he was also in rehab working on himself, which was difficult enough. He didn't need to be dealing with my shit, too. More than anything, I wanted to see him, to be in his presence. It had been too long. "I'm coming to see you tomorrow."

"Something's wrong..." His voice deepened. "Tell me what's going on." I loved his concerned tone. It was the sound of someone who truly cared about me.

I wanted to crawl into his lap. I wanted him to hug me and tell me everything would be all right.

"I was just missing your voice," I said. "That's all."

"Bullshit." He didn't buy it. "What did Hart do?"

I leaned back into the couch again and tucked my legs underneath me. "It's nothing, Brady."

"You think I can't handle it, don't you?" I heard his breathing slow, as if he was trying to force himself to stay calm. "You *know* I can, Rae."

I sighed. "His mom came to the house this morning. Hart wasn't home so it was just us. She thought I was the maid, Brady. He didn't tell her about me, or our relationship. She was so fucking mean." I could have used some weed to dull the pain of thinking about our encounter. But I had nothing on me to smoke, and talking to my best friend in rehab didn't seem like the right moment to light one up, so I went to the fridge for a beer. "She doesn't think I'll ever be good enough for Hart. And she kept making comments about my scar."

"Are you fucking kidding me?"

"Nope. Not at all."

"Screw her, then."

"It's not that easy."

"You haven't told Hart any of this, have you?" He knew me too well. He could tell there was more. "I bet you left his house and went straight to my dad's. You're sitting on his couch right now, aren't you?"

I set the beer on the coffee table while I sat back down. "Yup. I'm here and...I can't go back there. Not after that bitch put me in my place."

"I know you're working for Hart now. Dad told me. If he messes everything up for you, I will kill him." I loved that he had my back, but that was the opposite of what he should have been feeling, considering how his anger had damaged things for him in the past. "Those bank deposits are important to you, and losing that job means you won't be able to make them anymore."

I took another sip, tucked my legs against my chest, and rocked...*back and forth*. "I'm sorry I didn't tell you."

He huffed. "I know why you didn't tell me, and you've got nothing to be sorry for." His voice turned gentle. "Does he know what's coming in six days?"

He remembered. Again.

"He didn't even know that Darren had died. I told him as little as possible."

"You're afraid to tell him about it." It wasn't a question.

I shrugged. "I've never had to tell anyone before. Everyone around here already knows."

"Listen, what his mom said is really fucked-up, but you can't hold Hart responsible for that. He might have a good reason for not telling her about you, like maybe he knew she'd react like the Wicked Bitch of Bar Harbor." I laughed at that. "Before you get all crazy, find out what that reason is. It'll hurt if he says something you don't want to hear, but you've been through way worse. You're stronger than you give yourself credit for."

I had never heard him be so rational before. "Wow. This rehab thing is really working for you, Brady."

He laughed. It was a beautiful sound to hear. "No matter how it goes down, Rae, I'm here for you. That will never change."

He was right; I could handle whatever was going to happen

between Hart and me. And I did need to talk to Hart before I assumed to know his reasoning, though I wasn't sure I could do that today. I needed to get my emotions under control first.

Six days was affecting me in the worst way. Even worse now that Gerald had left me the voicemail.

I didn't want to take any of that out on Hart.

"Thank you," I whispered.

"You knew all of this already. You just needed to hear me say it."

"I miss you so much, Brady." Tears rose without warning, but I smiled through them.

"I love you, too. I'll see you tomorrow?"

"Nothing could keep me away," I said.

I held the phone in my hand even after we'd hung up, feeling the warmth of it as though it was Brady's hand in mine. Then I pulled up Hart's name and hit the button to start a text. I composed it carefully, making sure it wouldn't come across as a screaming accusation.

> **Me:** *Won't be coming to work today and I won't be back to the house tonight.*
> **Hart:** *Are you okay?*
> **Me:** *Not feeling so great.*
> **Hart:** *Do you need to go to the doctor? I can take you if you want…*

I should have known he would have asked that. He wanted to take care of me—as always. It didn't make sense; he was so caring, so giving, and yet he hadn't felt secure enough to share our relationship with his family.

> **Me:** *No doctor needed, but thanks.*
> **Hart:** *Then what can I do to make you feel better?*

He could have ensured his mom knew who I was, that she hadn't mistaken me for Maria or Mary…or even Marlene. My hands shook as I thought about the way she had looked at me, and the tone of her voice when she spat those ugly words.

Yes. I definitely needed more time to cool off before I spoke to him.

Hart: *?*
Me: *Doubt I'll be into work tomorrow either. Not sure if I have sick days yet so just hold my pay until I come back.*
Hart: *Rae, what the hell is going on? I'm worried about you now.*
Me: *Don't be. I'll text you tomorrow morning.*
Hart: *Call me instead. Please.*

I let him have the last word.

Several hours later, Shane walked through the door, carrying two plastic grocery bags and a twelve-pack. There had only been two beers in his fridge; I'd already downed both. He placed the bags on the counter and removed two beers from the case. He twisted off the caps, handed me one and joined me on the couch.

"I lied to my boss for you today," he said.

We both took a sip, mine a little longer than his. "I'm sorry, Shane. I never wanted you to get in the middle of this."

Since I was sitting in his usual spot, he took the one next to me, reclined into the cushions and put his feet on the other side of the table. We'd sat like this many times over the years. It had been a while, though. Too long, probably.

"You know I'd do anything for you." His calm, compassionate hand went to my shoulder. "Shit gets messy when it involves my job, though."

"You won't ever have to lie for me again—I promise. Everything between us will all be fixed soon…however it ends up."

He nodded. "I stopped by your uncle's store to get the groceries and beer. He asked about you and said you haven't been in lately to visit him." His fingers squeezed gently. "I know you've got your issues with him and your mom, and I understand why, but he's shaken up over Darren's birthday, too." He exhaled, the beer on his breath mingling with the other scents in the room. "Maybe you should just pop in there and say hello, just to put him at ease."

The last time I'd seen him, I was asking for a job. "I'll go over there soon. I don't want him bugging you."

"I don't mind that part. I'm just thinking that when he lost Darren, he also lost you." I had never even considered it that way. "Seeing what Brady's going through, I can sympathize with the way he's feeling. I know he wasn't your uncle's son, but Darren meant something to him and the loss had to devastate him." His hand pressed down a bit harder. "Remember that Irving is innocent in all of this."

Shane was right. My uncle had no idea what Gerald's involvement had been; he was guilty of nothing other than being related to *him*. But it was enough of a connection to have made me uncomfortable for all this time. And there was a good chance my uncle had stayed in contact with him. He might have been the one who'd given him my new number—innocently enough, but still.

I rolled my head toward him. "You're right. It's just hard. All of this is so fucking hard."

His hand dropped on top of mine, the warmth of it soothing me. "Every year since it happened, I've told you the same thing, and I mean it as much now as I did the first time I said it: we'll get through the next six days together."

I was so lucky to have him.

THIRTY-ONE

S hane and I met in Bangor at the rehab center for our visit with
Brady. "Are you okay this morning?" he asked as we walked
through the parking lot. "I didn't see you before I left the house."

I purposely avoided mentioning Hart. I didn't want to know if
he'd asked about me, or if he'd pressed Shane for information. I
had already put him in the middle, though I hadn't wanted to. I
also didn't want him to feel like every conversation had to be
about Hart. So I answered simply, "I am," gave him a long, tight
hug, and headed into the reception area.

It had been more than two weeks since we'd last seen Brady. So
much about him had changed in that time. The bruising on his face
was completely gone; his skin had a warm, golden tone now. There
was confidence in his step as he made his way to our table. He
stood upright, his shoulders level, and his smile reached all the
way to his eyes. When his arms wrapped around me, I could feel
all of his strength.

"I'm glad you haven't lost any more weight," he said, noticing
as much about me as I had about him. "I was worried you'd be
even skinnier than the last time I saw you."

"I've been eating a little more." That was to say, I'd been eating enough to maintain, such as the pizza Shane had fed me the night before. I'd kept the two slices down, and a few beers. It was strange to not have it all come back up afterward.

"Hopefully when this is all over, you'll gain it back like you usually do. You can't let this shit with Hart and his mom screw that up for you. You need to get healthy again...*five days.*"

"Five days," I echoed, nodding against his chest, taking in the scent of his shirt. The smell I remembered was lingering there, beneath the fabric softener and the subtleness of his cologne. The same pine-and-comfort scent of Shane's house.

Brady broke free and hugged his dad, and the three of us sat down at the round table. Shane's eyes never left his son. Neither did mine. It had been too long since we'd seen him so healthy, so alive. We wanted to know everything: how he was doing, how he'd been feeling, what he was learning, and what kind of progress he was making. We didn't have to ask much; Brady read the questions on our faces, and the answers began pouring out of him. He used real, raw words, not the insincere anger we were used to hearing from him.

He had finally found a point of balance.

It allowed him to listen to his demon, to understand it and come to terms with it in a way that kept him in control as much as possible. I couldn't help but notice how the whites of his eyes gleamed, how his hands stayed still and folded in front of him.

"You seem comfortable," I said. Not just in his skin, but in accepting the depth of what he'd been dealing with, and what had happened as a result.

"I think I am," he confirmed. "There's a lot to it, and it's complicated. I don't want to spend our whole visit explaining it to you. I'm too happy to see you to do that."

"We have plenty of time, son," Shane told him. "Whenever you're ready to share it with us, we'll be ready to hear it."

Maybe for the first time ever, Brady's eyes told me he understood what that would mean from here forward. "Thank you." He clamped onto my hand firmly, confidently, even as mine shook within his grasp. I noticed the contrast then, how he'd risen above while I'd been sinking deeper.

I had twisted even further from the light, and he had spun right into it.

"Dad," he said, "do you mind if I talk to Rae privately for a minute?" I blinked and came back to the moment. "I don't mean to shove you off like this, but I'd like to talk to her about some serious stuff." He winked at me.

Shane paused and smiled warmly, like he was proudly watching his son look after his daughter. "Of course. Whatever you want." He took his phone out of his pocket and checked the screen. "Looks like things are getting a little hairy on the jobsite, anyway. Perfect timing." He gave Brady a hug that lasted longer and meant more than any embrace they'd probably ever shared. He looked at me. "Will I be seeing you at the house later?"

I nodded. "Nowhere else I'd rather be."

He squinted. "Somehow, I don't quite believe that. Drive safely and text me when you get to the house." He rubbed Brady's head. "I'll talk to you tomorrow, son."

Then it was just Brady and me, sitting together by ourselves for the first time in what seemed like forever. I drank in those blue-ocean eyes I had so desperately missed—eyes that were so much more clear and knowing than I was used to. "I seriously doubt you want to hear about my sex life with Hart, so what is it that you couldn't say in front of your dad?"

His hand leapt to his chin, his nails scratching at the sand-colored stubble covering it. "Like I mentioned earlier, I've been breaking a lot of things down in therapy. My feelings and shit. Things I've said and done in the past. I've come to some conclusions, and I wanted to be honest with you about something."

I didn't like the feeling that rose in my stomach. It made my hands shake and my knees bounce underneath the table. He had never sounded like this before—not when he was sober, and definitely not when he was fucked-up.

Suddenly, he sounded like he'd grown up.

I clasped my hands together. "Okay."

His eyes softened, though the intensity of his stare remained. "You've always been there for me, Rae. It didn't matter how high or drunk I was, who I slept with, who I chased or fought. You never left me. I can't say that about any of my boys. They may have been there, but they weren't *there*…not like you." I watched his chest rise and fall, his vision drifting down toward the table. "There was this one time when I got really drunk in front of Drew, and…" He hesitated.

Shit.

Just the sound of her name doubled the tremble in my stomach.

What the fuck else had she done?

"Whatever it is, you can tell me," I assured him. "We'll be fine on the other side of it."

His eyes met mine again, and I could see his uncertainty. "I was telling her things I shouldn't have even been talking about and…I told her Saint had grabbed you before I'd gotten the chance." His confession stunned me. "My feelings were confused then—they had been for a while. There are different kinds of love, and I was mistaking one for another. I learned that in here."

I tried to smile, but I couldn't. I couldn't even fake it. "What are you trying to say?"

"You've been my constant for all these years, like a shadow, only you never stood behind me. You stood beside me, always, never ashamed or embarrassed of the things I did or the shitty decisions I made. You've been amazingly loyal to me."

There was a knot in my throat and no matter how hard I swallowed it wouldn't go away.

"You've done the same for me," I whispered.

"I realize now that Saint never took you away from me. I was worried for a while that Hart would, but I know you'd never let that happen. We're deeper than that, you and me. I mean, yeah, you'll end up spending more time with him, and you'll continue to live at his house instead of mine. But we're *us* no matter what. I used to think whoever you were dating was going to get all your love, and you wouldn't have enough left over for me. I know now how wrong I was."

My eyes were wet, and my lips had begun to shake. "You're right, Brady. It never happened, and I would never, *ever* let it. You and Shane are my family. I would never leave you and never stop loving you." I reached across the table and squeezed his hands with all the strength I had. "*Never.*"

He lowered his face and pressed his forehead against the back of my palm. I could almost feel the emotion flowing from his skin. "I have so much regret, Rae, about so many things." His lips brushed the tips of my fingers.

"You know I do, too."

I didn't have to go into detail; Brady knew exactly what I was talking about. There was one thing in my life that I wanted to take back. The night I had gotten my scar, the night I had left the house and returned too late. If I had only come back several minutes sooner or had never left at all, the last five years would have been completely different.

He lifted his head, and I saw how red the whites of his eyes had gone. I was sure mine looked the same. "I'm not going to tell you that none of it is your fault," he said. "I've been saying that since the day you moved in with me, and you've been repeating those exact words, and our stubborn minds are going to believe what they want. I'm going to make you a promise instead: I'm not looking back anymore. I can't afford to. There's too much shit behind me, shit that can easily drag my sorry ass straight to Caleb's and put four pills up my nose. Ahead is the only direction there is for me. And I hope you understand it's the only direction for you, too."

I respected that. I would have done *anything* to be able to move forward like he planned to do. But I didn't know how to stop looking over my shoulder, especially when Gerald was leaving messages on my phone, or while I still cringed every time I thought about Hart's hands coming anywhere near my face, or while the thought of going inside my mom's house made me want to tuck into a corner and rock back and forth, and never stop.

He squeezed my hand until I met his eyes again. "Can you promise me the same thing?"

I wouldn't lie to Brady; I wouldn't even attempt it. He'd be able to see through my lie, anyway. I understood completely where he was coming from, but we weren't in the same situation. His trouble had arrived in the form of a demon he'd fought long and hard to gain control of. Mine had come in the shape of ghosts that I had no chance of exorcising from my life.

The scars ran too deep for that.

"No," I told him. "I can't."

"You haven't hit rock bottom." He didn't phrase it as a question. He was right not to.

I shook my head. "I think I can see it from here, though."

He fixed my gaze and held my hands firm. "Do you know where I was when I called you to come and get me?" I didn't know if I was ready to hear this. "I woke up in the basement of some house in Bangor. I still don't know how I got there…the last thing I remember was being in Boston. I couldn't open my left eye; blood was running into the other. Every muscle in my body had either been kicked or punched. I have no idea what happened to me." His voice caught. He closed his eyes and shook his head. I knew whatever had happened to him was bad, but I hadn't really expected this. "I was naked, tied to a chair with my hands behind my back. My legs were wet because I'd pissed myself. In the back of my mouth, I could still taste the bitterness of the last pill I'd snorted. And it was all I could think about—not that my entire body ached, or might have been broken beyond repair, or that some stranger was standing in front of me with a bat in his hand or that I was bare-ass naked and covered in my own urine. All I wanted was more of what I tasted."

"Brady…" I whispered. It hurt to speak that word. Everything hurt. I was aching for my best friend.

"I was there because I owed money—a shit-ton of fucking drug money. Turned out I knew a few of the guys in that house and they said I was good for it, so they let me go under two conditions: I have to give them my truck, and I have to pay back what I owe them within two months. Once I do, I'm starting over." His eyes were filling. "That was my rock bottom, Rae...I don't have another one in me."

Brady had blown through his savings before he took off for Bangor, so I knew he didn't have the cash to pay them. And he loved his truck; he'd worked so hard to pay it off. It broke my heart to know he had to give it to them. I figured he'd be getting out of rehab and starting his life completely fresh. I hadn't considered he'd be starting it indebted to drug dealers.

"How much do you owe?" I asked.

His clear blue eyes showed fear. "With juice, close to fifteen."

"That's nothing—"

"Not fifteen hundred, Rae. Fifteen *thousand*."

It felt like all the air had been kicked out of me. "Shit, Brady."

"Shit is right."

I swallowed and shook my head until I was able to get my emotions under control for him. "We'll figure this out."

"They gave me a break once, but guys like this don't fuck around. You saw my face...they're capable of doing much worse. If I don't figure this out, they'll kill me."

I couldn't accept this as part of his reality. "Nothing is going to happen to you. I won't let it."

He laughed, his nervousness and grief rained through the sound of those chuckles and soaked my bones. "Unless I pay them off, there's nothing you can do to stop them from coming after me."

I needed to be closer to him. So I slid forward and wrapped my arms around his neck, burying my face in his shirt. "We'll find a way to pay them off just let me get through these next five days."

I truly hoped we could figure this out.

THIRTY-TWO

I was sleeping on Shane's couch, tucked beneath a cozy blanket with the early morning darkness surrounding me, when I felt a pair of hands touch the outside of my thigh. They rubbed in circles, traveling to my waist and dipping to my knee. I knew the touch, without seeing the hands it belonged to.

Hart.

I smelled him before I even opened my eyes. The lavender from his house clung to his clothes; the sharpness of cedar and musk carried on his exhale.

I sat up abruptly. "What are you doing here?"

He didn't move. He stayed on the floor, kneeling in front of me as he reached over to turn on the lamp. "You know why I'm here. The question is, why are *you*?"

I hadn't asked him for space—I hadn't asked him for anything, in fact. I hadn't answered his texts or his calls, and I hadn't sent any more of my own, either.

That was wrong of me. I knew that. But Brady's news only added to everything I had already been feeling. It was too much.

Four days was all I could handle.

Brady had been able to come clean and tell me everything that

261

had been holding him down. Was I ready to do the same with Hart?

"The morning you let me sleep in, your mom came to the house." Ready or not, there it was. By blurting it out, I didn't have a chance to second-guess my decision.

He bit his lip and tapped his fist lightly against my knee. "It all makes sense now."

I focused on his fingers. It was too hard to look at his eyes. "I've had a lot of accusations thrown at me over the years, Hart. Many of them I've deserved, but the things she said to me..." I paused, trying to figure out the right way to continue. I couldn't repeat what she'd said; that would have only made me more emotional. I didn't think that would help us at all.

"She thought you were the maid, didn't she?" I nodded and finally looked into his eyes. He knew exactly what kind of cruelty she was capable of, which made my stomach hurt even worse. "She did the same thing to my last girlfriend."

I couldn't believe he'd said that. "If that's supposed to make me feel better, it doesn't."

I hated that she'd thrown me into the pile with all the other ex-girlfriends. He had a past—both of us did—but it really stung to be lumped together with everyone else, as if I wasn't any more important than those other girls. Maybe it hurt more than it should have.

And it made me feel like I was on the bottom of that pile.

He shook his head, leaning in so our faces were closer. I had no choice but to continue staring at him. "I'm sorry, I didn't mean it like that. I was testing to see how far she'd taken it. Obviously she went all the way and probably said things far worse than I'm imagining."

I pulled back and rested against the cushions. "Are you sorry for the things you *didn't* say?"

Confusion crossed his face. "What would that be?"

"I don't know...maybe that we're a couple. That the maid isn't your assistant, but your *girlfriend* is since it's their company I work for, too." My voice was starting to rise. I couldn't stop it. "How about that the person picking you up for those meetings was your mom? Dammit, Hart! My head has been all over the place wondering who she was and what you weren't telling me."

He gripped me behind my knees, like he was going to pull me into his lap. A wrinkle creased between his brows and the muscles in his jaw began to flex. "It's because of my ex that she's like this. Katrina basically ruined any trust my mom had in the girls I date. Mom will get over it, and she'll treat you right—I'll make sure of that."

"You hid me from her, Hart. How do you think that makes me feel?"

"I was trying to protect you, Rae. I knew how she would be, and it sounds like she did exactly what I was afraid of, regardless." His gray eyes had taken on a charcoal cast as they filled with emotion. "I should have told you—I realize that now. And I should have told her about you, it just happened so fast. I thought it might have been too much, too soon."

I appreciated everything he had said up until the last part. It threw my stomach right back into motion.

"What about *us*?" I asked. "Are we too much, too soon?" I held my breath while I waited for his answer.

Hart shook his head. "They're my parents, Rae. My ex put them through a lot. I have to take things slowly with them."

I brushed the tears away before they had a chance to rain down. "What did she do, exactly?"

I wasn't sure I wanted to hear this, but if it answered questions about how his mom had treated me, then I needed to. I doubted anything he was about to say would make me like her more. Maybe, instead, it would help me understand her.

"Katrina worked at one of the salons I was opening. She knew my mom very well. You could say she was her protégé. Mom was pushing hard for us to get together. After a few months, I was getting ready to go to a new location, and Katrina didn't want me to leave...she thought getting pregnant would make me stay. She went as far as pulling the used condoms out of my trash and emptying them—"

"I get the point."

"She couldn't seem to let go. So she went to Mom and dragged her into the whole shitty situation. Needless to say, it didn't end well."

When I tried to lift my knees up to my chest and rock, he wouldn't let me. He forced me to keep my feet on the ground. I knew why, and I knew he was right.

I had to get through this without *back and forth*.

"Your mom thinks I'm after your money. She probably thinks I'm going to start emptying your condoms, too..." If she only knew we'd stopped using them, I'd be even farther down her list. "At this point, there's nothing I can do to show her I'm not a gold digger. I'm living in your house, I'm working for you...I'm sleeping with you. She has everything she needs to distrust my intentions."

"She has more..."

"More?" How much more could there possibly be?

I'm afraid you and your scar simply don't fit into his clean, perfect world.

His head cocked. "The reason she came into town was to look at two more locations in Maine."

"But you have Bar Harbor, Bangor and Portland."

"I want a few more."

"And why is that?" I didn't need more puzzles. I needed something truthful, something

I could trust again.

"Because I don't want to leave you. Your family is here and I don't want to be the one who drags you away from them." Family was such a loaded word and it could have meant many things. I wondered how he'd ever understand how dark and chaotic it was for me. "I may not have confirmed our relationship to her, but she isn't stupid. She knows why I've kept her away from the house, and why I'm pushing for more spas in Maine."

"No wonder she said those things to me. She hates me."

"She's *wary* of you. That's all. She'll come around—trust me."

I thought again about the way she'd looked at me, what she'd said about my scar and how she'd treated me when she thought I was the maid. According to Hart, she'd probably known who I was the whole time. She was just toying with me to be a bitch. That only made it worse.

"Do you think anyone will ever be good enough for you?"

He slowly leaned forward and brushed his lips over mine. "You. Only you. That has always been the answer."

I truly cared about him. I wasn't sure I had ever felt love for someone I had dated, but I knew my feelings were deeper and stronger than ever before. I wanted it all—everything I'd had for the last week, and everything I thought we might be able to grow into.

Maybe it wasn't the right time for that.

"Maybe I should move out and look for another job. Do something to prove to her that I'm not after anything but you."

His hands tightened over my knees as he slid me off the couch and into his lap. I wrapped my arms around his neck; my legs straddled his waist. "*You* are not the issue here; I won't let you do that, so don't even think about it. Things have been a mess at the jobsite since you've been gone. Shane's crew needs you. I need you —at work, at my house..." He pulled my hand off his neck and pressed it against his chest. "In my heart."

I felt something inside me start to soften, stir. It lessened the resistance I'd been building up. "I won't leave the spa, then."

His eyes scanned mine, drawing my doubt to the surface. "I don't want you to leave my house, either, Rae." I tried to protest, but he spoke right over me. "But you're not giving me all of you. Haven't I proven how crazy I am about you? That even though you try not to show me your scars, I think you're absolutely beautiful regardless of them. What you did, what you didn't do, what happened to make things the way they are—I don't care about any of that. I just want to be with you."

He was right.

Every word he had spoken was the truth. I felt completely protected whenever I was with him, cared for. Loved, even. So why did I have such a hard time sharing this part of my life?

Why couldn't I let him into the darkest part of me, and flood him with my truth?

Even I didn't know the answer to that.

"Soon," I whispered. It was all I could offer him.

His hands moved to my shoulders. He dipped his head so our eyes aligned. "Give me something, Rae. Something...*anything*."

I swallowed a mouthful of air and dug my nails into his skin. "Darren's birthday is in four days. I just have to get to that without falling apart. Then I promise I'll tell you everything." Part of me regretted those words as soon as they left me. The other part wished I had already told him.

"That's fair." He slid me a few inches closer so my chest pressed against his. "But you're going to stay at my place, aren't you?"

Home.

"I...I don't know."

"If you're not comfortable there, then we'll move out."

That was a huge sacrifice for him, one I didn't feel he needed to make. "I don't want that."

He was trying so hard—I could feel it in the way he held me, the way he breathed, how his forehead tensed. His hands wanted to reach out and stroke my cheek, my skin. He resisted. "You don't want my place, you don't want us to have another place. What can I do, Rae?"

"Help me find a place of my own."

There was a gaping pause before he spoke again. "I can find you a rental by tomorrow."

A rental was temporary, like every place I had ever lived in. I needed something more stable than that. A place no one could take away from me as long as I kept paying for it.

"Not a rental," I said. "I want to buy a house. My house."

"Do you know how much money that would take?"

"I have the money." The last deposit I'd made had brought my total to almost twenty-five-thousand dollars. If I found something small and not on the water, that would hopefully be enough for the down payment. My salary would more than cover the mortgage. "And you can live with me there."

"Then let's find you a home."

It was a word that couldn't live on its own.

"No," I said, "let's find *us* a home."

In my belief, everyone who lived in a perfect home would be safe. The hands inside would never harm anyone else. Days wouldn't be counted down as a means of getting past the darkness. No one was scared; no one was scarred. The walls withheld the storms. In a perfect home, there was nothing inside but pink and sparkles and twirling. And endless sunshine.

My stomach churned at the thought of all that.

I would never find perfect. Shit, I *hated* perfect.

But maybe there was a home out there for me, and Hart would be able to help me find it.

As long as it kept the storms out, that would be enough for me.

THIRTY-THREE

I sat on my bed with my legs crossed. Loose white sheets of lined paper lay in front of me, along with my chemistry book, open to the periodic table of elements. The family laptop was beside me as I searched for the answers I was looking for. It was complete bullshit that this assignment was due tomorrow, and we'd only been given one day to complete it. It should have been illegal to have chemistry first period, anyway. Even the smarties in my school needed a minute for the coffee and half-assed shower to set in before they could understand anything the teacher was lecturing about. Really, the only thing I could focus on that early in the morning was how his rug was a different color than his sideburns. What element plus what other element would equal an explosion was completely lost on me.

And Google wasn't telling me what I needed to know. The empty search window yawned at me.

I yawned back.

It was late. I'd snuck out to meet the boys and had returned well past midnight. Now it was close to one in the morning. My eyes were shot, and I was way too high for this.

Darren was probably sleeping, but he'd woken me up plenty of times to drive him somewhere, or to make him something to eat, or to help him with his English since he had a math brain. That boy was helpless sometimes. He'd live on vanilla lobster ice cream if he could. But he rocked his science classes so I knew he'd be able to help me with this.

I crawled off the bed and tiptoed out of my room. Mom wasn't home, and I didn't want to wake Grandpa as he slept on the couch. Darren, Mom and I had the bedrooms.

The living room was literally his "living" room.

I snuck through the hallway. It was pitch black, and silent. As I moved closer to Darren's room, the silence turned to something else.

Strange noises came from behind his door. His bed was squeaking. It wasn't super-loud, but loud enough that it seeped through the walls and the door. And there was breathing. Heavy breathing.

Was my brother beating off? And was I really standing outside his room listening to it?

Nasty shit.

Just as I was about to go back to my room, I heard another noise above the others: a voice that didn't belong to Darren. It was deep and crackly from years of smoking…

Grandpa?

What was he doing in Darren's room?

The bed squeaked. The breathing grew louder. The voice moaned.

It wasn't possible.

My mouth watered at the thought of what might be happening, and my stomach started to churn. I wrapped my fingers around the doorknob. Slowly and silently, I twisted it and pushed the door open.

Darren's room was dark. But the floodlight above the garage trickled in through the window by his bed. I could see everything that was happening.

The sight made acid rise in my throat.

Darren was on his stomach, naked from his waist down, his face buried in a pillow. Our grandpa was on top of him. Grinding into him from behind. Moaning as he moved back…and forth.

Back and forth.

I was frozen. My feet wouldn't move; my hands wouldn't reach out to push him off my brother. I couldn't scream. And I couldn't believe what I was seeing. I couldn't process it. I didn't understand it.

How could he do this?

His hands were visible in the light as they pressed Darren into the bed and held him captive. The same hands that had stroked my head; the same fingers that had smoothed my hair every night before I went to sleep. They were the same hands that now restrained my brother like shackles to keep him from getting up while he violated Darren over and over again.

I needed something sharp. Something that could hurt him.

Kitchen. I needed to get to the kitchen.

My body was still numb, but I felt the ice inside start to break. Acid burned as it hit the back of my throat. I pushed it down.

Kitchen, I reminded myself. I had to get to the kitchen.

Sharp, I repeated. I needed something sharp.

I took a step back and heaved. I ran to the bathroom, just making it to the toilet in time. Heave after heave came, until I was empty.

"Are you feeling okay, sweetheart?" Grandpa asked from outside the bathroom door. "I heard you throwing up all the way in the living room."

Liar.

He wasn't in the living room. He was in Darren's room.

Raping my brother.

I saw him. I saw what he was doing to my Darren.

And I hadn't stopped him.

There were tears streaming down my face and my stomach was telling me it wasn't quite done and my body was barely stable enough to stand, but I pushed myself to the corner of the bathroom. I crouched down and curled into a ball and wrapped the shower curtain around me, and I rocked.

Back and forth. Back and forth.

"Rae, honey, please answer me."

Back and forth.

"I'm okay," I said. I pulled the shower curtain even tighter and tucked my face into my knees.

The doorknob wiggled and began to turn. "Let me in, baby, you might be coming down with something."

"No!" I shouted. "I don't have a temperature. It's something bad... something I ate. I'm fine...just fine." My voice wasn't my own.

He sighed. I heard the metal relax as he let go of the knob. "Come wake me if you need me, okay?" I said nothing. "Oh, my good girl, I hate knowing you're feeling so sick."

I uncurled from the shower curtain and heaved into the toilet again.

"Rae, I'm here, it's okay...you're okay." Hart's voice encircled me like a cloud bank. His body wrapped around me from behind, his thumb gently rubbing the base of my neck. He drew circles over my skin—soft, tender circles that were meant to calm me.

They didn't.

I was unable to purge myself of Gerald's hands.

Of my grandfather's hands.

The rain I heard pouring down on the roof above us only complicated things. It matched the intensity of the storm that had been brewing within me for years. Five years, to be exact.

It had finally broken open.

I wiggled out of his grip and sat up in the bed, curling in a ball with my back leaning into the headboard. And I rocked.

Back and forth.

Shock drained from his eyes, turning into concern. "Did I do this?" he asked. I didn't answer.

Back and forth.

"Rae, what happened to you? What did you see in your dream?"

I tucked my face into my knees and slammed my back into the wood behind me. Then I pitched forward and did it again. Every impact shot through me like electricity. The pain was welcome.

It took away the emotional edge that cut into my heart.

It disconnected me little by little from the scene playing again and again in my head.

"Rae…" Hart's hands pressed into my knees. I rocked harder. "All I want to do is make you feel better, and I don't know how to do that right now."

There was nothing he could do.

Hands.

I couldn't get my grandfather's hands out of my head.

Back and forth.

My hair fell over my shoulders as I rocked. People couldn't compliment my face so they always said I had pretty hair instead. But that was where his hands had been: in my hair…stroking it, smoothing it.

The scene of my grandfather attacking Darren had been branded into my soul. His hands went from being tools of comfort to weapons of my brother's destruction. I couldn't remove that memory from me. *His hands were in my hair.*

It felt as if they were still there, and had been all along. I couldn't get them out.

Although I'd never tried before…

I unrolled from the shape I'd curled myself into and headed for the bathroom. Hart followed me, his footsteps echoing my own, his breathing as labored as mine. I yanked open every drawer, dragging through their contents until I found what I was searching for: scissors. I picked them up and held their cold steel against my cheek. I slid my finger and thumb into the holes and spread them wide open.

Hart stood ready to reach in, to save me from whatever I was about to do. I doubted he knew what that was.

I pulled a section of my hair away from my cheek, feeding it between the blades as I watched myself in the mirror. Light glinted from their surface and accented the groove of my scar, as if to remind me: *The truth will always be written on your face.*

I screamed at my own reflection.

Hart jumped beside me. I saw his hand reach for my shoulder, pausing just short of touching my skin. "Please tell me what you're doing here, Rae…what you're going through." His breath hit my cheek as he spoke. It was the only impact his words made.

I felt the blades resist as I squeezed them closed.

Something inside my lungs began to loosen.

I spread the blades open and pushed them closed again.

A flurry of golden hair drifted through the air, falling over the sink, the rug I stood on, my feet. I grabbed another handful and did it again, and again after that.

So many scars…so many memories.

So much rain.

"Rae, baby…"

My stomach fell calm, even as I watched the rain reflect off the windows behind me. Down it fell, just like my hair. Just like me. I kept going until I felt I'd cut away everything that held the memory of my grandfather's hands.

I wasn't renewed, or reborn. Or whole, even.

But something in me had released. It was the grip of my grandfather's terror, which had held me for so long.

I turned and faced Hart, my hair jagged now, the uneven edges stopping just below my chin. "Touch it."

He shook his head, the steel gray of his glistening eyes as sharp and clear as the blades in my hand. "I can't…"

I'd scared him. I could see it. After all my resistance, all my withdrawing whenever he'd reached out to touch my head, he didn't know how to do it now.

I placed the scissors on the counter and reached forward. Clasping his hand gently in mine, I carefully brought his fingers up to my hair. I was as scared as he was. But I wasn't going to live in this storm anymore.

We'd leave it behind. Together.

"Touch it."

When I felt his hand against my locks, I let him go. My eyes closed. My lungs filled and emptied as I gasped. He held still. "Touch it," I pleaded.

His fingers worked their way between the strands, cradling my head, closing together and opening again as he let my hair slide against his palm. He pushed it back, out of my face...away from my scar. It tingled with every motion. My heart beat, steady and thunderous in my chest as panic evaporated from me.

I opened my eyes again. "Touch me."

He was crying.

"Touch me...*please.*"

Those words would replace my *back and forth*. They set the tone for how I would move forward. He still had no idea what had caused all of this; there was so much to tell him, if I could even bring myself to say it all. I knew I needed to say it, and I knew he needed to hear it. He wanted to help me overcome the anguish I couldn't let go of, and I wanted to allow him that. I had spent every other relationship trying to heal whoever had the most pain.

I realized at that moment: that person had always been me.

I didn't want it to be that way anymore.

Hart was my chance to heal *myself*, to finally let go of the storm.

"Please...touch me," I begged.

His hands slid down, out of my hair and over my jaw. He cupped my cheeks tenderly—both of them. My mouth didn't water; I didn't tell him to stop. I didn't seize or convulse or spasm with pain. I let everything go and gave in to the beauty of his skin against mine. It was the first time I'd ever let anyone touch my scar.

It felt like salvation.

I watched him lean down, his lips moving to where his hands had been, beginning at the edge of my chin and kissing their way up. Long, slow, sweet kisses over every inch of my cheeks. I felt his tears mingle with mine. "I love this face," he whispered. "All of it." He pecked his way around the spiral, stopping in the middle to linger over the jagged edges, as if to tell me they didn't exist. Then he went around again. He moved up to the corner of my eye where the scar began and worked his way to the side of my lip where it stopped. He paused, his eyelashes ticking my skin as he blinked, his breath creeping down my neck. Seconds slid between us like the slowing of the rain. "I love *you*."

My eyes welled again. I closed my lids as the tears dripped down my cheeks. Holding the bottom of my face with his hands, he gathered every drop.

I was raining, and he was catching me in his hands.

Hands I loved, to replace the memory of the ones I didn't.

Three days.

"It was pouring the night it happened…just like it is now."

My voice didn't surprise me this time, even if my choice of words had. I lay in bed against his shoulder. His hand rested on my cheek, his thumb tracing those same comforting circles. "My mom was working the night shift, so I told my brother and my grandfather that I was spending the night with a friend. But I wasn't."

A strange feeling came over me as I spoke. I felt like I was floating. Instead of being caught in the memory, it was like I was watching it play out before me.

"I waited in my car at the end of the street. The rain was pounding against my windshield. It was so loud…so fast. The wipers could barely keep up." I glanced at the window across the room. It was the same sound, the same speed hammering against the glass now. "I just sat and waited. I don't remember how long I was there. It felt like forever. And when I felt like I'd given him enough time, I went back inside. Quietly. My clothes were soaked. My hair was heavy, drenched. It stuck to my face, kept getting in my eyes. I took my shoes off so they wouldn't squeak. I left a trail of rain behind me as I walked. I stood in the hallway. The lights were on this time…"

I was raining again.

I couldn't help it.

Hart kissed the tip of my nose. "It's okay," he said, smoothing away my tears. "Let it come."

So I did. And when it had passed, I told him more. "The door to Darren's room was open. I saw my grandfather in there again, like I had the first night...the night I found him raping my brother." I heard Hart's breath as it caught in his throat.

Mine remained surprisingly calm.

I was telling Darren's truth as much as I was telling my own. I had to do this for both of us.

"I'd told myself it wouldn't happen again—that I would do whatever I had to, to protect Darren from that evil fuck. When I'd asked Darren about what I'd seen, he told me it hadn't happened, that I hadn't seen what I thought I had. But I knew the truth. And I knew how frightened he must have been, and how that man must have terrified him into keeping his mouth shut. I could only imagine what kind of threats he'd made. I had to catch my grandfather in the act, so he'd know he could never do it again...so he would pay for what he had done to my brother.

"And there he was, in Darren's room again. I pushed the door open a bit more so he would see me. I was ready to pull him away, to knock him on the ground and beat the life out of him. He was standing in front of Darren's desk. His hands—those nasty fucking hands—gripped the chair behind him for support. He faced the middle of the room, his back to me. I didn't see Darren anywhere. My heart was beating so loudly, I thought for sure he'd hear it and turn around. Then I saw his shoulders shudder. He moaned and sniffled and wiped his face. He didn't seem to hear me, and he still didn't turn around. I couldn't take it anymore. So I yelled at him, *'What are you doing to my brother, you sick bastard?'* He jumped. I'd startled him. He finally turned and faced me, moved toward me... and as he moved, I saw Darren, lying on the bed. His eyes were closed...he was sleeping, I thought. *No, not sleeping.* His face was blue, and a belt was fastened around his neck..."

Hart's cheek pressed against mine. I felt his tears on my skin.

"He'd hung himself." I'd never before said how he had chosen to do it. I'd always said *Darren was dead* or *my brother committed suicide.* The impact of those words kicked me in the chest.

"I'm so sorry, Rae." Hart's voice was small, a rasping whisper against my forehead.

"'This is your fault!' I'd cried out. It was the only thing I could think to say. *'I tried to save him,'* was his response. I stared at my brother's body, lying on the bed where my grandfather placed him when he'd tried to keep it from happening. But he was too late... and I was too late, too."

This is all your fucking fault! I'd said again. That time, I wasn't sure if I had been saying it to my grandfather or to myself.

I watched the rain, preparing myself to tell him the rest. "Seeing Darren there destroyed me in an instant. I had to get away —not just from his room, but away from the house, from that vile man. I just had to get out. So I ran. Back through the door and down the front steps. Into the storm. No shoes. The wet grass squished under my feet as I sprinted across the lawn and over the sidewalk. I just ran." I could feel the water under my toes again, even though I was safe and dry in bed. I could feel my hair *drip, drip, drip* in my eyes as I ran. "I saw it...the car. I saw it from the corner of my eye. Its headlights, the slick shine of the glass and metal. I heard its tires. I was in the middle of the street, and I could have kept going, but I didn't want to." Suddenly, the drifting feeling was gone. I wasn't watching my life from a distance anymore. I was back in my body, telling my truth. Finally letting the rain fall. "I wanted it to end for me like it had ended for Darren."

Nobody had ever heard this part of the story.

When I'd told Shane and Brady and my mom what had happened, it was a slightly different version. I'd said that everything had happened so fast, that the rain was so heavy I hadn't seen the car coming until it was too late and didn't have enough time to get out of the way.

Some of that wasn't true.

I knew exactly what had happened, and what I wanted to happen next.

"So I stood in the street, and I closed my eyes, and I rocked back and forth as the car came," I said. "I let the storm take me wherever it wanted to."

Instead of taking me, the storm shattered me and left me where I was.

Maybe it was what I had coming, even more than death.

I hadn't helped Darren with the pain he was forced to keep hidden, so maybe I deserved to wear mine on my face, and carry it in my soul for the rest of my life.

"Your scar…" Hart said.

I nodded. "I was in the hospital for a few weeks. There were broken bones and surgeries, nothing as severe as what the windshield did to my cheek. But none of it mattered. Darren was gone, and I was…not."

"I'm grateful you survived."

I stared into his eyes, tears blurring my vision. My sorrow turned him into a watercolor. "Then you should thank Brady the next time you see him. When I was in that hospital bed, I was willing to let it all go, not at all grateful to have survived. My mom couldn't get through to me. Or the nurses. But Brady never left my side. He made me live again, even when I didn't know how it would be possible. So when I say that he and Shane are my family, this is what I mean."

His brow folded, and I knew he understood how much they meant to me. "What happened to your grandfather?"

Anger flushed through me. My hands began to shake. "My mom said he waited at the house until the ambulance came. Then he got in his rusty old pick-up truck and took off. He left a note apologizing, the fucker. But he still left my mom with her son dead in his bedroom and her daughter broken in the middle of the street."

His lips brushed over mine. They couldn't cool the rage.

"His note explained how he couldn't handle the guilt of what had happened to either of us. He played the victim."

Hart nodded. "And your mom?"

"When I was strong enough, I told her the truth." I exhaled heavily. "She chose not to believe me."

He tilted my face to meet his gaze, reading my eyes again. "Her son killed himself and her daughter was crushed by a car, and she didn't believe you when you told her the reason?"

I shook my head. "She chooses to be mystified about what made Darren commit suicide, she writes it off as *teen angst*. It's complete bullshit." Besides my uncle, we were the only family we had left, and her denial had ruined our relationship. "The most painful time of the year are the weeks leading up to Darren's birthday…it's three days away." His eyes showed even more understanding. "I can't keep food down very well, and I don't sleep without dreaming of dark things."

"Of Darren and the accident."

This time, he was wrong. "No. I dream of my grandfather's hands."

He glanced down at his fingers on my face. "Did he…?"

"No—he never did to me what he did to Darren. He was actually a source of comfort before I knew what he really was. He used to brush my hair, and rub the top of my head…run his hands along my cheeks. The same hands that violated my brother and drove him to kill himself." These were my ghosts, the hands of a man I considered to be beyond evil, and they haunted me at their will.

"It makes sense now." His voice was as gentle as his touch. I didn't cringe or ache to push his hands off my face, even as I realized how much touch they were offering. Rather, I wanted to press them harder against my skin. "And now I understand why you did this to your hair."

I nodded. "I'm purging my ghosts."

"I'm going to help you however I can, Rae. I promise."

I believed him. "It was all my fault. If I'd been strong enough to confront my grandfather as soon as I knew, or if I'd taken Darren and left, things would be different now." I'd never fooled myself into believing I could start over and leave all this behind. But I'd always held onto the idea that I could have done things differently.

Hart kissed my fingers. "This wasn't your fault—none of it. You were a kid. Your grandfather is the one to blame."

It was too much for me to believe.

"Look at me," he insisted. I couldn't do it. "This wasn't your fault." He said it again, as if repeating himself would drive away the guilt. I'd failed Darren, and had been trying to make up for it ever since. I was the caretaker in every relationship, to the point of sacrificing myself. The more wounded they were, the more I felt I could fix them.

But none of that would ever bring my brother back.

"*Look at me, Rae,*" he repeated. I let my eyes drift from his stomach up to his chest, until I was looking into his cloud-gray eyes. He knew everything now, more than anyone did. I couldn't imagine how he felt about it all. "Thank you."

That was too much. "For what? For pulling you into my shit storm without telling you why it even existed? For taking my insanity out on you instead of explaining the reason behind it?"

He shook his head. "Thank you for trusting me with your pain… and thank you for letting me back into your life, against your better judgment…and thank you for finding a way to love me, even when you thought it wouldn't be possible." In all the time I'd spent holding the men in my life together and keeping them from falling apart, nobody had ever really said *thank you* before. And now, the man who was putting *me* back together was the one thanking me, when it should have been the other way around.

I was overwhelmed.

His lips pressed against mine. Everything inside my body poured out in our kiss: the regret, the desolation, the utter despair at having carried my pain alone for so long.

Everything I could never give to anyone else, for fear of having to tell them the truth.

I'd never gotten over Hart being taken out of my life; my feelings for him had been buried under layers of scar tissue. I'd never faced the reality of what had happened to Darren when he'd been ripped away from me; that piece of my soul had gone numb. And I hadn't gotten used to the idea that Brady was moving in a different direction, drifting away as he worked to clean himself up.

Having love removed from my life without warning was something I'd gotten used to.

Even more than the ragged spiral on my face, this was my scar.

THIRTY-FOUR

D ue to my confession to Hart, I had to make an appointment
at a salon the next morning, so I met Shane at the rehab
center instead of driving with him. It meant I wouldn't have as
much time with Brady, which I hated. It had only been a few days
since I'd seen him, yet so much had happened in that time. There
was so much he and Shane needed to hear—so much that, for the
first time, I was eager to share.

I walked in the front door and pulled off my beanie, running
my fingers through my hair. They only brushed through five or six
inches before I reached the ends. The hairdresser had cleaned up
the length and added in some layers. It had never been this short
before.

It made me feel lighter.

A part of me was even starting to feel free. Not completely yet,
though.

Two days.

I stopped at registration to fill out the usual paperwork and
have my bag searched. It was the same routine every time I came
here: the tech moved behind me and asked me to spread my arms
and legs. She started at my wrists, ran her hands to my shoulders,

down my sides, around my stomach, and over each leg. In the past, I'd cringed at the pat-down; even though it was a woman's hands, she'd always gotten too close to my neck, threatening to wander to one of my forbidden places. I didn't stop breathing when she touched me today. I didn't scrunch my body together like I was on the verge of sneezing. I just let her do her thing.

"Great haircut," she said when she was done.

I looked over my shoulder and smiled. It was genuine. "It is, isn't it?"

I passed through the door that lead to the rec room. Brady and Shane were sitting at a table off to the side. They weren't alone. There was a girl sitting with them, with her back to me. Her long espresso hair flowed over her shoulders and down her petite frame.

I didn't need her to turn around to know who it was.

"Rae, you're here…" Shane said nervously, standing up and meeting me before I made it to the table. "I didn't think you'd be coming so soon," he whispered. "I was hoping Drew would be gone by the time you arrived."

"Why is she here?"

His hands clamped my shoulders. "She came to talk to Brady. We had something we needed to tell him…together."

They had something *they* needed to tell him. *Together.*

And Shane hadn't told me what it was?

But he told me everything when it came to Brady. This was *my* family, not hers. So why did I suddenly feel like an outsider?

"Should I leave?" I asked, not caring whether or not she heard me.

Shane frowned. "I know she's not your favorite, but this is something you need to hear. It might change the way you feel."

"Doubt it," I mumbled.

"Please come sit with us?" He held out his hand and wiggled his fingers.

I needed to hear whatever it was, so I took his hand and followed him over. He pulled out a chair for me next to Brady. But

Brady didn't even glance in my direction. His eyes were trained on Drew, and Drew's eyes were fixed on him. He didn't even seem to be breathing.

Drew slowly looked at me. "Hi, Rae."

I ignored her. "So what's going on here?" I asked roughly.

Brady's stare gradually shifted over to me. "Turns out Drew is... uh...my sister."

My stomach dropped and my jaw hung open. I didn't even try to close it. "She's your *what?*" I was louder than I needed to be.

Shane blushed. "It's true."

"Why am I just hearing about this now?" I couldn't help the accusatory tone.

"I'm just hearing it now, too," Brady answered. "Drew figured it out, but Dad didn't want her to tell me until he thought I could handle the news."

"How long have you known this, Shane?" He'd been with Drew's mom? I could hardly digest it.

"A few months. We found out while I was renovating Drew's house."

My stare shifted between the three of them. They all had the same eyes and similar coloring and their faces were shaped the same.

She wasn't the outsider.

I was.

"I know this is a lot to take in," Drew said, "but I—"

I spoke over her. "Shane, why didn't you tell *me?*"

"Please don't be upset, Rae. I really wanted to tell you, but Brady needed to hear the news first. I wasn't comfortable telling anyone until he knew about his sister."

The thought of her being *that* to Brady sent a chill through me.

Was I concentrating on the wrong thing here? Maybe the fact that he hadn't told me yet wasn't as important as how this was going to change us. Drew and I didn't get along; with Brady getting out of rehab soon, I imagined he'd be spending a lot of time with her...his *sister*. Things were about to get really messy.

"He's been doing so well," Shane said, "*we* thought it was the right time to tell him."

We.

Drew had been a surprise member of the family for less than a whole season and already she was helping Shane make decisions. Everything was so complicated. It made my stomach feel even worse than it had before. There were issues between me and Drew, and between Brady and Saint. And now, everyone was family.

"There's more," Brady said.

"Oh, I can't wait to hear it." I glanced up from the table and met his eyes.

"Dad talked to Drew about my situation. She's going to lend me the money to pay the dealers."

"She is?" I may not have been related by blood, but I still had a voice in this family, and there was no way I was keeping quiet about the money.

Brady eyed me warily. That meant he'd heard the edge in my tone. "Isn't that awesome, Rae?" he said carefully.

Drew gazed at him. "I really want to help."

I glared at Drew, with her arms crossed over her chest like a shield and her happy eyes and her smirk. She couldn't have possibly known what was coming. "How did that become your decision to make?" I asked her.

"It wasn't, Rae," Shane said, sounding stunned. "She offered to help, and we accepted. We thought you'd be as relieved as we are."

But she wasn't the one who could fix this...*I* was.

"There's no way I'm going to let that happen," I told her, raising my voice. "I don't care what your intentions are. Brady is *my* family. I've been here for him for all these years, not you. *I* was the one he called when those assholes had beaten the shit out of him. *I* held him while he trembled and puked his guts out. *I* made him feel safe—*me*, not you. I'll be..."

I stopped myself from saying...*damned if you get to be the one who fixes him.*

I hadn't broken the pattern. I was still trying to fix Brady, when I really needed to fix myself. Somehow, I couldn't let go.

"You have no fucking idea what he's been through or what he needs," I said instead. I turned to Brady. "I have the money. Every cent will come from me. You don't need Drew."

"What?" Brady asked, before it registered. "Rae, no..."

"Brady, *yes*." I stood firm.

"Unless you're planning to buy a home, you don't touch that account—do you understand? That's what it's for: *your* home."

He and Shane had taken me to the bank to open the account, sometimes tagging along when I made my deposits. Shane gave me a check every year for my birthday just to add to the balance. Spending that money on a place to live would give me something that was mine, but it would never replace the way Brady and Shane made me feel.

They were more than just my family.

"*You're* my home," I told him. I glanced at Shane. "You are, too." I felt my lips tremble. "You carried me out of that hospital bed when I'd thrown everything away. You were the only one who would look at all my ugliness, and you've been carrying me forward ever since. It's been a horrible time. *Horrible.* I've made mistakes everywhere, and so have you. But we've loved each other right through it all." It was becoming clearer the more I spoke. "It wasn't just me taking care of you, Brady; it was you taking care of me, too. I realize that now. You're the closest thing I have to a brother..."

It hit me then: something in me believed that by saving Brady, I'd also be saving Darren.

It was such a fucked-up thought.

But it was another piece of truth I had to face.

"I need to do this for you—and I have the money to do it. So I'm going to be the one to fix this." I glared at Drew again. "Not *you*."

Before any of them had a chance to speak, I turned and ran for the door.

A house was just a house to me now. Brady was the home I needed to keep safe. I would figure out another way to buy a place to live, another way to stand on my own. Another way to heal myself.

Brady needed it more than I did.

I sat in my car, composing myself before starting it up. I jumped when my phone rang. *Unknown* showed on the screen. My hand reached for it on impulse. I stared at it while it rang, trying to feel something other than rage.

It was time for this to change.

I answered the call, but said nothing, waiting for him to speak. "Rae?" The raspy voice I hated so much jittered in my ear. "Rae, are you there?" I wanted to hear what he would say, how he would try to convince me that I hadn't seen what I'd seen, that I didn't know the things I knew about him. About what he'd done to Darren. "We need to talk, Rae. You can't run from me forever."

It all came barreling out of me. "Don't you *ever* fucking call me again, old man!" I screamed. "Do you understand me? *Don't you ever...fucking... call me...again!*" I hung up and threw my phone on the floor as hard as I could.

All at once, I felt the storm pulling me back in.

THIRTY-FIVE

I stood in front of the bathroom mirror with only a towel wrapped around me. I'd just gotten out of the shower but had forgotten to use conditioner, so my hair was a tangled mess. I didn't have the energy to get back in, squirt the liquid onto my hand and run it through my strands. It could stay tangled and sloppy for all I cared.

I looked at my phone, at the time and the date, and I breathed.

It was only six in the morning.

Today.

I had nowhere to be. No reason to clean my body. No cause to flee the bed I shared with Hart other than worrying that my tossing and turning would wake him. I hadn't slept a minute the whole night. I'd watched the reflection of the moon shimmer over the ceiling until it disappeared down the wall. Then I moved on to the stars that shined through the skylight. I'd traced their patterns, followed their slow arcs across the dark sky until the tightness in my chest became too much. I had hoped the shower would loosen it, though I knew nothing would help. Not taking deep breaths; not smoking a joint. Not talking to Brady.

The void within me couldn't be filled.

There was a red circle on my chest where the water had beaten down. It was the entrance to my broken core, the place where it hurt the most. My short golden locks couldn't cover it anymore, couldn't soothe it. It ached even more with each passing second.

I just wanted to see him one more time.

I didn't want to say good-bye; I could never have said that to someone I loved as much as Darren. The thought of it was ugly and jagged, red like my scar. No, I wanted to tell him how sorry I was for not protecting him from Gerald. I wanted to wrap my arms around him and hold him, to shield him from the evil that lived in our house.

I thought back to the last time I'd held him. It was after I'd seen him being ravaged by that horrible man. Darren was fourteen at the time—an eighth-grader—so I drove him to school. We had a quiet moment in the car. I wanted him to know that I knew what was happening without torturing him any more than he'd already been. So I tried to keep things simple. "Everything cool with you?" I asked.

He shrugged. "Sure."

I glanced at him as he gazed out the window. "You're not really convincing me."

He didn't look at me. "It's all good, Rae. Just…school stuff. Homework."

My heart trembled. He was trying so hard to be brave.

"You know," I told him, "we've never had a dad to take care of us. That really sucks, I think. And Mom is always working." I didn't mention Gerald. I was hoping if I gave Darren the opportunity, he'd bring him up. He said nothing. "So if anything is going wrong or bothering you, you know you can always come to me, right? That if you didn't know how to deal with something, I'd help you with it however I had to. I'd do anything for you."

He shrugged again. "There's nothing wrong, Rae. Nothing I can't handle on my own."

My heart was hammering now. I didn't want him to feel alone anymore.

The light changed to green, so I began to drive. I pulled into the school lot and parked. "Listen to me, Darren..." I paused, trying to think of a delicate way to say this without scaring him. "I know what Grandpa did to you."

His head snapped around, and his eyes widened.

"I saw him the other night...when he was in your room."

He didn't say a word.

"We need to tell Mom."

"No!" he shouted. "Don't do that. Please...you can't, Rae...you can't. Promise me, please. *Promise me!*"

He was frantic. It gave me a true sense of how much fear he was living in. My heart was breaking for him. "Okay...okay. I won't."

He stared out the window as his breathing starting to calm. He tucked his hands under his knees. "Nothing happened anyway, so there's nothing to tell." He was lying, that was why he still wouldn't look at me. "You didn't see what you thought you saw, Rae." He took another breath. "You're wrong..."

I let the silence settle between us. There was nothing he could say that would convince me I was wrong. I knew what I saw, and he needed to know I was going to protect him regardless of what he was willing to admit. "I will never let him do that to you again." Our eyes slowly filled with tears. "I will *never* let him do that to you again," I repeated.

He hesitated for a second. Then hugged me, tightly. So hard, I could feel my ribs buckle. "You can't tell Mom," he whispered. "Please." Then he jumped out of the car.

It wasn't long after that that I saw him on his bed, asphyxiated with his own belt.

That was how I remembered him, even when I didn't want to. But every year on his birthday, I forced myself to imagine what he might look like if he were still alive. How tall he'd be, how handsome. If he'd still have only three freckles under his left eye or if there would be more. What a fantastic young man he'd be, if only...

If only.

I traced my scar, remembering the sacrifices I hadn't been able to make for him. Maybe he'd been more fortunate to have escaped. "Happy nineteenth, Darren," I whispered into the mirror.

"Happy nineteenth, Darren," Hart echoed.

The sound of his voice made me smile. It was the only happiness I could have hoped to find on a day like this.

I turned around, watching him lean against the frame of the door, dressed in only a pair of thin cotton sweatpants. "We're not staying home today," he said.

"We're not?"

He shook his head as he walked over to me. His nose grazed my cheek, as though he was taking in my scent before he kissed the center of my scar. "We're going out to commemorate Darren's birthday."

Commemorate it? It was enough just to survive it.

"Don't you do that every year?" he asked.

"No. I usually just smoke pot all day and hope to pass out at some point."

He smiled. "So what would you do if you weren't high?"

I shrugged. "I don't know." I'd never been asked the question before and didn't have an answer ready.

I wasn't sure if Hart's silence meant he was thinking of something, or if he was waiting for me to say more. He just breathed on my neck and held me quietly.

Finally, something came to me. "I'd like to see his grave," I told him. "I haven't gone back since the funeral." I hadn't been able to, though I'd tried several times. Each time I'd been alone by choice. I thought it was what I needed to do; it just ended up being too much. I never made it past the entrance of the cemetery.

Hart smiled. "Then that's where we're going."

Several inches of snow covered the ground as Hart and I walked through the gate of the cemetery. A sidewalk circled the whole property; several shorter paths weaved among the graves, through different patches of plots. We stayed in the middle, taking the narrower aisles that led to Darren's section. Hart's hand clung to my mitten-covered fingers. His body was pressed closely to mine. I couldn't feel him, even though I knew he was holding it tightly.

After the second hill, my pace began to slow. Hart's arm wrapped around my shoulders and he pulled me into his chest. His smell was stronger than the pine in the air. I could tell he was trying to use his warmth to thaw me.

"I should have brought you a blanket," he said.

My whole body shivered. "I'm not cold."

"We can stop if you need to." He pressed his lips against my temple.

"No. I'm good." I knew my feet were moving, but it felt like he was lifting them for me and placing them back on the ground, like he was carrying every ounce of my weight and keeping me softly fogged, so the realization of where we were wouldn't hit me all at once. And while he was busy with me, I kept my eyes on the ground, staring at the different footprints that had been pressed into the snow. So many shoes and boots and sneakers had walked this path before us. Probably would after us, too. I wondered if their hearts hurt as badly as mine.

I knew how close we were getting, even without my eyes following the names on the graves that we passed. I remembered all the stones that surrounded his plot, even only having been there once. When the prints in the snow weren't enough, I began counting my steps. When we were only feet away, I stopped and glanced at Hart. "It's that one," I said. My head nudged toward the stone in front of us, but my eyes remained on his overcast gaze. My emotions seemed to be reflecting back at me from within his vision.

"How are you?" he asked.

I opened my mouth to answer, but nothing came out. Not even a sound. Just a drop that started at my bottom eyelid and fell to my cheek. He caught it before it reached my chin, cupping my scar as his mouth brushed over mine. It was a tender kiss full of breath, encouragement and hope.

It was the pause I needed.

"I think I'm okay."

I faced forward again, my side pressing against him as I took the final steps. When I came to a stop, the wind seemed to as well, a pocket of serenity hovering over us. It wasn't warmth, but it wasn't cold, either. It was a quiet, steady storm that held in place as I read the words on his headstone.

DARREN RYAN.
SON. BROTHER. FRIEND.

Fourteen short years of life from start to finish, and now he lay in front of me, underneath a mound of snow and dirt, in a box that would never be opened again. How was that even possible?

Had he really been gone for five years?

I closed my eyes and leaned my head into Hart's shoulder. "I miss you, Darren." Hart's grip tightened around me. "I miss you so much…" I opened my eyes and watched my exhale cloud from my lips.

"I remember the way he used to look at you," Hart said. "The way his eyes watched you when you spoke, admiring you, eating up every word you said."

I smiled at the thought. I remembered that, too. But I remembered more…

"I let him down."

"No, you didn't, Rae." Hart's arm wrapped over my stomach. "He knew he could go to you with anything and that he could trust you. But his pain was something you couldn't fix."

Aside from Darren and Hart, everyone else in my life had wanted to be saved at one point or another. I had watched Brady reach his rock bottom after falling again and again. But Darren didn't stand a chance. He was a little boy victimized by someone he trusted. He *started* at rock bottom.

He had nowhere else to fall.

"I just don't understand, Hart, why didn't he let me try?"

"Maybe he didn't know how to get through his fear. Maybe he was afraid of what would happen to you if you tried. You can torture yourself forever, but you'll never know for sure." He was right. "He didn't feel like he had a choice. But you do, Rae—*you* have a choice. You can either spend the rest of your life holding out for answers you'll never get, or you can spend it remembering how much love there was between the two of you and live your life in honor of that."

I thought about the conversation I'd had with Brady. He'd said that once he paid off his dealers, he would never look back again. No dwelling upon the regret, no wishing for a do-over. He was going to find acceptance and move forward. Could I do that? Would the memory of the love between Darren and me be enough to let me move on?

"I..." As my vision left the stone and slid to Hart's face, something in the background caught my attention. It was a splash of red from the road ahead of us. The street ran around the back side of the cemetery, rising several feet above and overlooking the hills of tombstones. After Darren's death, I'd refused to drive on it, even if that meant taking a longer route. I'd heard only a few cars pass us since we'd arrived. It was all background noise. But now, I couldn't drag my eyes away from the red pick-up truck as it passed. It was an old model—old and familiar. There was rust over the door and all along the cab. It disappeared behind a row of trees before I was able to see the driver.

It was just a coincidence, I told myself. So many men in Bar Harbor drove pick-up trucks, including Shane and Brady, and lots of them were old and red and rusty.

Gerald's truck had been all of those things, but there was no way he was here. Not today. Not at the same time I was...

"You okay?" Hart asked. "It looks like you just saw a ghost."

My ghost. His words were more terrifying than he realized.

A coincidence, I repeated in my head.

I shifted toward him slowly, my eyes following. "Love," I answered finally, "that's all I want to remember between Darren and me." I wanted everything else to go away, especially my memories of that man.

"I think that's the right decision."

"I know it is." My voice wasn't any louder than a whisper.

He looked toward the stone and tipped his head, trying to encourage me to take a step forward. It was difficult, but I did it… and then I took another, and another, until I stood over Darren's name. I filled myself with breath, and I knelt down on the snow. I wrapped my hands around the top of the stone. It was freezing. My eyes filled and my vision blurred. My fingers ached for his warmth, for the feel of his skin against mine—not Hart's… Darren's. This wasn't anything like embracing my brother. But it was the closest I'd ever be able to get to him. I glanced over my shoulder, wondering how alone I was now.

"I'm right behind you," Hart said. "And I'm not going anywhere."

I closed my eyes and rested my face on the stone, on the side that held so many memories of Darren. The scarred side. My skin tingled against the cold.

I didn't speak. I just let the thoughts flow in my head, and in my heart.

I'm here, Darren. Finally. I know it took me a while. Too long, really. I tried to come before…I just couldn't do it. I didn't want to see you here, to think of you as a headstone. And I didn't want you to see the place I was in. It was ugly and it had been for years. Things are changing, though. I'm changing. I'm getting better. I'm…

Hart's voice worked its way in. "Rae…"

I turned to face him and saw someone else walking toward us. No—not walking, it was more of a limp. His legs seemed to be dragging his body along, like they were the only part of him that could still bear weight where the rest had fully deteriorated. My stomach began to churn as I studied him. He wore old brown slacks and a thick flannel shirt. A winter hat was pulled over his gray hair. His face was so stony, so grim. I couldn't bring myself to look at his hands...I'd seen them too much in my nightmares as it was.

I started to shake.

Hart leaned in and whispered, "That's him, isn't it?"

I stood as briskly as I could, so he couldn't take me by surprise like he'd taken my brother. "Yes. That's Gerald, my...grandfather."

THIRTY-SIX

I n the years since Darren's death, I'd dreamt of the horror this
man had caused, of the terror his hands were capable of. I'd
never thought to rehearse what I'd say to him if I had the chance to
see him again. I never thought I would. I had no idea what to
expect now that it was happening.

I was seething. "You don't belong here," I said harshly. "You
need to leave before this gets ugly for you." Hart clutched my arm.

"He was my grandson." That was all he offered.

I hadn't heard him speak in person in so long. The voice
brought everything back. He stood at a distance, with his hands
clasped and resting against his thighs. The sight of them made the
churning in my stomach even worse. I thought I'd be the same
quivering, nervous mess I'd always been when he'd haunted my
memory. But standing before him, next to Darren's grave, remembering everything he'd put my brother through and everything I
couldn't save him from, I found strength I never had back then.

I was the storm now.

"After what you did to him, he is *no one* to you."

Before Gerald had left, I hadn't gotten the chance to confront him about what he'd done to my brother. If he ever wondered how much I knew, he didn't have to question that now.

Hart slid past me and stood in front of Gerald. "Get the fuck out of here." He was shouting, towering over Gerald's weakened frame. The old man didn't budge, so Hart said, "If I have to drag you out of here, I will."

He'd aged so much since the last time I'd seen him. His back was hunched; his arms were plagued by tremors. Coarse white hair covered his cheeks, and skin hung slack over his eyes. I had loved that face once. I'd kissed it every night before bed and looked forward to seeing it every morning. Looking at it now, all I felt was hatred and disgust.

He exhaled a raspy breath. "I just want to talk to you, Rae. Before I can't anymore."

"What does that mean?" I spat.

"I'm sick."

"That's for fucking sure," Hart said.

Gerald coughed, hacking so loudly it sounded like he was going to throw up. He removed an inhaler from the pocket of his flannel and took a deep puff. He finally stood straight again, but still looked like he was about to pass out. "I don't have much time left." He coughed again, this time into a handkerchief. There was blood on the white cloth. "I'm dying, Rae. I just need to make my peace. So let me speak to you real quick, and I'll leave you alone forever."

"You think that's a reason for me to talk to you—because you're dying?" My voice sounded even angrier as it came through my lips than it had sounded in my head for the last five years. "You can't possibly believe that I care about anything you have to say."

"You're right," Gerald replied. "I don't believe that."

Hart kept his eyes locked on the old man. "Say the word, and I'll drag him out of here before he can say anything else."

Hart was trying to protect me. But as much as I despised that man, I needed closure. I would hopefully get that by hearing whatever he thought was important enough to track me down and say. From the looks of him, this was probably going to be my last chance to hear it.

"It's okay. Let him talk."

Gerald put his inhaler back in his pocket and crumpled the handkerchief. His face spoke of his physical pain. In anyone else, it would have inspired sympathy. I had none for him. "I understand why you hate me, and you've got every reason to feel that way. There's nothing I can say to defend myself." He took long, deep breaths between thoughts. "I live every day knowing what I did to that poor, innocent boy."

"So do I," I told him. I gazed at Darren's headstone. "He doesn't, though. He doesn't live any day knowing anything anymore."

Gerald shook his head, his eyes softening and gleaming. "I deserve what's coming for me. I'm dying, slowly and painfully. And alone. No one feels bad for me, and no one should."

"It doesn't seem like enough," I said, taking another step toward them. By Hart's posture, I knew he wouldn't let me get much closer. "I'm actually relieved to hear that you're dying." It sounded so gross coming out of my mouth, but I did nothing to stop myself from saying it.

"I understand that." He wobbled on his feet. Hart noticed and tightened his grip to help steady him. "I've been calling so I can apologize. Thought I might catch you here today."

"Wow...that's quite a coincidence."

"No. I come here every year on this day."

Suddenly, even Darren's grave felt tainted by this man's presence.

"What makes you think you deserve to mourn for the boy who *you* drove to suicide, Gerald?" It barreled out of me.

"I know I can't fix the damage I've done, and I can't bring that boy back to life and make him hurt any less. But there hasn't been a day I haven't punished myself for what I've done."

"You want to punish yourself? Then call the police and tell

them you molested and raped Darren Ryan before he committed suicide. And tell my mother what you really did, while you're at it." He said nothing. "Tell her that her daughter isn't a liar, and that her son didn't just kill himself out of *teen angst*, as she calls it, but because her father was sexually abusing him." The words brought tears to my eyes again.

His stare dropped to the ground and he fell into another coughing spell. This time, he used the back of his hand to wipe away whatever rose. There was blood on his lips when he finally pulled it away. "I can't. And that makes me weak, I know."

I had no sympathy for him whatsoever. "No. It makes you evil."

"That, too."

It still seemed so casual to him, so removed. It was tornadoes and typhoons tearing my life apart on a daily basis, and it just didn't seem to be the destructive force for him that it should have been. I needed him to know exactly how much it had impacted me. "I was going to kill you, you know." The sound of my confession shocked me. It was something I never intended on telling him, or anyone. It finally felt like something I needed to admit out loud. I couldn't carry it out, but I could make sure he knew that the thought had been with me. "The night Darren died, I was coming back to the house to put a knife in your chest."

Hart cringed when I said it.

My voice was getting louder. I didn't stop it. "I knew what you had done to him, and I wasn't going to let you ever do it again. But I didn't get there in time." My whole body had gone numb. I couldn't believe I was still standing, or that the tears hadn't started streaming. "It should have been *you* with that belt around your neck. *You* should have had the blue lips. *You* should have had the lifeless body. *You* should have died for what you did, not him…not Darren." I reminded myself to breathe, drawing huge gusts of frigid air into my lungs to steel myself. "I thought for sure if I ever saw you again, I would do it. But I don't have that impulse anymore." I sized up his withering form. "By the looks of it, you'll be gone soon anyway. You don't deserve my concern, or my vengeful thoughts. You deserve nothing from anyone anymore."

He nodded, as if he knew he couldn't argue any of what I'd said. "I hope you haven't let the past stop you from living."

I wasn't even going to dignify his comment with an answer. "You will never come and visit my brother's grave again, do you understand? You will die with this as your last memory of him, and me." Hart's fists clenched as he waited for Gerald's response.

But the old man did nothing. He just nodded and turned on his heels, dragging his body slowly down the sidewalk in the direction he'd come from. The tension broke, and Hart's arms were suddenly around me again, pulling me into his chest. The tip of his nose circled around my cheek as he kissed the center of my scar. "Are you all right?"

I kept watching the back of Gerald's head until he disappeared from my view. Then I tilted my face up to Hart. "I'm not sure." If the storm I lived in still had motion, I was now in the eye. Everything had fallen still and silent. "I think I'm okay."

Hearing Gerald admit what he had done did give me some relief. Knowing he was dying and probably would be gone soon helped a little bit, too. But something still felt unfinished. Unresolved. It had nothing to do with Gerald. It had everything to do with me.

And Darren.

"I need you to take me somewhere," I said.

"Anywhere you want, we'll go."

It was the second time that day my choices had taken me by surprise. "I want to go to my mom's house."

THIRTY-SEVEN

"**A**re you sure you want to do this?" Hart asked.

We were in my mom's house, where I'd only been briefly in the five years since Darren had died. I came home briefly to recuperate after the accident, and I left once I could walk on my own. And now, I was outside the door to Darren's bedroom.

It was time.

I'd called my mom on the way over, to tell her I was coming. Finally. She'd wanted this for so long, and I hadn't been able to bring myself to do it. I'd kept my key and let myself in. I was relieved she wasn't there; it made things slightly easier as I got past the initial shock. There was only one person I wanted with me, and he held my hand the whole time.

"I'm sure," I answered Hart as my fingers clutched the knob. "I have to do this. I have to go in and face what I ran away from. It's the final step, I think." I hoped.

I truly thought it would be the closure I needed, something to stop the countdown from repeating each upcoming year, and the dread...and the hurricane of guilt and pain that overtook me every December. I needed to move on. And to do that, I needed to stand in the two places I'd been avoiding all this time. I'd already been to his grave.

Now I needed to be where he'd lived…and where he'd died.

Slowly, I opened the door, letting the air rush out before I stepped inside. I scanned the whole room. It was as if time had stood still. Nothing had changed, really. The blinds were still half open. Two of the posters drooped; their tape had worn off. His clothes were on the floor in his closet. His math book sat on his desk, loose-leaf papers next to it, with equations written all over them. I'd avoided looking at the bed, the last place I'd seen him just before I'd run away.

I couldn't run again.

I took deep breaths, squeezed Hart's hand, and lifted my gaze.

I thought I would see him as I had that night. His body in the middle of the mattress, the spot where Gerald had told the paramedics he'd placed Darren after lifting him off the rafters. His bluish skin and his eyes lifeless in his swollen face.

That wasn't what I saw at all.

Darren and I sat on his bed, talking about Driver's Ed and how he wasn't ready for that quite yet, even though he'd be eligible in a few months. "I'd rather have you drive me around," he said. That made me feel necessary, and loved. Then he randomly placed his hands in the air as if they were on a steering wheel and rested his foot on an imaginary gas pedal. "Guess who I am." His hand dropped from the steering wheel and reached across me as though I were a passenger.

"You're not mocking Mom, are you?" I asked.

"Of course I am." He even mimicked her voice and pretended to dig around in something that was supposed to be on my lap. It was her purse…she always kept it there. "Did you take my makeup out of this bag, Rae? How many times do I have to tell you to put my makeup back after you use it?"

"Mom…" I said, playing along. "I didn't use your makeup."

"Never mind," he said. "I found it." Holding an invisible tube, he lifted it to his eye and drew a line on his bottom lid. Using both hands now, he steered with his knee, his attention not even on the road.

I laughed so hard, I snorted. "Darren, she did that exact thing the last time I was in the car with her. She didn't even wait for a red light!"

"Watch the wheel while I blend my shadow, won't you, honey?" he said.

My laughter only got louder. Darren had her mannerisms down, and he sounded so much like her. He even puffed the back of his hair when he finished with the eye shadow like she constantly did when she was driving.

"Darren, stooooop," I yelled, gasping for breath.

He finally dropped the act and glanced over at me, his giggles almost as loud as mine. "Will you teach me when I'm ready, instead of her?" he asked. "So I can avoid the whole makeup lesson?"

I smiled at him. "Whatever you want."

His face fell, and he grew solemn. "I love you, Rae."

He could always surprise me by saying that.

"I love you too, Darren." It was a murmur.

I shook my head and blinked as hard as I could, coming back to the present. Seeing once again the dent in the comforter that his body had left reminded me of the moment I had found him there that night. There was no laughter then.

But there had been laughter. In this room, in this house.

In our lives.

I had to carry the laughter forward now, and the love. I had to leave the rest in the past.

"You're so strong to be doing this," Hart whispered. He stood behind me, his hands on my waist, holding my body against his. That was exactly where I wanted him. Comforting me. Calming me.

Healing me.

"I really wasn't, until you helped me find the strength," I replied.

It was true. I wasn't sure I would have gone to the cemetery or come back inside this house again if I hadn't been with Hart. Brady gave me the comfort I needed to hang on, but neither he nor Shane had been able to get me to go there. Hart gave me courage to move on.

With his help, I was starting to find myself again. Or maybe I wasn't finding myself at all...maybe I was becoming someone new. And in the exact spot where I'd left myself behind all those years ago, I was meeting her for the first time.

I glanced around his room as more and more happy memories returned. I knew it wouldn't take another five years for me to come back. This was our home, and Darren's room, the place where those memories had been made. I'd said good-bye to all of it once, allowing Gerald's vile influence to take it away, my guilt robbing so much of my time and happiness.

I wasn't going to allow that anymore. I deserved happiness.

My mom had been in the house for a while, but hadn't come to find me yet. I knew from her hanging back that she was giving me space to process all the emotions I would feel when I finally opened Darren's door. I appreciated that. But now I needed some closure with her, too.

I slid my fingers into Hart's grasp and walked into the hallway, stopping in the doorway of the kitchen. Mom was standing at the coffeemaker, waiting for the pot to fill. There were three mugs on the counter, next to a bowl of sugar, creamer, and artificial sweetener. She didn't know how I took my coffee—I learned that when I'd met her at the café—but at least she was trying.

"I saw his grave today, Mom."

She hadn't heard that word in her house in so long. I watched her eyes close, her chest rising and falling as she turned toward me. "It's a nice stone, isn't it?" We were easing into things. I could almost see her thoughts processing. "Hart, I'm so surprised to see you." She smiled as warmly as she could. "You're all grown up."

Hart smiled at her. "It's nice to see you again."

My mom beamed at him, and at me. There was a gentleness to her that I hadn't seen in a while, a streak of vulnerability in her eyes. It felt wrong to have spent so much time resenting her, so much time away from her. Anger and guilt had caused that. But I'd dropped my shield the second I'd walked into this house.

"Coffee?" she asked.

Hart and I moved over to the table, and Mom followed right behind us with a tray. Hart mixed my coffee the way I liked it and placed it in front of me.

I watched her sip and swallow, taking in her face and all its detail. There were black bags under her eyes, and her cheeks were too thin... just like mine.

"It's been hard, hasn't it?" I asked, breaking the silence.

She slowly looked up from her mug, her brownie colored eyes meeting mine. "I think it always will be."

She was right. I thought about telling her that Gerald had come to the cemetery and everything I had learned from his visit, including his health. But there was no point. He was a pathetic man and it wouldn't change anything between my mom and me. If he wanted her to know his confession, he would have told her, too. For all I knew, he had.

"Rae, I need to tell you some things," she said, suddenly turning serious, as if she'd read my mind. Her eyes began to fill, her hands straining around the ceramic cup. "When you told me what had happened, what you'd seen..." She paused, her chest rising and falling even faster than before. Her knuckles turned white, and her teeth pressed into her lip to keep it from trembling. "You have to understand, a police officer called and said my son was dead, and my daughter was on the way to the hospital where I was working. Then I learned that the man I'd trusted with the most important things in my life had left them broken and disappeared. It was too much to process. All the guilt, all the pain. I couldn't protect you, and I couldn't deal with the aftermath. And then you told me about Grandpa..."

It was so familiar; I'd been doing the same for the last five years, refusing to visit Darren's grave or his bedroom, hiding those thoughts in a cloud of smoke. I was trying to fix and protect others because I hadn't been able to fix and protect him.

She was caught in the storm as much as I was.

"I understand," I said.

Her fingers reached across the table and tangled in mine. "I know you weren't lying...I know you wouldn't have done that." Years of pent-up pain poured out in our tears. "And I don't want another birthday to pass without having you here to commemorate it."

"I don't want that either," I said.

She came across the table and clung to me, sobbing. We had come to an understanding. An unspoken promise. We were no longer going to look back; we were moving forward—finally—and we were going to do it together. I doubted the month of December would ever feel normal again. And I knew there was no possible way that the hole Darren's absence had left in our lives would ever be filled. But if we helped each other through it, maybe it didn't have to be so destructive anymore.

Without realizing she had done it, Mom pressed her cheek against my scar. I was filled with a comfort I wasn't expecting. There was no anxiety, no dread. Just the healing warmth from my mom, which had been missing for so long. The silence between us was peaceful and calm.

We lingered in that for a while.

And when I finally walked through the house on my way to the front door, Hart clung to my hand. I paused at the bottom of the steps and slipped off my shoes. Then I let him go, and I carefully strolled over the grass. In the places where the snow had melted, I could feel the frozen blades between my toes. He didn't ask what I was doing. He knew. I had to experience *all* of that night, each moment lived anew, all leading to an outcome that didn't leave me battered by my own torment.

He opened the passenger door for me as I hopped over to the

curb. "There's a towel in the backseat. You can use it to dry and warm your feet," he said.

"I know. Don't ask me how, but I know." I seemed to know where everything was in Hart's life. It reminded me that he was always taking care of me. And it made me smile, a genuine smile, not the kind that clouded over a long-held pain, but to my commitment of finding real happiness.

I fastened my seatbelt and leaned back into the headrest, thinking about my future with Hart. Once the spa in Bar Harbor was complete, we'd be heading up to Bangor. Then we'd move on to Portland where we'd rent an apartment downtown. We hadn't spoken about that part yet; it was something I had just decided. I'd never lived in a city before; I'd never lived anywhere except Bar Harbor. Suddenly, I had a desire to change that. Maybe one day we'd come back here to run the spa. Maybe we'd stay in Portland. Or maybe we'd move into his condo in Boston.

It didn't matter where we lived. Distance wouldn't take my family away from me, or my home. Like Darren, it all lived inside me, and something as basic as geography couldn't change that.

Hart started the engine and shifted into reverse, staring through the glass before he turned toward me. "Looks like a storm is coming in."

I closed my eyes and sighed. Of course it was. Rain would be so fitting for Darren's birthday. Maybe it was a sign.

Maybe it was tears.

Or maybe it truly was just rain.

THIRTY-EIGHT

We'd stopped at a pub for dinner and didn't get back to the house until after nine. I hadn't smoked all day. I hadn't ordered a drink at the restaurant, even though Hart had a few beers while he ate. I didn't want any of it. I wanted to keep my mind completely clear and remember every detail of Darren's birthday. So much had happened, more than I ever expected. Surprisingly, I was calm.

Still, it didn't seem right to end the first day of my new beginning in the same way we spent most of our evenings, flipping through a magazine or zoning out in front of the TV. I wanted to peel back what had kept me from being fully honest and intimate with him. I wanted to show him every part of my skin, to be fully naked before him and know that he loved me as I was, scars and all.

He leaned against the kitchen counter, swiping his finger across the screen of his phone. I lifted it out of his hands and brought his fingers up to my lips. "Thank you for today." I kissed his knuckles, one at a time.

He smiled. "You don't have to thank me. I'll do anything for you. You know that."

He had proven that to me again and again. But that didn't mean I would stop thanking him. I wasn't just grateful for what he had done today, but for all the different ways he had changed my life since he'd come back into it. I had almost not let him in. Thankfully, I had…and he was here.

And he was all mine.

I tugged on his hand and pulled him up from the counter. "Come with me."

A wrinkle creased his brow, and his smoky stare intensified. "Is something wrong?"

I didn't answer. I just turned my back toward him and led him down the hallway to the bedroom. *Our* bedroom. Once inside, I moved him in front of the mattress with the back of his knees resting against the bed and sat him down. Concern flickered in his eyes until I lifted my sweater over my head and dropped it on the floor.

"You don't have to do this, Rae. I'm not expecting anything from you."

"That's not what this is about." I removed the tank top that I wore underneath. My shoes and belt were next. I continued to strip until I stood in front of him wearing only my bra and panties. "You saw all of me today, more than anyone has ever seen. Now I want to give you the rest."

His eyebrow hitched. "You haven't given me this part already?"

I smiled, turning my head so my scarred cheek faced him. "Not like this."

His hands slowly moved through the air and cupped my cheeks, gently pulling me down to the bed. I straddled his waist while I kissed him, tugging off his button-down and the T-shirt he had on underneath. There was the faintest taste of beer on his breath…and something else. Something hot and erotic. Something I wanted to suck off his tongue.

With his chest finally bare and only a pair of boxer briefs covering the rest of him, I lowered my lips. Licking my way across his defined chest, I was able to take in more of his scent. Cedar and musk filled my nose, the smells I'd grown used to, and a subtle splash of his body wash. I could feel the pounding of his heart as I moved toward his nipple. Biting down on the end of the rod that pierced it, I held the little ball between my teeth, and gently pulled.

Air burst through his lips and ended in a moan. "God, I want you, Rae."

I met his gaze. "You have me, Hart. All of me."

My teeth released, repositioning to take his whole nipple this time, and then I used my tongue to flick the end of the rod. His hands went into my hair, pulling the strands while I sucked. I opened my eyes and glanced up at him, watching the passion spread across his face as I yanked down his boxer briefs. He needed more of my mouth, so I dropped my head until I reached the tip of his cock. I wrapped my lips around him, only able to take half of him in. So I used my hand to cover the rest. His hips jerked forward and rocked back. We were moving in the same rhythm, meeting for each stroke of my mouth as he filled the air with the deepest sounds.

His hands suddenly found me again. "I can't wait any longer. I have to taste you." He cinched the skin under my arms and flipped me onto my back. His mouth devoured mine as he ripped my panties off. But he didn't stay on my lips for long; he moved gradually, his tongue covering every inch of flesh until it rested between my legs, licking the spot that throbbed. I knew he took satisfaction in my sounds, and in the way my body wiggled and bucked beneath him, so I made sure he knew exactly what he was doing to me. And though I didn't use words every time, he understood what I was saying, and he didn't let up for a second.

My thighs closed in response to the sensation of his fingers filling me and his tongue flicking across my sensitive spots. He pushed them open again. Just as I'd given into his horizontal licking, he switched to a vertical motion, then he stopped and sucked the tight bead into his mouth. I couldn't take it anymore.

"Hart," I panted. "I want to come with you inside me."

Part of me thought I'd have to beg; he'd made me do that in the past. But in one swift movement, he slid up my body and wrapped his hands over my cheeks. His mouth found mine as his tip rubbed against my entrance. The slightest movement would have sent him in.

We both kept still.

His thumb ran around my mouth and stopped in the center of my scar. "I love this." He moved his thumb and kissed underneath it. "And this." His lips traveled to the corner of my eye where the scar started. "And especially this." He dropped down to the edge of my lip where the scar ended.

That was almost too much to take. "Why?" I asked.

"Because it's where your strength lives."

I knew then he had me forever.

He straightened, staring into my eyes, his mouth right above mine. He slowly kissed me. "I love you, Rae."

I remembered the last time his mouth had danced over my face. This time felt different. It was deeper, more intense. I was filled with a sincere longing that I wasn't sure I had ever understood until that moment.

"I love you, too," I whispered.

Nothing between us was rushed anymore, not even after he'd finally entered me. Our bodies moved together, our hips meeting in the middle, briefly separating, and pushing right back. His lips never left mine, kissing me with such passion. It felt like he was cleansing my soul. His hands stayed cupped to my cheeks, holding my scar as if it was something sacred. The warmth began to spread through me.

I felt as if I'd finally stepped into the brilliant, beating light of the sun.

EPILOGUE

"This..." Brady said, pausing as he glanced at his dad. Hart, my mom, and I looked on anxiously. "This...tastes like *shit*. How the hell did Darren eat this every day?"

I laughed and covered my mouth with the back of my hand to keep the vanilla lobster ice cream and gummy bears from flying out. Brady was right; it did taste like shit. The five of us had each gotten a single scoop in a small cup, along with Darren's favorite topping. I could tell it wasn't just Brady who was having a hard time getting it down. Still, we'd all finish every drop.

We had to. It was Darren Day.

This was something Hart had invented shortly after Darren's birthday. December seventeenth was too painful of an occasion to celebrate the way my brother deserved. Hart thought choosing a different day would make it easier on all of us. The seventeenth of June seemed to be perfect—not just because it was his half-birthday, but also because summer was Darren's favorite season. Now that it had arrived, we were starting the celebration with vanilla lobster. Batting cages were next.

He would have loved it.

Mom popped a gummy bear into her mouth and ground it

between her teeth. "I'll never forget how your brother used to beg you and Hart to bring him here."

I laughed again, sticking my spoon into the creamy mound. "On our way out, if you were home, he used to go through your car and steal all the change from your ashtray so he could afford the large instead of the medium cup."

Her eyes gleamed as much as her smile. "So that's where it all went."

I glanced at Hart, watching him try to work through the bite in his mouth. "An extra scoop of gummy bears was fifty cents more, and he never had enough so Hart used to pay for that."

Hart smiled at the memory. "And after ice cream, he always wanted to go to the pub," he said. "That gave us a chance to eat something substantial. Fries with ranch—that was all he ever ordered."

"He put ranch on everything," Mom said.

"And was skinny as a bean pole anyway," Shane said. "Didn't matter how much crap that kid ate, he never gained an ounce."

"That's because he played so much ball," Brady said. "Every time I was at your house, he asked if I'd play toss with him. That kid was so much better at baseball than me. Didn't matter to him, though. He just wanted to play and hang." Brady's smile fell. "I miss that kid."

"Me, too," I whispered.

"We all do," Mom said.

"He was a good egg," Shane added.

"A 'good egg,' Dad?" Brady asked. "Really?"

We all laughed.

"Yeah. A good egg, and a good kid." Shane's eyes glistened. "A good brother, and a good son."

As a mist of silence passed over the table, I felt my phone vibrate from my pocket. A text message from Christy filled the screen. Last I'd heard from her, she'd broken up with pink streaks —who'd turned out to be quite the jealous type—and was moving back to Maine.

Christy: I'm in town again, girl. Wanna meet for drinks?
Me: I do! How about tomorrow? I'm tied up today.
Christy: Whoa! Rope or handcuffs? Suddenly, I like Hart even more than before...
Me: Ha! Neither. :) I'll text you in the morning. Let's plan for some shopping. I need more of your bras.
Christy: A day all about tits. Sounds perfect to me ;)

It was good to see her silliness again. I was glad she was back.

My eyes met Brady's as soon as I looked up from my phone. With every day that passed, he appeared stronger and healthier. He'd taken me up on my offer and had used my savings to pay off the dealers, but he insisted on making payments to me every month. He was still camped out with Shane, working with him on the spa up in Bangor and learning how to live again—sober this time. And he wasn't looking back, which meant he had new friends, new hobbies, and weekly NA meetings.

I was so happy to watch him as he moved toward his new future.

His bond with Shane was more solid than ever, and the one he had with me was just about perfect. We were even closer now.

Brady wasn't the only one who'd changed.

Since Darren's birthday—and the news in February of Gerald passing away—my mom and I had really started to work on our relationship. Hart and I were working at the Bangor spa too, which meant I wasn't able to see her as much as I'd like. But I called her on my way back to Bar Harbor most nights, and we chatted the whole commute. And at least once a month, Hart and I went home for dinner.

Home.

That was what her house was becoming again. Every time I returned, I started to feel more comfortable. As a rule, Darren's door remained closed until I opened it, which I did on a regular basis. Maybe one day, we'd both be at a place where it could always remain open.

My mom's house wasn't the only place I now called home. I hadn't yet purchased a place of my own, and I was in no rush to. Therefore, Hart's house had become *our* home. We'd be moving to Portland once the Bangor spa was finished, and we'd agreed on going to Boston after that, so buying a place had lost some of its significance. I had finally realized I'd had a home all along. It was with Hart and my family.

"Dinner is at eight tomorrow night," Hart whispered.

My eyes fixed on his stormy gaze. "I thought your mom said seven?"

He winced. "She changed her mind at the last minute...is that okay?"

I rolled my eyes, but nodded as he texted his reply. The woman hadn't fully softened to the idea of her son and me, though she had stopped putting me down and now called me by the right name instead of the slew of others she had used. And she no longer burst into the house whenever she pleased, mostly because we'd changed the locks. Hart assured me things would get better between the two of us. I didn't need his assurance; I could feel her walls breaking a little more each time I was with her.

Mine were, too.

I sat by the window, letting the sun touch my skin, allowing it to illuminate my scar. I didn't cringe or cower or worry about what anyone thought of it. That didn't concern me anymore. Instead, I watched the people I loved celebrate the one we'd lost, the one whose presence had filled me, and whose absence had nearly destroyed me but had ultimately pulled me back together. I realized then that my scar didn't compare to my strength. And because of it, happiness had found its way back.

I was finally ready for it.

If you enjoyed *Pulled Within*, check out *Pulled Beneath*, which is Drew's story.
(http://amzn.to/2gU5MWA)

ACKNOWLEDGMENTS

Jesse Freeman, Tess Thompson and Allie Burke, you're my family, my inspiration, my virtual tissues. You make every day better and I love you all so much.

Melissa Mann, Michele Esterkes, David Bohmiller, thanks for being my rock. Your unconditional support and love means everything to me.

Brian, Codi, Bella, and my parents, I'm reminded each day how lucky I am to have you. Not just within reach or a phone call away, but as muses and role models and as my family. I couldn't do this without you. Love, love, love.

Bloggers, I can't thank you enough for all that you do for me. So many of you have been with me since the beginning, sharing in this wild journey, and supporting me in every way you can. I wish I could hug each of you. Just know that I love and adore you all and I appreciate you so much.

And lastly, my readers, you're truly amazing. You force me out of bed, you send me running to my computer, you make me smile when I least expect it. I'm honored and humbled and most often speechless by your compliments. Thanks for loving my words. Thanks for demanding more. Thanks for accepting me.

ABOUT THE AUTHOR

Best-selling author Marni Mann knew she was going to be a writer since middle school. While other girls her age were daydreaming about teenage pop stars, Marni was fantasizing about penning her first novel. She crafts sexy, titillating stories that weave together her love of darkness, mystery, passion, and human emotions. A New Englander at heart, she now lives in Sarasota, Florida, with her husband and their two dogs. When she's not nose deep in her laptop, working on her next novel, she's scouring for chocolate, sipping wine, traveling, or devouring fabulous books.

Want to get in touch? Visit Marni at…
Website
MarniMannBooks@gmail.com

MARNI'S MIDNIGHTERS

Getting to know my readers is one of my favorite parts about being an author. In Marni's Midnighters, my private Facebook group, we chat about steamy books, sexy and taboo toys, and sensual book boyfriends. Team members also qualify for exclusive giveaways and are the first to receive sneak peeks of the projects I'm currently working on. To join Marni's Midnighters, click HERE.

NEWSLETTER

Would you like to qualify for exclusive giveaways, be notified of new releases, and read free excerpts of my latest work? Then sign up for my newsletter. I promise not to spam you. Click HERE to sign up.

ALSO BY MARNI MANN

STAND-ALONE NOVELS

Signed (Erotic Romance)

Endorsed (Erotic Romance)

The Unblocked Collection (Erotic Romance)

Wild Aces (Erotic Romance)

Prisoned (Dark Erotic Thriller)

THE PRISONED SPIN-OFF DUET—Dark Erotic Thriller

Animal—Book One

Monster—Book Two

THE SHADOWS SERIES—Erotic Romance

Seductive Shadows—Book One

Seductive Secrecy—Book Two

THE MEMOIR SERIES—Dark Fiction

Memoirs Aren't Fairytales—Book One

Scars from a Memoir—Book Two

NOVELS COWRITTEN WITH GIA RILEY

Lover (Erotic Romance)

Drowning (Contemporary Romance)

Made in United States
Orlando, FL
22 July 2023

35341738R00200